love
and
lingerie

USA TODAY BESTSELLING AUTHOR
LACEY BLACK

LOVE AND LINGERIE
Rockland Falls Book 2

Copyright © 2019 Lacey Black

Cover Design by Y'all. That Graphic.
Editing by Kara Hildebrand
Format by Integrity Formatting

This book is a work of fiction. Any reference to historical events, real people, or real places are used fictitiously. Other names, characters, places and events are products of the author's imagination, and any resemblance to actual events or places or persons, living or dead, is entirely coincidental.

Published in the United States of America.
ISBN-13: 978-1-951829-60-5

love
and
lingerie

LACEY BLACK

Chapter 1

Harper

Saturdays are my favorite days.

That moment where the world is starting to move about town, open signs are flipped, and the bright sun starts to filter through the large windows. But not today. Today, the sun is nowhere to be seen. That should be an indicator of how the rest of the day is going to go. Yet, evermore the optimist, I flip the sign on the front window and prepare to greet the day.

Kiss Me Goodnight is my home away from home, the premiere destination for whatever your heart desires. I have subtle satins, sexy laces, daring leathers, and even a few pieces that may cause you to question your particular brand of kink. But we're more than that too. I stock handmade lotions and soaps, locally made shampoos and conditioners, and perfumes from a small independent business that got their start in the family kitchen.

But I want more.

I have ideas.

Just no space to make it happen.

Sure, I've checked into a couple of other available buildings in the square, but neither of them are what I'm looking for. Neither of them have the proper space for my vision. It wouldn't be a solid move upward, but more lateral. Plus, they both face the north and are shaded by a huge oak tree that would eliminate the early morning sun warming up my boutique. Those spaces just don't feel right.

The best option is to buy the building that's pieced directly between Douglas Hardware and myself. It's been empty forever, the owner never even entertaining an offer to sell. She's rented it a few times, but nothing ever stuck. It's a small space, barely five hundred square feet, but when you add that to my existing eight hundred square feet, it would make for a wonderful place to spread my wings and grow. Yesterday's conversation with my loan officer comes back to me, along with the dollar amount he approved to lend, if my offer is accepted. Then, there was the trip to the realtor's office and the earnest money I delivered to make said offer. It's starting to come together.

I smile as I glance around my business and complete my customary two-twirl spin by the front door. I built this myself, with blood, sweat, and tons of tears. It wasn't easy, that's for sure. Not when the old men on the city council wanted nothing to do with a "dirty sex shop" coming to paint a bright red A on the town square's sweater vest. But this isn't a sex shop. There isn't a sex toy to be seen, outside of my own nightstand drawer. This is about seduction, self-confidence, and feminism. Empowerment, that's the word I like to use. Hell, I even have it on my company business cards.

Grabbing my nonfat, caramel mocha and the white bag containing my morning blueberry crumble muffin (my little sister is seriously the best baker ever), I slip behind the counter and fire up the computer. It's slow to boot on this gloomy Saturday, so I keep chugging my sugary coffee drink and wait it out. When the machine is finally alive, it starts to blink back at me. The cursor. Right there at the top of the screen. Blink. Blink. Blink.

I start to click like a madwoman, because, when all else fails, just start stabbing your mouse with your index finger. Yet nothing seems to happen. I recall Samuel's control-alt-delete trick, pressing all three buttons at the same time and waiting, fingers figuratively crossed. I rip into the muffin, shoveling my first bite into my mouth in annoyance—not at the breakfast treat, but at the situation. After a few long seconds, it starts blinking again, mocking me with its inability to do its job.

So I kick the tower under the counter.

Blink. Blink. Blink.

Nothing. Works.

"Dammit!" I bellow, cursing my super cute strappy sandals and their failure to cover my now aching toes properly.

Grabbing my phone, I fire off a text message to my older brother, Samuel, who will surely come to my computer crisis rescue. He's the oldest of us four Grayson siblings and takes his role very seriously. He's also the most anal-retentive man I've ever known. He's our resident negotiator, computer guru, and town government buff. Plus, if you ever need lengthy contracts reviewed, he gets off on that shit. Well, I don't know that for a fact, because—eww, he's my brother—but you get my drift.

I fire off a quick text message.

> **Me:**   Computer at work won't turn on. Help?

He replies right away.

> **Samuel:**   Getting ready to bury Mr. Crosswell. Should be done by one.

Did I forget to mention Samuel is a funeral director? Oops. My oldest brother spends his days and nights with the dead, which is actually quite fitting, considering he's the most awkward of us all when dealing with the living.

> **Me:**   One?!? *insert whiney GIF*
> What am I supposed to do until then?

> **Samuel:**   Do it the old-fashioned way. Carbon copy receipts and a calculator.

> **Me:**   That sounds horrible! *insert crying emoji*

Samuel:	You'll survive. Sales tax is seven point two-five percent. Don't forget that. Otherwise, you're paying it out of pocket. Keep your receipt copies and I'll do a spreadsheet when I get there.
Me:	You've ruined my Saturday.
Samuel:	I did no such thing. Besides, you get to create a spreadsheet and input numbers. This will be fun.
Me:	Said no human being ever...
Samuel:	Gotta go. The dead wait for no one.
Me:	Was that a joke? Did you seriously just crack a funny? I'm so proud of you, Sam-I-Am! *insert happy wiping tear gif*
Samuel:	Goodbye, sister. Get your receipt book out of the back of the drawer. It's underneath the daily deposit sheets beside the inventory folder.
Me:	Boy, you know how to have a good time, buddy.

He doesn't respond. Slipping my phone into my back pocket, I stare at the offending electronic device one more time, secretly praying for it to magically fire to life. When nothing happens but that damn blinking cursor, I groan loudly and reach for my mocha, clipping the cup with my fingers and sending it flying. The plastic lid on the top pops off, spilling four dollars of premium Joe all over my new sample packets of lotions and perfumes.

"Son of a bitch!" I bellow into the empty store at the exact same time the bell chimes above the door, notifying me of a customer.

"Well, what did my mother ever do to you?" Mr. Douglas asks with a wide grin as he enters.

"Oh my gosh, Mr. Douglas, I'm so sorry you heard that. You know I wasn't referring to you...or your mother," I apologize profusely, reaching for a roll of paper towels and giving him a look of regret. The truth is, however, his mom really is a grumpy ol' bitty. Annie Douglas is a snippy, snarky old woman who most of the town gives a wide berth to. They also helped spearhead the lynch mob that tried to delay my building permits and license approval. They didn't feel a sex shop was the ideal business to have located beside their precious hardware store.

Little did they know, they are two very different things that can actually work hand in hand...

"Ehh, you're fine, dear. Mother is rather bitchy most days. And how many times do I have to ask you to call me Bud?" he asks, hands in his pockets and a friendly smile on his face as he approaches my counter. "Oh, dear, what did you do?" Bud reaches for the paper towels and helps blot up the mess.

"I'm having an off morning. First my computer died, and now I spilled my coffee all over the new samples," I tell him, dumping the small packets out of the basket.

I run in the back quickly and rinse out the container. While it's drying, I head back up to begin the daunting task of hand cleaning all of the small samples. When I reach the front, Bud is there, wiping each one down and setting it aside in a new basket he found under the counter.

"You don't have to do that," I tell him, reaching for a stack and starting to clean.

"I don't mind, dear. Plus, I might as well get used to having some free time. I've decided it's time to retire."

I stare wide-eyed at the man who runs the hardware store. He has definitely aged some over the last two years, but he seems to be doing fine health-wise. "Are you...okay?" I ask, choking up a little on the thought of Bud being sick. He seriously is the sweetest, kindest man I've ever known. In fact, I've sort of placed him in the position of father figure, considering my own dad is too busy traipsing around the world with his new wife. The one who's my age.

"Oh, I'm fine. Great, actually," he says, throwing his paper towel in the trash and leaning against the counter. "Kitty and I have been thinking about getting one of those RV things and doing some cruising.

I smile. "I can see you both doing that."

"Well, now that she's retired from the school, I think it's time to take a step back from the hardware store. I have a great group of guys who work there, and they'll be able to take the reins and keep it going strong."

Again, I offer him a warm smile, which he returns. It's amazing that a man as genuine and caring as Bud can come from a pair of grumps like Annie and Ernest. Not to mention he and Kitty birthed the spawn of Satan himself. Thinking about their son, Latham, gets my blood pumping in a whole different way. He's a jerk, an ass, and the last time I saw him, I might have punched him in the gut and slammed my heel into his foot.

"Anyway, I just stopped over to tell you the news. I'm going to help through the end of August to train my replacement. Then, we're off to see the countryside," he adds, pushing his glasses up his nose and flashing me another grin.

"I'm happy for you." I truly am. Kitty was the first official customer I had when I opened my doors, and Bud delivered fresh coffee cake to me that very afternoon. Something about the ivory and navy bra she chose and how it...complemented her skin tone nicely.

Right...

He heads toward the door, but stops before he can exit. "Oh, I'll send my guy over shortly. He's a wiz at computers."

I stand there, stunned, and eternally grateful for the gesture. "Thank you, Mr. Douglas."

"Bud," he reminds me, as he waves and slips out the front door.

I straighten up the front counter, rearrange the new line of panties on the front display table, and dust the shelving that houses my bath and body products. I desperately need more space. I have so many amazing ideas and items I can offer Rockland Falls, but unless I want to hang it from the ceiling, I'm about out of options. I can't even search space-saving display ideas on the Internet because my computer is down.

Sighing, I reach for my phone and send off a quick message to my sister. Marissa is probably having sex, lucky bitch. Not that I'm envious of her relationship with Rhenn, but more that she gets some regularly, and from a smokin' hot man to boot.

Marissa met Rhenn two months ago when our family's bed and breakfast caught fire. He was the electrician hired to rewire the house during the reconstruction phase, and the sparks definitely flew. I convinced her to have a little no-strings sex with the man, which ended up being the best thing that happened to either of them. They fell in love. Rhenn relocated, from his hometown about three hours away, to be closer to my sister, and they've been sneaking in amazing everywhere-sex as often as possible.

See? Lucky bitch.

The bell chimes once more and I quickly put my phone away. Two young women enter the shop, each holding the signature cup from the coffee house down the street, laughing, and carrying on. I'm instantly jealous of their caffeine-infused goodness, sad I had to go and spill mine. Maybe I can talk my bestie, Freedom, into making a quick coffee delivery.

"Good morning, ladies. How are you this morning?" I offer to the new arrivals.

"Excellent," the blonde coos. "My friend is getting married in a few weeks and we need something sexy and naughty that will make her new husband drool." Her friend giggles, nodding her head in emphasis.

"Well, you're in the right place. I have just the thing," I state, leading them to the section I consider honeymoon worthy. The bride ends up buying a set to wear beneath her wedding dress, as well as something for the first night of their honeymoon, while her friend purchases some of the fun, bold new boy-cut cheekies I just got in last week. Even with having to handwrite their receipts and basically wanting to jab a pen in my eyeball because it takes so long, it was a great first sale of the day.

Unfortunately, the rest of the morning doesn't quite go the same. A few customers come in to browse, one with a young child in tow who knocks over the mannequin displaying a negligée, and then proceeds to throw a temper tantrum that results in him swiping all the bras off the table beneath it. While I was cleaning up that mess, another potential customer complained about the thin lace on some of the panties and said it never holds up in the wash. Both ladies left (and fortunately, the kid, too) empty-handed.

By noon, my stomach is growling. I got distracted by the lack of computer and taking care of the few customers who shopped that I never finished my muffin. When I finally dig it out of the bag, it's already drying out, considering it's missing its top, but that doesn't stop me from shoveling the entire base into my mouth as if I haven't seen food in a week. I can barely even close my mouth when I hear the bell chime above the door.

I try to chew quickly and not choke at the same time. My mouth is so packed with muffin goodness, it's practically impossible to close my trap and keep half-chewed food particles from flying from my face. Why I thought it was a good idea to shove the entire thing in my mouth is beyond me. Maybe because I've always had killer mouth skills? That makes me snicker.

And almost choke.

"Well, well, well, if it isn't Harper Grayson."

My entire body goes rigid, my jaw ready to drop open, but since it's already hanging open, that doesn't take much effort. I whip around and come face-to-face with the boy—or man—who made my life hell back in high school. He's leaning against the counter, all casual and cocky like, as if he owns the joint. But it's the stupid, wicked smirk that makes my heart start to pound in my chest. I simultaneously love and hate that fucking smirk.

Latham Douglas.

"Satan," I say through a mouthful of muffin. Or at least I try to say it. I'm not sure if he understood a word I said, though. The vindication only lasts a second.

"Still shoving things in your mouth, I see," he says, making my cheeks slightly blush. I hate him.

"Still the biggest asshole around, I see," I finally retort when I swallow the food in my mouth.

"And to think I was being a gentleman and bringing you lunch," he says, making me snort in disbelief. "I guess if you don't want this chicken salad on wheat my mom made, I can just throw it in the trash," he adds, leaning his massive body over the counter in search for a trashcan.

"Don't you dare," I practically growl, narrowing my eyes into little slits of death. In one quick motion, I dive for the bag, barely getting my hands on it before he pulls it out of my grasp and holds it above his head.

"Is that any way to greet a friend?"

Again, I snort – in a total ladylike way, mind you. "Friend? I don't usually want my friends to fall off a bridge into shark-infested waters while wearing nothing but lead-filled shoes, covered in ribeyes."

He throws his hip against the counter and leans on his elbow. "So you've thought about me naked, I see."

"I'm still plagued with nightmares."

Latham laughs, a deep, sultry sound that does something to my body I try to ignore, but it's hard to try to kill him with your eyes when your panties are getting wet and your nipples are starting to throb. "You haven't changed a bit, Harper," he says, looking around the store for the first time. I watch as he pushes off the counter, thankfully leaving the sandwich *and* fresh mocha on the counter as he goes.

Unfortunately, it's not the door he's heading toward. It's my red lace thong and matching bra set that's displayed perfectly on a tabletop mannequin. "This is nice," he says, reaching up and rubbing his hand down the plastic ass.

I stomp around the counter, sandwich and coffee completely forgotten, and smack his hand. "Quit fondling my mannequin."

As I right the panties, making sure they're displayed impeccably, I feel his eyes burning into me. When I glance his way, they're raking over my body, devouring me with the easiest of glances. Of course, my body starts to heat to volcanic devastation level and I find it hard to do my job with steady hands.

Hard.

Yep, my brain went there.

So do my eyes.

They immediately drop to his groin, drinking in the impressive bulge in the front of his fairly tight, flawlessly fitting blue jeans. Dammit, why must they fit him so perfectly? He clears his throat, and my eyes fly up to his. Those stupid brown eyes are as smooth and rich as milk chocolate. "See something you like?" he smirks.

"No. I see something I despise," I retort, turning my back on him and heading to the counter. That sandwich is calling me.

Latham doesn't take the hint and follows me, returning to his casual stance. I ignore his presence, unwrapping the homemade sandwich and taking a massive bite. "Hungry?" he asks, watching as I eat, eyes alive with mischief.

"Starving," I reply, making sure to talk with my mouth full.

He leans in close, maintaining eye contact, and whispers, "Have I ever told you watching someone eat a sandwich like it's their last meal on death row is the sexiest thing I've ever seen?"

I almost choke. It's painful to swallow. "I hate you," I grumble when I can finally move air through my throat.

"Feeling's mutual, Sweetheart," he chastises, rearranging the sample packets I had just displayed mere hours ago.

"What are you doing here, anyway? In the market for a new lace thong?" I ask, taking a much smaller, more ladylike bite of my sandwich.

"Guilty. My other one is starting to show some age. I've had it for...years." Something in the way he says it causes my eyes to meet his. I wish I wouldn't have. They're all-knowing and smug, and I... I...hate him!

Leaning forward, I whisper, "I want those back."

"Never. Those are my favorite pair."

I gasp, flush a totally unflattering shade of red, and stare across the counter at the Devil himself. I can't believe he went there. He just had to talk about that one time...

"Anyway, as much as I'd love to stand here and chat about the old days, I have work to do," he says, pushing off the counter and coming around like he owns the joint. I don't move, which means he has to slide between me and the countertop, our bodies practically touching, our eyes locked on each other's.

"What are you doing?" I whisper, trying to find the words and hating how much he affects me.

"Working. Dad said you have computer troubles," he says as he turns and grabs my tower.

"What? You're the new guy?"

He doesn't even glance my way, just pulls out a small screwdriver from his pocket and starts to take apart my machine. "That's me."

"But...but, what do you know about computers? For all I know you're about to sabotage my entire operation!"

He looks my way, continuing to unscrew the first of several. "Sabotage your panties and bras?" he asks, his eyebrows furrowing together and the corner of his plump lips turning skyward.

"Well, my inventory and accounting system," I respond, uncrossing my arms over my chest and reaching for the tower. "Give me that. You probably have no idea what you're doing."

Latham turns his back and blocks my movements. "I'll have you know I was in communications when I was in the Army. My job was to set up intel and comms in some of the worst parts of the world, Sweetheart. I can fix anything. Your little computer filled with panty prices and shipping orders isn't going to be too hard."

I stand up straight. I knew he was in the Army, but his dad rarely talked about it. Even though he was proud of his son, it was hard for him to discuss the fact he was always away in some foreign country and rarely came home.

When I don't say anything, he stops what he's doing and turns my way. "You gonna let me do this or not?"

Not wanting to give in too easily, I wait several seconds before replying. "Fine. For your dad."

Latham gazes up at me, his eyes locked on mine. "Fine. I'll be done in a few minutes. I'm pretty sure your hard drive is fried anyway."

Great.

That's just par for the course on this lovely Saturday. And to think it's just past noon...

Chapter 2

Latham

I CAN SMELL HER.

Her sweet, succulent scent drifts over to where I crouch on the floor, teasing me with its toxic fumes and sassy disposition. Okay, so maybe not quite that dramatic, but the woman is still as maddening as ever. I've never craved taking a woman over my knee as badly as I do with her. And now I'm adjusting my tight pants. Stupid dick recognized her immediately, even if it had only one little taste so many years ago.

Harper leaves me working on her computer, heading off to do whatever it is she does in this place. As soon as I stepped inside, all I could picture was that very woman wearing every piece of material she stocks. Fiery red to match her personality, seductive blacks, and innocent whites. Every single piece, I want to see displayed on her perfect body.

Age has only enhanced the beauty of Harper Grayson. She was always the most beautiful girl in school, but thirty-two-year-old

Harper? She's a fucking boner-inducing knockout. Long red hair I'd love to wrap my hands around and those fuck-me blue eyes. She's the perfect combination of sin and sexy.

Jesus, listen to me.

Drooling over the woman who'd rather feed you to sharks than spend five minutes catching up with you after more than a decade. I'd say it's definitely time to get laid. Entirely on their own, my eyes turn and catch her just off to the right, reorganizing what looks like a black leather bustier and garter belt.

My boner has a boner.

I turn back to the job at hand, wishing I had something else in my hand right now. Her ass, maybe. Definitely my cock. Even though I'd rather find someone else to take care of this little problem I seem to have, I'm pretty sure I'll be jerking off in the shower later tonight, only with images of the sexy lingerie shop owner next door keeping me company.

When I try to power up her computer, the hard drive does nothing. In fact, if I listen closely, there's the lightly knocking noise coming from the unit. That tells me one thing: it's deader than hell. I put it back in its place and recover the side, leaving the screws off. "I have bad news," I holler, catching her attention and bringing her back to where I squat. "Your hard drive is definitely done. You can replace it, but it's almost just as easy to purchase a new tower."

"Shit," she mumbles, closing her eyes and worrying her bottom lip. My cock twitches.

"This unit looks a few years old," I say, standing up beside her.

"I uh, I got it refurbished when I opened the store. The computer store assured me it would be good for a while."

"And it could have been. Refurbished units aren't always bad. How long have you had it?" I ask, crossing my arms over my chest and leaning against the countertop. I don't miss the way her eyes drop to my arms, taking in the hard lines, detailed muscles, and hint of my tattoo.

"Two years."

"Well, since you probably don't know how long it was in use before it was reconditioned, I'd recommend a new unit then. I'll pick one up when I go to Harriston later this afternoon. If you have a computer backup program, I can get you up and running by Monday."

She just stares at me. Her eyebrows are pinched together, and it looks as if she's trying to piece together a puzzle. "Why?" she finally asks, skeptically.

"Why? Why what?"

"Why would you help me? You hate me."

False. I've never hated her.

"I don't hate you."

"You told me you did."

"You told me the same," I remind her.

"But...I do hate you," she states, though the look in her eyes is all I need to know. She doesn't hate me at all.

"Then we can call a truce for the weekend. After I get you up and running, you can go right back to hating me."

She squints, yet the vivid blue in her eyes still shines brightly. Reaching out her hand, she extends it toward me. "Deal."

I take the offered hand, and reply, "Deal." The moment her hand is held tightly within mine, an electric current zips through my body. Her touch is most definitely deadly.

I don't wait for her to say anything, just slide my screwdriver back into my pocket and turn toward the door. "Wait! Don't you need money or something?" she asks, walking toward me.

"You can pay me back when I know how much it is."

She nods, so I turn back to the door, pulling it halfway open before she stops me again. "Wait, how will you get a hold of me?"

Glancing over my shoulder, I look her straight in the eye. "I know where to find you." Then, I throw her a wink, because I know it drives her crazy (and not even the good crazy, like the kind that makes you want to lock up all your sharp knives) and head out the door, a little extra bounce in my step.

I knew running into Harper Grayson was going to be entertaining, but I didn't think I'd enjoy it this much.

A smile breaks out across my face as I walk the short distance to my family's hardware store. Pulling open the old, heavy door, whistling a happy little tune, I bypass the front counter and head down the hall to my dad's office.

"What has you in such a good mood?" he asks, a knowing smile on his own face.

"Nothing, old man," I reply, sitting down in the chair and putting my feet up on his desk just to aggravate him.

Dad takes a swipe at my boots. "Next month you can put your filthy boots all over this desk, but until then, back off. It's still mine."

I laugh, putting my feet down on the floor. "Tell Mom, Harper says thanks for the sandwich."

Dad wrinkles his eyebrows. "I don't recall Mom making Harper a sandwich. I thought I brought that in for you."

I shrug. "You said she spilled her coffee, so I grabbed her a new one and dropped off my sandwich. When you said she works there by herself most days, I figured she might not have time to go out and grab lunch."

"Mmmhmm, that all that's about?" Dad asks, his smile turning all-knowing.

"That and I looked at her computer, since you already offered up my services. It's fucked, by the way. I'll pick her up a new one when I go to Harriston later to sign those papers."

Dad watches me, eventually nodding. I'm not sure what he sees in front of him and I don't ask. Some things are better left unsaid. "Anyway, I'm going to head up front and start to transfer the inventory to the new system. Dale should still be able to use the old system while it's importing into the new."

"Sounds good. Let me know if you need anything," Dad says, turning his attention back to the stack of papers in front of him.

I make my way up to the front, ready to refamiliarize myself with the business I grew up in. When I was young, it was my grandpa who owned the hardware store, then eventually my dad. Now, it's my turn. Dad plans to retire within the next month, which means I have mere weeks to learn everything I can about running a successful business. I have plans for it, some of which I've already run past him. That's why I'm off to Harriston this afternoon. To get the ball rolling on the biggest project of them all.

Purchase the small building between Harper's store and ours.

It's perfect for the expansion I've been envisioning for Douglas Hardware since I got my papers to leave the Army, anticipating the return home. After fourteen years, I was finally saying goodbye to that part of my life, ready to step into this role at the helm of my family's business. It's a great space that'll add just enough room for the extra inventory lines I've wanted to carry.

Nothing's going to stand in my way of making this place bigger and better.

Nothing.

I knock on her door, some boy band shit filtering through the open front door. A dog starts to bark instantly, heavy pads scrape along hardwood floors. "Who's here?" Harper asks her dog in one of those voices all women use to talk to babies and puppies.

"Oh, it's you," she grumbles as she reaches the front door. She's probably looking at me through her screen door, but I don't notice. The only thing I notice is the way her tight white tank top molds to her voluptuous tits. "My eyes are up here," she deadpans, crossing her arms over her chest to shield them from my eyes.

Joke's on her, though. She only pushes them up higher.

"Eat him, Snuggles," she says to the dog at her ankles.

"But if your dog eats me, who will get your new computer up and running for you?" I ask, bringing the bag up and shaking it.

Harper sighs, rolls her eyes, and opens the screen door. As soon as I step through the entryway, the owner of the deep bark jumps at me, excitedly, tongue hanging from his open mouth. "Down, Snuggles."

"Snuggles?" I ask, glancing her way as she closes the door behind me.

She crosses her arms again defiantly; basically ensuring I'm going to have wet dreams about her and her magnificent tits later tonight. "So?"

Glancing down at the dog, I pet his floppy head, drool streaming from his happy little face. "He's awfully ugly to be a Snuggles." Harper gasps. Snuggles whimpers, as if he understood me.

"You're mean. I can't believe you said that. Besides, Snuggles is a lady," she baby-talks, bending down and giving her dog some love. The dog wags her butt before leaning forward and licking her owner's face.

"I can't believe you named your dog Snuggles. She's going to have a complex for the rest of her life," I say, kneeling down and whistling for the dog to come. She does, letting me know even though she's young, she's trained.

"Traitor," Harper mumbles as she stands up and glares daggers down at me.

"She's definitely a pit bull, but what else? I can see a little something else mixed in," I ask, keeping my eyes on the happy puppy while offering a scratch behind her ears.

"Boxer."

"Look at you," I mock in a singsong voice. "A face only a mother could love." The dog doesn't seem to mind the insult though. She just leans her head into my hand, ensuring I continue to scratch in all the right places.

"Reminds me of you," Harper says.

"Oh, Harper, don't be a spoilsport. You know you love me too." Again, with the stupid baby voice that I didn't even know I could make. Of course, on me, it just sounds like someone is squeezing the shit out of my balls.

Speaking of balls...

"No, Devil, that's where you're wrong. I hate you," she says matter-of-factly.

Standing up, I look down at the sassy, yet incredibly sexy woman. She's tall for a female, about five ten, and has that perfect model frame. Not too skinny, like a beanpole, but with curves in all the right places. Actually, come to think of it, I think I recall my mom talking about a few modeling gigs she did back in the early days when I first enlisted. "There's a fine line between love and hate, Sweetheart."

She stares at me, shoulders squared, and not backing down for a second, but doesn't say anything for several long seconds. "So, about this computer. You have a new tower in that bag?" she asks, glancing down at the big bag on the floor.

"I do not," I answer, reaching for the bag and pulling the new laptop out. "I wasn't impressed with their units, so I moved on to these."

Harper snickers. "You said units."

Rolling my eyes, I reply, "Always a little girl, aren't we?"

Standing up tall, she glares. "There's nothing *little* about me."

I know she doesn't mean it like that, but I'm a guy. I'm. A. Guy. With a very active dick (though, thanks to military life, it hasn't quite seen as much action as it would like), so when my eyes start to rake over her luscious body, I have to admit she's right: there's nothing *little* about her. Except maybe her waist. But her tits – damn, those tits – and her hourglass hips and long legs and big personality...

"You're right. Your mouth definitely isn't little. It's quite...big. Plus, there's your ass. I know it's a lot bigger than it used to be." Why do I say it? Because I love getting a rise out of her. Much like the rise she evokes in my pants.

Harper gasps, her eyes narrowing down into little slits. I almost smile in anticipation of what jabs she's about to hurl my way next. "And look at you, asshole," she stutters, glancing up and down my body as if trying to come up with a good retort, yet coming up empty. "Never mind. I'm not stooping to your level of idiocy and immaturity."

"Idiocy? Immaturity? And here I thought I was your hero, coming to rescue you from the computer-killing virus you probably downloaded from looking at porn at work."

"I don't look at porn at work. I'm not a sixteen-year-old boy!"

Again, my eyes fall to the tight tank top. "Nope, definitely not a boy."

"Stop looking at my chest!"

"Stop drawing my attention to it!"

Harper growls, throwing her hands up in the air. "You're impossible. Let's just go to my store so you will stop insulting my dog and staring at my boobs."

"Oh, don't think I won't still look at your boobs at the store, Harper."

"Shut up," she mumbles, calling Snuggles into the kitchen and letting her out the back door. I watch from the front entry, glancing into the living room when she moves out of sight. It's cheerful in neutral colors, yet with splashes of purple and blue accents that just speak of the woman who lives here. The couch is tan with a matching recliner, and the walls are a slightly darker beige. The flooring is an espresso walnut that looks damn good in the brightly lit space. Top that off with a stone fireplace, flagstone mantel, and a decent sized television that puts my little thirty-two incher to shame.

What draws my attention right now is what's sitting on that beautiful mantel. The first photo is a family picture of Harper and her siblings. They're standing with their mom in front of their family bed and breakfast where she grew up. They're stretching a red ribbon across the porch, with Mrs. Grayson and Marissa, together, holding a large pair of scissors. The entire family is smiling proudly at the camera, obviously getting ready to cut the ribbon. It's a recent photo, so I make note to ask Harper about it.

The photo next to it is her holding a little boy. He's probably four or five years old, with a big toothy smile and striking blue eyes that remind me of Harper's. The resemblance is uncanny, yet the shape of the eyes and nose are different. If I had to guess, I'd say a relative. Another photo to ask about.

The final picture is a younger Harper standing with Freedom Rayne, her spunky best friend. It was taken on the beach, both girls posing for the camera with blinding white smiles and barely-there bikinis. I remember the first time I realized those two were friends. We were in early grade school, and even back then, they were as different as night and day. The fact they're still so close actually makes me a little nostalgic that I lost touch with so many of my own friends after high school. But the week after I graduated, I was off to boot camp, rarely to return to my hometown. Most of my old friends went off to college, got married, and started popping out kids. I was in foreign hot zones, setting up communications for our troops and using my computer skills to do a few things I'm not at liberty to discuss.

"Ready?" she asks, joining me in the living room, Snuggles hot on her heels.

"Yeah," I reply, clearing my throat. "How is Free?" I ask, nodding toward the picture.

"You'll see for yourself in about ten minutes," she says, grabbing her purse and heading to the front door. I notice instantly she added a blue sweater over her tank top, which hangs off one shoulder and hits just below her belly button. Thank God for the white tank top underneath or she'll see exactly what my body thinks of hers the entire ride to her store.

Her very sexy lingerie store.

"Afraid you can't control your urges if left alone with me?" I ask, meeting her at the front door and waiting for her to walk through first. My mom raised a gentleman, but also because I can stare at her ass a little more.

Sorry, I'm also a guy.

When we're both on the front porch and her door is secured, she turns to me with evil in her eyes. "No, I'm afraid if I kill you, I won't be able to dispose of the body by myself." Then she gives me a big, wolfish grin and heads off to her car. I'm left standing on her porch, a stupid smile plastered on my own face. I've missed sparring with Harper.

Just don't tell her that.

The drive up to her store is short. Most businesses in town aren't open on Sunday, which means the only foot traffic are those coming in and out of the diner just up the block. The hardware store isn't open, but that's something I plan to change. Even if I have to work that day myself. The only option for purchasing building materials is to drive to Harriston about thirty minutes away. It's proven most home improvement projects are completed by the homeowner are done on the weekend. Yet, Douglas Hardware is only open on Saturdays from seven to one.

It's something that's going to change.

Especially when I purchase the building next door and bring in more merchandise.

I park in front of the hardware store, planning to head there after installing Harper's new laptop, and meet her at her lingerie store. Kiss Me Goodnight. It's definitely an interesting name for a business, but it fits her. It fits the vibe she's going for within the walls of her place. It's not just super sexy lingerie (though she has plenty of that too), but it's casual pajamas and body products too.

Inside smells amazing. Like warmth and sweetness, with a hint of seduction, all rolled into one. A total chick place, but I get it. It's totally her. Just as I set the new laptop down on the counter, the front door bursts open in a frenzy of chaos and lavender. Free. Her name is Freedom Rayne, born to tree-hugging, vegetarian hippies who changed their own last name when they were married.

"I brought coffee with soymilk and honey and goat cheese fig muffins!" she exclaims as she sweeps in, her long flowy skirt billowing around her bare ankles.

"Goat cheese?" I ask, standing up and staring down at the food as if it were about to bite me.

"Don't knock it until you try it, Latham Douglas. It's like sex for your mouth," she sasses, making Harper choke on her coffee with soymilk.

"My mouth does love sex," I boast, reaching into the pan and grabbing a muffin. Both ladies watch as I bring the sweet treat (if you can really call goat cheese and fig a sweet treat) to my mouth, shoving the entire thing inside in one solid bite.

"Damn, your mouth does love to devour," Free coos, leaning her elbow onto the counter and staring up at me with a smile. "Harper, isn't his mouth amazing? He just shoved that entire thing in there and actually makes it look sexy." She bats her eyelashes my way and smiles wickedly, but I already know it's totally for show. Free isn't into me anymore than I'm into her. It's just a game that I'll happily oblige.

When I swallow the surprisingly delicious muffin, I lean forward, setting my own elbow on the counter and say, "You should see what I can do with my tongue."

I hear a gasp, but not from Free. No, this one comes from Harper, who just so happens to knock into the display shelf of lotions, setting them all flying like a crazy game of dominoes. "Get a room!"

"Ehh, I don't think Lath can handle what I would offer," Free says, shrugging to her friend and throwing me a wink and knowing smile.

"I believe you speak the truth, Freedom Rayne."

"I love the way you say my name, Lath. With just a hint of that southern North Carolina drawl, I bet you get all the ladies worked into a tizzy."

Before I can reply with a smart-alecky quip, Harper stands up from collecting the goodies she knocked down, places her hands on her delicious hips, and glares at both of us. "Can you stop stroking his already massive ego, please? I brought you here to help me bury the body, not flirt with him."

"You want to stroke my massive what?" I ask, turning my predatory smirk her way.

Harper rolls her eyes so hard I'm pretty sure she just saw her brain. "Puh-lease, I'd rather not discuss whatever tiny, itsy-bitsy, little *thing* you want stroked."

I swear, her mouth makes me so hard.

Instead of retorting and calling her out on her lie, as I'd love to, I send a wink her way and dive into the laptop box in the bag. Pretending to ignore her, I get busy setting up her new system, which, thankfully, her old one backed up every night off-site *and* at the end of every day with an external hard drive. I'm not sure who was computer savvy enough to make such a suggestion to Harper, but it was definitely a solid business decision. Most businesses don't think to have two forms of backup, my own included. That's another thing I'll be changing when I officially take over the hardware store.

When the backup is installing, I finally glance up and notice Harper and Free. They're over by the far south wall, pointing and discussing something. Weird, considering that wall butts against the empty store between hers and mine. Maybe she's going to add some displays to that wall. Right now, she has a small unit that houses baskets of sexy panties.

Needing to stretch my legs, I make my way to them. Neither of them hear my approach, a product of my time in the military, and their words become clearer.

"I love that idea. Open brick on this wall with an arched doorway between the two. That'll be beautiful," Free says, painting a picture for her friend.

"Oh, I dig that. I know there's brick between that store and my own. I hope it's in good enough shape to use that in the addition," Harper adds.

My brain zeroes in on their words. Addition? Open brick between stores? What the hell? Does she want to buy the building between Kiss Me Goodnight and Douglas Hardware? It sure as shit sounds like it, but when I met with my realtor in Harriston yesterday afternoon, he assured me I was the only bidder making an offer.

"Plus, that extra space will allow you to add that aromatherapy line you were telling me about," Free says, pulling my attention back to them.

"Yes! I have so many great ideas for the new space. I can't believe I made that offer. I'm terrified and so excited at the same time," Harper beams, practically jumping for joy right there where she stands.

Made an offer?

I'll be dammed if I'm going to sit back and let her have that space. I've already put feelers out with a few contractors on opening up the wall between my building and that one to give us more space. *I* have ideas, *plans* for it. She thinks she's going to just *get* it?

She's got another think coming.

Chapter 3

Harper

"YOU'RE ALL SET," LATHAM SAYS, pulling my attention away from the plans Free and I are making.

I don't even have the property yet, but that isn't stopping me from envisioning just what I'd do to the space if my offer were accepted. When I made it, my realtor assured me I'd know whether it was accepted or if a counteroffer was made. The good news is she thought I was the only one being considered by ol' Mrs. Morton.

The anticipation is killing me.

"That didn't take long," I say, spinning around and meeting him back over at the counter.

"It was a simple reinstall, thanks to your up-to-date backup. You can have a quick look, but it appears that all your files transferred easily enough. Your accounting software is finished, and the add-on for inventory is completing now," he says, turning the laptop my way. "I recommend keeping it plugged in to the

Ethernet cable while you're here, but your Wi-Fi should work fine if you take the laptop somewhere else in the store or to your office."

"I do like the idea of being able to take it mobile," I concede, not really admitting he may have been right in his suggestion. I hate that. "How much do I owe you?"

Latham pulls a receipt out of his jeans pocket and hands it over. I glance at the dollar amount, inwardly groaning that I have to take the money out of what I've been saving for the property next door, but knowing it needs to be done. If I would have hired a computer expert to work on it, the cost may have been dramatically more.

"How much for your time too?" I ask, setting aside the boxing gloves—figuratively speaking, of course. Though, the idea of donning a pair does have some appeal... At the end of the day, I am grateful for his assistance, and he deserves to be paid appropriately.

"I don't need your money, Harper."

"I'm going to pay you for your time," I retort, crossing my arms. His eyes immediately dip down to the cleavage I know is on display. Even though I covered up with this thin blue sweater, it still hangs dangerously low in the front. I may or may not have had that planned when I threw it on earlier.

"How about you pay me with a kiss?" he says breezily, offering me the stupid cocky grin that does things I try to ignore to my lady parts.

"I'd rather kiss a pig," I throw over my shoulder as I head off to my office, leaving him standing there chuckling.

I write out the check for one hundred dollars over the amount on the receipt. If anything, he deserves a little payment for the Sunday time he spent here, fixing my computer issues, instead of doing whatever the hell it is he does on Sundays. I jot the check details down in the ledger and make my way back to the front of the store. Latham is standing at the counter again, casually leaning against it as he chats with Free. He's smiling easily, and not that evil, demonic one he always gives me. It's light and free, and I can't help the slight bubble of jealousy that surfaces when I think about Latham and my best friend.

"Here," I say a bit too hastily, thrusting the check in his hand. His eyebrows furrow together in question, but he doesn't say anything. In fact, he doesn't even look at the check. He shoves it in his pocket, never taking his eyes off mine for a second.

"Thanks."

Crossing my arms, I stand up tall and square my shoulders. "Aren't you even going to look at it?"

"Do I need to?"

"I wouldn't short you, if that's what you're asking."

"I didn't think you would."

"I paid you more."

"Why?"

"Because you spent part of your Sunday here instead of doing...whatever you would have done today."

"You mean I was here, with you and Free, surrounded by lady's lingerie *instead* of watching football in front of the TV, while drinking beer and eating chicken wings?"

"There's no football in July," I argue. I'm rewarded with a smile.

"You have a point, Harper. Then, my next option would have been of the entertainment variety, if you know what I mean. I have a list of lady friends a mile long."

"Pig."

He barks out a laugh, the sound going straight to my core. My panties are pretty much ruined by this point. "I guess you'll never know," he says with a wink and moves. As he slides behind me (I refuse to move, by the way), his warm breath fans against my neck and goose bumps pepper my skin. His lips are mere inches from me and heat floods my veins. "Just say thank you, Harper."

"Thank you, Harper."

He chuckles, but doesn't move. I can feel the heat of his body practically pressed against my back. It takes everything I have to not lean into his massive body. But this is Latham, I have to remind myself. The devil himself, and he's probably using all of his sexual wiles to get under my skin.

It's working...

No, it's not!

"I'll see you soon, Sweetheart," he whispers, his lips grazing ever-so-slightly over the back of my neck. I shiver instantly. He places a scrap of paper in my hand, but I make no movement to see what it says. I'm not sure I want to know.

"Stop calling me that," I reply, my own voice a little raspy.

"Never," he says loudly, as he finally moves past me, and heads to the door. Without saying a word, he waves at Free and slips through the entry, pulling it tightly secure as he goes.

"Damn, that was hot. Did you just orgasm?" Free asks, her eyes wide with shock and excitement.

"What? No!"

"You didn't? I just about did watching. He sooooo wants you," she coos.

"Shut up," I grumble, ignoring the slight bubble of excitement that seems to plant firmly in my chest at the prospect.

Free laughs, making herself useful while I check out my new laptop. The software is completely installed, and the moment I move the mouse to waken the screen, a password authorization pops up.

Password?

I type in my first name. Nothing. I add my last name. Still doesn't work. I try the name of my store, but that gets denied too. I start to get a little irritated – okay, a lot irritated – as I try word after word after word. Nothing works. Leave it to Latham to password protect my new laptop and not tell me what the magic word is, the infuriating, frustrating, pig-headed man!

I'm just about to call Free over for help when I think about that little slip of paper he placed in my hand. I didn't want to give it a thought before, but now? Now, I find myself digging into the pocket of my shorts and pulling it out. His handwriting is horrible, yet familiar, as I glance down at the single word scrolled across the pink Post-It.

He didn't.

I type that word into the password box and click enter.

My home screen immediately appears, and so does my smile. Leave it to Latham to force me to type out that one word multiple times a day. That word I hate, yet secretly love at the same. That single word I will forever associate with the man who could drive a nun to drink and turn to prostitution.

Sweetheart.

When I leave the store a few hours later, I notice Latham's truck still parked in front of the hardware store and a few lights on within. He's been there since he left my business, probably catching up on his own weekend work. I'm sure he has a lot to learn if he's going to take over the helm of the family company by the end of next month. I know he worked at the hardware store while in high school, but he left so quickly before college for the Army and hasn't been back since.

I make a rash decision; one I'm probably going to regret in the long run.

I buzz across the street to the diner and order two specials to go, along with two large sweet teas. I don't know if he still drinks tea, but it's sort of a staple down in the South, so I'm guessing it'll be fine. When the food is ready and placed in a white bag, I head back across the street and knock on the door. The first time, he doesn't hear me, so I knock a little louder the second time.

Latham appears from the back office I know is his dad's, a concerned and surprised look on his face. When he unlocks the door, he asks, "Is everything all right? Is the laptop giving you troubles?"

"No," I state, clearing my throat. "I was leaving work and noticed you were still here. It's dinnertime, so I thought I'd grab you a bit of food." I hold up the bag, practically thrusting it into his chest.

"You bought me dinner?"

"I bought myself dinner and since you were still here, grabbed a second order. They were having a sale, actually. Buy one, get one free. It was free."

A smile crests his lips. "Aww, if you wanted to have dinner with me, all you had to do was ask."

"Shut up," I grumble, pushing past him and stepping inside his family business.

I can hear him chuckle as he locks the door and follows me into the office. The desk is covered in a few catalogs for product, as well as what looks like a blueprint design for construction. Latham swiftly swipes it away, rolling it up and throwing it on the table behind the desk. He makes quick work at clearing off a spot to set the food down and takes the container holding our two teas from my hand. "Sit," he directs, motioning the chair beside me.

"No, I can see you're busy. I'll just take my food home and eat."

"Harper, stop being difficult. You might as well enjoy your food while it's still warm," he says, setting a cup of tea on the desk in front of my chair.

"I have to go feed Snuggles," I reply lamely, knowing I fed her before I left for the store earlier today. I only pray Latham doesn't remember, but of course, he does.

"You fed that mangy mutt before you left. She'll be fine for another fifteen minutes," he says as he pulls the two Styrofoam containers from the bag, placing one in front of me and the other in front of him. "What is this? It smells amazing."

"Chicken-fried steak with mashed potatoes and gravy," I answer, my mouth starting to water.

"Seriously?" he moans as if I just said the best thing ever. "I've missed Hazel's chicken-fried steak so fucking much." Latham pulls open his container, drops down into his chair, and stares down at the food.

I'm already shoveling my first bite into my face. "Are you going to eat it or make love to it?" I ask, not evening caring that my mouth is full.

"I haven't decided yet," he whispers, slowly grabbing his fork and cutting off a piece of meat. He dips it in the mashed potatoes and gravy and shoves the entire piece into his mouth. "Holy shit," he groans, his eyes rolling into the back of his head. His full lips move, his jaw flexes, as he slowly chews the food. "Best fucking food ever."

We're quiet for several minutes as we both eat our food. I can feel his eyes on me, though I don't look up to confirm. There's something so...natural and civil to sit here with him, without throwing eye daggers and hateful words. I'm not sure I like it. At least not enough to draw attention to it.

"So," he starts, closing up his empty container and reaching for his sweet tea, "what have you been up to the last fourteen years?"

"Fourteen years, has it really been that long?" I ask, almost absently, as I close up my own empty container and toss it into the trash.

"It has," he confirms, kicking his worn boots up on the top of his dad's desk.

"He's going to hate that," I say, referring to the boots.

"I know he will. He'll notice the dirty scuff marks as soon as he gets in tomorrow morning," he says with a chuckle.

I sigh, not really wanting to answer his previous question. Not that there was anything wrong with it, but I guess I just don't have any major accomplishments I can dote on for the next half hour. In fact, my life has been a big blob of nothing for the most part, and for the girl who was voted most likely to achieve everything in high school, I can't help but feel a little saddened by my lack of, well, anything. "A little of this and that," I go with casually.

He stares at me, as if reading my inner, private thoughts. "This and that? Didn't I hear something about modeling?"

I can feel the warmth in my cheeks. "Checking up on me while you were gone, did you, Satan?"

He shrugs. "Mom mentioned it to me. Where'd ya go?"

I clear my throat and take another drink of tea. "New York and a short stint in Paris." My mind instantly goes right back to that moment in time. A nineteen-year-old naïve girl, alone in the city, with big hopes and dreams.

"What happened?" His voice is deep and rough, as if he can already tell there's more to this story he won't like.

I shrug and paste on a small smile. "It just wasn't for me."

His eyes pierce mine, dark and demanding, but I don't give in. I never talk about that time in my life, and I'm not about to share it with someone like Latham. "I'll let that slide for now, but eventually, we'll come back to it."

I don't like the way he says that, as if he *knows* for a fact we'll be talking about more personal details in our lives soon. Nope, not going to happen, Latham Douglas. "Anyway, so how about you? What was it like in the Army?"

"It was hard, at first, but I enjoyed it. I miss the camaraderie and the discipline of it all, but to be honest, I'm happy to be home."

"I bet your parents are happy too."

"My mom cried for an hour after she opened the door and found me standing on her doorstep with my bags in hand," he says fondly, which makes me smile. I can just picture Kitty grabbing onto her boy and refusing to let go. Even if her son is an ass, she only ever saw the good in him. I'm sure it's there, buried deep down.

We sit there, neither one of us really saying anything more. It's weird, ya know? I haven't threatened to decapitate him, and he hasn't tried to give me a noogie or wet-willy. Maybe two people really can grow up and actually get along?

"So, how's the nightly headgear going? I see your teeth finally pulled together so you're not so buck-toothed."

Maybe not.

I sign loudly and way too dramatically. "I haven't worn head gear in about two decades, Satan. How's the tube sock fetish? Did your mom ever get the crusty ones under your bed clean?"

He just smirks. "Thinking about my Johnson, are ya?"

"Only about cutting it off."

"Sounds kinky. I didn't realize you were into that sort of shit."

"You're impossible," I say with an eye roll.

"Are you seeing anyone?" he asks. Now that gets my attention.

"Are you asking me out?"

"Hell no. I'm trying to figure out if some pencil-pushing nutbag is gonna beat down my door for talkin' to his girl."

"You're so dramatic. I'm my own person. No one tells me who I can or cannot talk to," I tell him decisively.

"Oh, I don't doubt it, Sweetheart. I just want to be prepared is all. I hate when I'm caught off guard and take a punch to the face." He gives me a hard look.

"That wasn't my fault," I defend.

"No? I believe it was your ex's fist that landed hard on my chin."

"It didn't even faze you. You threw two more right after."

Latham smirks. "I do recall. And, had fun doing it."

I can feel the moment we start to teeter too close to memories I'd rather forget. Standing up, I make sure my mess is cleaned up. "I should go."

"You don't have to," he says, making no move.

"I need to let Snuggles out."

With that being said, he finally stands up and walks around to my side of the desk. "Ahh, yes, the ugliest mutt this side of the Mississippi."

"You're mean. I hope she bites your balls next time she sees you."

"As much as I enjoy a mouth on my balls, I think I'd rather it not be hers." Something in the way he says that makes my face start to heat and my body start to sing.

"Anyway," I start, drawing out that word a little too dramatically, "I need to go."

"Yes, to take care of the dog."

"And because I don't want to be here when the poison starts to work," I say all sweet-like. Leaning in, I whisper in his ear, "I just hate messes." And because I apparently have no self-control, I inhale a nose full of his woodsy, sexy scent.

The look on his face is priceless. He stands up straight, his hand rubbing the back of his neck. "Poison?"

I pat his belly and give him a wicked smile. "I guess you'll just have to wait and see." Then, I turn on my heel and strut out of the office and to the front entrance, well aware his eyes are following me the entire time. I throw the double lock and pull open the door. "Oh, and Latham?" He meets my eyes, a guarded look on his face. "You might want to make sure you have a puke bucket handy."

With the final word, I flit victoriously out of the hardware store and to my awaiting car. My triumph is short-lived, however, when I slip inside, turn the key, and nothing happens. I try again. And again and again. Still, my car doesn't turn over. I smack my steering wheel, now angry and with a throbbing hand, and glance back up. Latham is standing there, a wide smile on his face, as he holds something up.

I realize immediately what it is.

He gives me a little wave, throws a bunch of sparkplugs in the air, shoves them into his pocket, and strolls back into the store.

Satan.

He wins again.

Chapter 4

Latham

FIRST THING MONDAY MORNING, I dial my realtor. Pete Benson and I were in school together, both playing on the football and basketball teams. We hadn't really kept in touch, but the minute I returned to town and my ideas for the empty space next door started taking shape, I reached out to my old friend for help.

"Hello?" he asks, his voice groggy from sleep.

"Did I wake you?"

"It's six in the morning. Fuck yes, you woke me."

"I've been up since four. We have a situation."

"There's only one kind of situation I want to deal with at six in the morning, Lath, and your ugly ass isn't it."

"There's another bidder for the property."

Silence. "What? How do you know that?" He's wide-awake now.

"I overheard a conversation I probably shouldn't have."

"We'll come back to that part, but are you sure?"

"Definitely," I reply, rubbing the back of my neck. "Can you confirm it?"

"Yeah, I'll make some calls. Probably not until closer to eight, but I'll get on it right away."

"Thanks, man."

"You prepared for a bidding war for this?" He's not asking anything I haven't wondered myself.

"Yeah, I'm ready."

Pete clears his throat. "Okay, then I'll call Mrs. Morton's realtor and see what I can find out. I'll call ya."

"Thanks. And Pete?" I ask, looking out the back window of the tiny apartment above the hardware store. "I'm not above playing dirty. I want that property."

"Consider it done."

We disconnect, and even though a part of me wants to gloat about my soon-to-be victory, a tiny part also feels something I wasn't expecting.

Guilt.

I push her and her plans aside, choosing to focus on the day before me. We have a truck coming in an hour, plus a new shipment of power tools later in the day. This is the perfect opportunity for me to get a jump on some of the other small jobs I've been noticing need tending to, like a little reorganizing of the painting supply area and even a few updates in the kitchen displays. I have a big to-do list, and it wouldn't hurt to head downstairs and get started before Dad and the rest of the employees come in.

Plus, if I surround myself with tedious, mundane tasks, maybe then I'll stop picturing the way Harper's red hair shone beneath the Sunday sun or the way her tank top molded to her perfect tits. The semi-woody in my pants tells me I'm full of shit, but a guy can hope, right?

A guy can definitely hope.

Mondays are a little busier than I anticipated. The temperatures are climbing fast, ensuring the afternoon will drop off dramatically. Everyone will either be inside, where their air-conditioning is cranking out the cool air, or they'll be at the beach. My personal vote would be for the beach, but there's too much shit to do to even consider enjoying a little sun and relaxation.

I'm helping a customer with new locks and a rekey project when the bell above the door chimes. I ignore the newcomer, since Dale is up at the counter to help. I continue rekeying, careful to make sure the grooves all match up. "This is the best brand on the market, so you should have no problems," I say to the man, handing him his new locks and updated keys. "But if you do, give me a call and I'll come out and take a look."

"I'd be happy to give you a call," I hear over my shoulder in a sweet, sultry voice. The male part of my brain (fine, it's all male) starts to perk up with interest.

Until I turn around.

And come face-to-face with Felicity Charles, the girl from high school who did everything she could to get in my back seat.

"Hey, Felicity," I greet casually.

Before I can move, she flings herself into my arms and practically attaches to my chest like a spider monkey. "Oh, Latham, it's so good to see you! It's been too long," she coos, batting her overdone eyelashes and licking her pouty red lips.

"It has," I confirm, gently peeling the customer off my chest. "So what brings you in today?"

"I need help!" she practically explodes with excitement and exasperation. When I glance over her blonde hair covered shoulder, I see Dale turning away and making a beeline back to the counter as if his ass were on fire.

Lucky bastard.

"What can I do for you?" I ask, crossing my arms over my chest and trying to give her my attention. I mean, she is a customer, after all.

"I locked myself out of my apartment again." She twirls her long hair around her fingers. "It's the second time this month, and that got me thinking, I should, you know, hide a key. Like under my flower pot. On my back patio. This way, it'll be there when I need it...or whenever anyone else needs it." Then she winks, and I inwardly groan.

"So, you need a key made and a hide-a-key box?"

"Yes! That!" she bursts, jumping up and down victoriously. Of course, I'm pretty sure the only reason she does is so I notice her tits. I notice, of course, because I am, in fact, a guy. But just because I notice them doesn't mean I want to play with them.

"Okay, well, let's get you all set up."

I quickly turn back around to the key-making station. I was making these back in grade school, so it was no problem to jump back on it and whip out a few keys earlier today, even if I hadn't had my hands on it in several years. Hell, I could probably make keys in my sleep.

With my attention completely on the task at hand, I startle when I feel Felicity press against my back. "What are you doing?" I ask over my shoulder, her dark eyes smiling brightly.

"I'm sorry," she giggles. "I'm just so excited you're home! Your mom and dad have been telling my parents all about your return. Oh, that reminds me. I need to grab that application while I'm here. I know it's just a formality, but your dad says I should fill it out ASAP."

Say. What?

"Excuse me?" I ask, turning off the machine and facing her. She hasn't moved so when I do turn, I'm basically pressing my chest against hers.

"The job, silly. Your dad said you're hiring. He offered it to me," she says with a shrug.

"Oh, uhh...that's...well, Dad hasn't mentioned that to me yet."

She waves her hand. "It just happened last night. Your parents came over for dinner and I mentioned that I needed a second job so I could move out. I'm waiting tables over at The Pump, and it's going well, but they can only give me Friday and Saturday night hours. Your dad mentioned you're looking for someone and gave me the job."

Are you kidding me right now? Dad just gave Felicity a job without even asking what my plans were? We had discussed hiring an additional employee, but hadn't decided anything. At least, I thought we hadn't. Technically, he's still the boss, but he's less than six weeks away from retirement. Whatever mess he just created, he's leaving for me to deal with.

And dealing with Felicity every day isn't something I signed up for.

Our parents have been friends since their youth, all going to school together, so I grew up with Felicity. She's high-maintenance as fuck, clingy, and way too needy for my liking. I think my parents thought we'd get together at some point in life, but I knew that shit wasn't happening. No matter how much she tried.

"Well, I start tomorrow. I can't wait! I'm so excited," she coos, twirling her hair with one hand and grabbing my bicep and squeezing with the other. "It'll be just like ol' times!"

Not really. I hated hanging out with her, yet she always seemed to weasel her way into my group of friends. She screwed most of them, and continually made her intentions with me clear. She even went as far as to show up naked in my bed one night. That was right before senior prom. A night I won't ever forget.

"Great," I reply, offering her a small smile. "So, here's your key." I reach for a key box beside the machine and hand it to her as well. "Let's go to the counter and get you rung up."

Dad pops out of his office when we reach the front, a friendly smile on his face. "Oh, Felicity, you're here."

"I am! I can't wait to start tomorrow," she coos, batting her thick, black eyelashes my way again. She leans across the counter, pressing her tits together and upward out of her shirt.

"We'll get you a few polo shirts. I'm not sure we have your size in stock, but I can order some," Dad says as he hands her an employment application. An application that's apparently just a formality at this point.

"Extra small!" she boasts. I'm pretty sure an extra small is going to barely contain the tits she apparently had worked on while I was away. I don't ever recall Felicity being so well-endowed in the chest area. Now Harper? She has the perfect, natural shape and size that keeps the fantasy coming.

And me coming too…

It takes way too long to get her out of the store, and when she finally does, I follow my dad into his office. "Really?"

"What?"

"Felicity? You expect her to get any work done here? She'll be too afraid to break a nail," I grumble, dropping down into the chair. I throw my feet up on his desk, just to piss him off.

"Listen, I didn't really have a choice. Darryl was telling me she needs a second job so she can move out of their place."

"Not my problem," I protest. "Wait, move from their place? She just told me she needed another key for her apartment."

Dad snorts. "Uh, no. She moved back home months ago and hasn't left yet. I think he's helping give her the little push out of the nest. I know she's not the best fit here, but he's my friend. And I do recall him helping you out a few times in the past," Dad says, referring to the time where he helped me restore my old truck. We didn't have the extra garage space, but they did. So I worked on my truck there on the weekends, and even used a lot of his tools.

"This is going to be a disaster," I gripe.

Dad laughs. "Probably. Just keep her busy at the front desk. She can clean and do some of the other organizing stuff you've wanted to do."

Dropping my head, I know I'm defeated. Dad's helping a friend, and giving his daughter a job. Now, I'll be stuck with her on a daily basis. "You know there's nothing there, right?" I ask, needing to make sure this isn't a setup.

Dad snorts. "Are you kidding? I saw the writing on the wall when you two were in high school. Your mom might need a reminder, but not me. That's not why I brought her here. Besides, I always had my eyes set on another when it came to you." I can see his not-so-innocent smile spread widely across his aging face.

"I don't want to know," I say, though I'm pretty sure I already do.

"She's a good girl, Latham. She's got a fiery spirit that brings out the best in you," he says as I'm walking to the door.

"Fiery because she'll try to light my ass on fire?" I throw over my shoulder, Dad laughing as I go.

"I like her," I hear him holler as I join Dale at the counter.

There's only one problem.

I like her too.

It's just after noon when the phone call I've been waiting for comes in. I excuse myself from the counter and head back to one of the storage rooms for a little privacy. "Hello?"

"Yeah, there's definitely another offer on the table."

"I thought you said I was the only one?" I ask, annoyed that the deal could possibly be in jeopardy, but more annoyed it's Harper who could fuck up my plans.

"As of Saturday, there wasn't. The attorney assured me the listing wasn't even public yet."

"Then how did she find out about it?" I growl into the phone, talking mostly to myself.

"She? Who?"

"You don't know?" I ask.

"No, I'm not privileged to that information. I'm only allowed to know that another offer has been made, not who made it."

Do I tell him or not? I mean, if he knows, then we can formulate the best plan of attack together. "Harper Grayson."

Dead silence.

"You there?"

"Yeah, did you say Harper Grayson? As in fucking knockout, with tits that would make a grown man beg, Harper Grayson?"

My blood starts to boil and my nostrils flair. My reflex is to bark and bite like a jealous man, but that can't happen. Not with Pete, who'll take every opportunity to razz and joke about how I reacted to his comments. So instead of saying what I want to, I go with, "Yeah, that Harper."

"Damn, man. She still as hot as ever? I remember in high school when you—"

"Listen, Pete, let's not lose focus. The goal is to still acquire that building. I need it for what I have planned for the store. I'm not going to let a woman selling thongs and body wash spoil that."

"Did you just say thongs? Does she wear them?"

I growl. "I don't know." I do know. "My point is the space would suit my needs better than hers. Make a bigger offer."

"How much bigger?" he asks.

I sigh deeply. "As big as you need."

Pete's silent on the other end. "You sure?"

Rubbing the back of my neck, I reply without even thinking. "Do it."

I've got the finance to back it up, but had hoped to be able to put some of that money into the renovation. It's going to take dough to knock out a portion of the wall and make the old space usable again. Not to mention what I've already budgeted for the new computer system and updated security. But if I want to make Douglas Hardware the place they come to for all do-it-yourself projects, then we need to make these changes. It's too easy to make the thirty-minute drive to another town, where the stores are bigger and the selection greater. I need to keep the customers in town.

Or the business I've grown up in may be no more.

Chapter 5

Harper

I JUST WAVE GOODBYE TO another customer when my cell phone rings. I recognize Mandy's name right away. She's a former classmate of mine who I reached out to when I heard about the building next door being for sale. She's also Mrs. Morton's niece, so she was able to give me a little more information about the property before it was formally available. She asked where I heard about it, but I never confirmed that piece of information. I'd never tell. It's a secret I'll forever keep.

"Hello?"

"We have a problem," she says in way of greeting.

"What kind of problem?"

"There's another offer."

Did I just hear her right? Another offer? How? When?

"I just got word this morning. Another offer came in from a realtor in Harriston."

"Harriston? I thought you said this building wasn't even formally on the market yet?" I ask, dropping down onto the stool I keep behind the counter.

"It wasn't. That's why I'm so confused on how you found out. Even *I* didn't know, and I'm not only her niece, but the listing agent."

I rub my temple, feeling the headache blooming. "What do we do?"

"You need to come back with a bigger offer. The one you gave is almost exactly what the other offer is. You need to stand out."

"I don't have that much wiggle room," I confess quietly. "My offer was already close to my loan limit."

"Then can you borrow money from someone? Your mom, maybe? You don't want to let this opportunity slip through your fingers, Harper. I mean, when you expand your product line, you'll bring in the extra income to pay the loans off."

At least that's the hope. Of course, it's never guaranteed. My new vision could tank considerably and all this extra work, time, and money would be for nothing. "I can't borrow from Mom. She's still recovering from the fire at the bed and breakfast. They put a lot of extra money into redecorating."

"Samuel then?"

"Maybe," I reply, knowing I could probably borrow a little from my oldest brother. He's always stressing the importance of proper savings and has been squirreling away part of his paychecks since he was old enough to get them.

"I need to go back with a new offer, Harper. What do you want to do?"

My heart pounds in my chest. I know what I have to do, but it's going to make it tight to do it. Part of that loan amount was so I could add the new lines. Every dollar I take from there means my inventory will be affected. "Add five. That's about what I was prepared to go, though I had hoped I wouldn't need to."

"I can do that. Five thousand is a good offer. I'll draw up the papers, stop by and have you sign them, and hand-deliver them to my aunt. She won't be able to refuse the offer, don't worry. She doesn't need the money, but still wants premium dollar for the building. You're already at her original asking price."

"I hope you're right," I whisper, letting worry and uncertainty settle in.

"I'll be in touch," she confirms, hanging up before I get the chance to say goodbye.

Everything I've been dreaming about is right within my reach. But now, someone throws a wrench in my plans, making an offer on a building that's too small for the average business. Who else could possibly know about the building being for sale? There's only one person I know of who knew, and he's the one who shared that tidbit of info with me. He swore me to secrecy, so I don't see him telling other people.

Who knows, maybe this is the kick in the ass I need.

Time to settle down, focus, and do what it takes to win this bid. That building is mine. I just need to make it happen.

At the end of the day, my little sister, Marissa, shows up with a smile on her face and a large iced coffee in her hand. "What has you all happy, happy today? Did you get some?" I ask, teasing my sister. Now all I have to do is sit back and wait for the inevitable blush.

She doesn't disappoint. "No," she says, glancing down and averting her eyes. So if she didn't just get some, it clearly is fresh on her mind. "I came to town to get a few things for tomorrow's breakfast and thought I'd stop in and see my favorite sister, but since all you're going to do is give me a hard time, I'll just leave." Marissa doesn't make a turn for the door, but continues to approach the counter.

"Where's your boy toy?"

"He's working. He's working a big job in Harriston, so he'll probably just stay at his apartment there tonight," she says with a shrug, but I can see the look of disappointment on her face.

Marissa and Rhenn have only been seeing each other a few months, but I can tell it's something bigger than either of them have ever experienced. What started off as a hot little fling, quickly turned into more. He ended up moving to Harriston, only about thirty minutes away from my sister, and transferred his job. Even though he has an apartment there, he spends almost every night in my sister's bed, getting up early and heading off to work. The only thing left hanging open is his dojo back in Jupiter Bay, where's he's originally from.

"A night apart will do you good. Give the ol' cookie a rest for once," I tease.

"Eww, don't say cookie."

"Muff? Honey hole? Sweet love wallet? Snake charmer? Flesh cave? Penis fly trap? Vagina?"

"You're disturbed. You've been hanging around Aunt Emma too much," she retorts, fighting a smile.

I can't help but laugh. "Yeah, that ol' woman is kooky as hell, yet quite entertaining," I reply, closing out my daily sales log and counting the register.

"I brought you this," she says, placing the super yummy iced coffee in front of me. Extra whipped cream, just the way I like it.

"Thanks," I reply, taking the drink from the counter and slurping up the delicious goodness. "Now, I'll have to spend thirty extra minutes on the stationary bike tonight."

"Spin class?" she says, making a horrified face.

"Yeah, at six. You should come."

"Yeah, I'd rather slam my pinky in a car door."

A bubble of laughter spills from my throat. "So dramatic. It wasn't that bad."

"It was horrible. I almost died."

"Did not, baby," I say, counting out the rest of the change and filling out the sales log. When it's complete, I attach the sheet to today's report from the laptop (which works wonderfully, I might add – just don't tell Latham). Once the deposit slip is filled out and everything placed where it goes, I turn off the lights and lock the front door. "Oh, I almost forgot to tell you. Someone else is making an offer on the building."

Marissa looks surprised. "Really? Who?"

"I don't know, but it came from a realtor in Harriston."

"That sucks. Can you counter?"

"Yeah, I increased my bid by five thousand. I hope it's enough because I don't have anything else to add."

Marissa reaches across the counter and takes my hand. "I could help. I don't have too much, but what I do have is yours."

My heart soars. "Thank you, but I'm not sure I want to do that. I don't want to owe everyone. I mean, what if the new venture doesn't take off the way I hope?" I ask, finally saying the main concern I've had since I found out about the building being for sale.

"It's going to do great, Harp. Don't worry about that. Everyone loves your store, and when you bring in more local product, they'll love it even more. It shows you care about the community and supporting local entrepreneurs."

I can't help but smile. "You're right," I state, standing up tall (and towering over my petite little sister). "This new addition is going to be badass."

"The badassest badass shop in town!"

That makes me giggle. "Badassest isn't even a word."

"It should be. We'll add it to the dictionary – right next to a photo of your storefront."

I laugh as I gather my purse, Marissa trailing behind me as I head to the back door. "Thanks for your support," I tell her, pulling her into a hug right before we push through the back entrance. The sun shines brightly, the air warm and heavy.

"You're welcome," she replies, turning and heading toward the corner so she can walk back around to the front of the store where her car is parked. "You know," she adds, stopping in her tracks. "Didn't you go to school with that Pete Hughes? I recall him being a realtor in Harriston."

With my keys in hand, I stop and give her my attention. "Oh, yeah. I forgot about him."

"Maybe you can give him a call to see what he knows?"

"Pete was good friends with Latham in school," I say absently.

Suddenly a piece starts to shift, clicking into another like a jigsaw puzzle.

No.

He wouldn't.

Would he?

"What?" she asks, a concerned look on her face.

Just over her shoulder is the back entrance to Douglas Hardware. Their building takes up half the block, with the lumberyard behind the alley and expanding to the back corner. "Latham."

Marissa glances over her shoulder to the sign above the door, realization setting in. "You don't think," she starts, but leaves it open-ended.

"I do think..."

"What are you going to do?" she asks.

"Win that bid."

With renewed energy and focus (and a lot pissed off), I slip into my car, make my way to the night drive-up window at the bank and throw in the deposit, then head to the gym. My mind is flying a million miles a second, but it keeps coming back to this one thing: no one else knew about the building being for sale.

Except quite possibly Latham.

No, it wasn't him who shared this tidbit of information with me in the first place, but his father. Bud might have mentioned it to his son, too. What if that was their intent? To start a bidding war between their business and mine. Well, the gauntlet has been thrown. I'm not walking away. I want that building. I want to expand my dream. I'm not about to let some jackass who sells paint and two-by-fours push me out of the way.

Latham wants a fight?

I'll give him one.

Of course, I don't know for a fact it *is* Latham who's bidding against me, but whatever.

As soon as I show my membership card to the front desk clerk (that's pointless, by the way, since we're in a small town and everyone knows everyone), I head back to the female locker room to change. I rent a locker with my membership to keep my workout clothes in, so I don't have to carry them with me every day. I change into a black sports bra, red tank top, and black bicycle shorts. When I'm cycling, I don't want bulky material chaffing my thighs, so I wear short, tight pants that cover all my bits and pieces, but allow me the movement I need. I slip on my favorite pair of Adidas runners, fill up my empty bottle with cold water, and head out to meet my class in the spin cycle room.

Unfortunately, my sour mood is further spoiled when I step inside and find my favorite machine already occupied. And not just by any newbie, but none other than Felicity Charles. The girl who did everything she could in school to get under my skin and take everything I had (boyfriends, mostly) for her own. She's an obnoxious Barbie doll of a woman, with just as much brains between her ears as her plastic counterpart.

"Oh my God, is that Harper Grayson? I haven't seen you in forever," she practically yells in the mostly full room of class-takers. Of course, the hairs on the back of my neck immediately stand up and my teeth start to grind the moment she draws out the last word, as if forever somehow has eighteen syllables.

"Hey, Felicity, how have you been?" I ask, trying not to give her my attention, as I look for an unclaimed machine. This class is wildly popular, and usually almost full, so it only takes me a second to realize there aren't many left available. Basically there are two: one directly to her left and one right in front of that one.

Grabbing the unit in the front row, I set my water bottle in the holder and head over for a hand towel. Before I can turn around and do a few stretches, her annoying voice pierces the air once more. This time, bellowing the one word that causes me to stop in my tracks. "Latham!"

Spinning around, I find the man I loathe standing at the doorway, a look of surprise on his face. His eyes meet mine, and even though I wish I wouldn't, I feel the intensity of that gaze all the way down to the apex of my legs. Stupid female hormones. Why must I be attracted to the one man who makes me want to pull my hair out and scream at the top of my lungs? He's the only one to ever get this kinda postal reaction out of me. Well, him and maybe Felicity.

"Are you joining us?" she coos, hopping off her machine and heading his way.

He looks like he's two seconds too late to make a break for it, but relents and gives her a smile anyway. "I was heading to the treadmill and some free weights," he says, glancing at her, but returning his eyes to me. I pretend not to care, instead heading to the front of the room to join a few others in stretching. I make sure to turn my back to him.

And squat.

A lot.

I know my ass is one of my best features, so why not use it to my advantage and show him what he can't have?

"Oh, you totally need to try spinning. It's the best workout you can get!" Felicity practically yells. I try to ignore them, but also can't help to glance their way. Of course, in order to do that, I have to look back at them while I'm stretching – from between my legs. Yes, they're upside down, but it still works. At least it did until Latham's eyes land on mine. Even from this position, I can see how dark and full of desire they are, and I can't help the little tingle of excitement that gives me.

With his eyes still locked on mine (which is really weird now because I'm bent over and looking at him from between my legs), a predatory smile crosses his smug face. "I'd love to join you."

Shit.

"Come on, then. There's an empty machine right next to me!" Before I can look away, she grabs his large forearm and pulls him farther into the room. The movement severs our eye contact, and that's probably for the best. I was starting to feel all warm and tingly for the devil, and that can't happen. Especially after the realization I had when I was leaving work tonight. There's no way I'm letting Latham anywhere near my libido, at least not until I have proof he's the one who made the other bid.

When I'm all stretched out, I return to my bike. Yes, the one positioned right in front of Latham. He gives me a confident, cocky grin, one I return immediately. "Hello," I say, turning around and giving him my backside.

"Hey," he replies, even though he can't see my face anymore.

"Good evening, friends! Are we ready for a workout?" Staci says into her headphones, the sound of her voice carrying through the speakers. "Welcome to Ladies Spinning to Pop Divas. Let's get those leg muscles burning, shall we?"

"Pop divas?" I hear Latham ask behind me as I start to move my legs, a victorious smile spreading across my face, just as Cher starts to blast through the sound system. "You've got to be kidding me," he grumbles.

"Oh, stop being a ninny," Felicity coos. "It's fun! And besides, after our workout, I'll buy you a drink."

I roll my eyes so big, I'm sure the instructor can only see white. Doing everything I can to push Felicity and Latham out of my mind, I start to move my legs, loving the way the burn starts in my calves and spreads to my thighs. I lean forward, positioning my forearms on the handles and start to push through the pain. I've taken this class for a few years now, and have no problems following Staci's instructions. It doesn't take long until we're pumping our arms and thrusting our hips upward, pedaling like hell and starting to sweat.

"Come on, ladies," Staci bellows, "and gentleman. Let's get those hips thrusting!"

I do as instructed, and even though the music is loud, I can clearly hear Latham's moan. It sounds almost...orgasmic.

"You okay?" Felicity asks, and I can't help but glance over my shoulder.

If the ass goes down and has a stroke from spinning, I kinda want to witness it. What I wasn't expecting was to find his eyes glued firmly on my ass. He's pedaling just as fast, thrusting his own hips upward in a manner that can only be described as sexual, and watching me move. A sliver of pride bursts through me, along with something else that settles between my legs.

It's also the first time I really notice his appearance. He's wearing a T-shirt with the sleeves cut off and basketball shorts, but it's the hard, corded muscles that draw my attention. Well, that and his tattoos. Yes, tattoos. As in multiples. There's several on his arms, which I'm surprised I hadn't really noticed before, but also one on his right calf. When he moves, they all jump and flex under the hardness beneath, making my mouth go dry and my panties wet.

"Focus, ladies!" Staci hollers, drawing my attention back to the front of the room. It made me realize I had slowed down considerably, wasn't even close to the same pace as the rest of the class. These are the kinds of distractions I can't allow myself to have, and that's exactly what Latham Douglas is: a distraction.

Returning my focus to the class and the workout, I catch back up with the instructor and pedal twice as hard, determined to not let him have one more ounce of my attention. It's hard though, when Felicity continues to annoyingly talk and compliment the Devil as if he were the spinning master. It almost makes me throw up in my mouth.

When the thirty minute session is finally complete, I sit back on my seat, letting my legs begin to slow their forward motion. I squirt a little water into my mouth, noticing how out of breath I am. I'm never this winded, yet I feel like I just ran a marathon in the rain. Sweat is definitely not attractive.

My legs are a little wobbly when I stand up, so I immediately start to stretch them out. As I'm bent over, a shadow falls over me. "Did you enjoy your first Ladies Spinning to Pop Divas class?" I ask without looking his way.

"I did. The view was phenomenal."

I glance up and meet his bright eyes. "Pig."

That only makes him laugh. "Guilty," he says as he takes a drink from his bottle. "I didn't know you took spin class, though I'm not surprised. Your ass is definitely well worked," he says, the sexual innuendo clear.

"Well, I do enjoy a good workout on my ass," I quip, giving him a smug smile.

"I just bet you do," he whispers, his voice deep and husky.

He takes a step forward, his large body impeding in my personal space, and my eyes look up to meet his. It's suddenly hard to breathe. He's right there, his body pressed against mine, when that annoying voice breaks the silence. "Are you ready, Lath?"

I jump back, stumbling into my bike. I'm saved from taking a tumble when his big arms reach out and grab me. Shockwaves of lust slam into me, filling my senses with his scent and his touch. My wide eyes meet his equally shocked ones, but that look quickly disappears. It's replaced by a cocky smile.

Righting myself and shaking off his hands, I say, "Well, *Lath*, you don't want to keep her waiting."

His smile slips a bit and his eyes sober. "Why don't you come with us?" he asks, the look on his face clear he doesn't really want to go have drinks with her.

"Sorry, I can't. I have to head home and take care of my dog," I say, grabbing my towel and wiping my neck. I reach for my water bottle, but don't see it in the holder. That's when I realize it's in the Devil's hand. The asshole has been drinking my water.

"Oh, too bad," Felicity says, clearly not upset at all I can't go. "Maybe next time."

"Yeah, maybe," I reply with a sweet smile. "Anyway, you two have fun," I add, reaching for my water. He doesn't hand it over right away. Instead, slowly brings it to his mouth and squeezes. He takes a long drink, his eyes locked on mine as his throat muscles work to swallow the liquid, before handing it back to me. I feel his gaze as I bring it up to my mouth and place my lips in the very spot his just sat. A shiver sweeps through my body.

"Well, let's go, Lath. We can celebrate my new position underneath you!" she exclaims, making me choke on the water I'm swallowing.

My eyes meet his as he pats my back. "You okay?"

"Fine," I gasp. Turning toward Felicity, I can't help but ask, "New position?"

"I'm Latham's new girl!"

"At the hardware store," he adds quickly, the slight hint of reservation in his voice.

"Yep. I start tomorrow morning and get to spend all day shadowing him and working beside him. It's going to be sooooo fun," she says, threading her arms through his and plastering herself against his side.

"Well, congrats to you," I say to her with a smirky smile. "I mean, there's no one better to sell wood and screws than you. You're an expert." Felicity's mouth flies open and Latham chokes on air, but tries to cover it quickly with a cough. "Anyway, you two have fun."

Chapter 6

Latham

"CAN YOU BELIEVE SHE SAID that? How rude! I mean, it's not my fault Joey cheated on her. Though, do you blame him? She's awful!" Felicity bellows as she slides into a booth bench I was just about to sit on. The moment she does, I switch gears and move to the opposite side.

"Joey?" I ask, hoping and praying she isn't about to say the one name I dread she's going to say.

"Joey Trudeau. They were dating, I guess. I mean, it's not my fault! I didn't know he was seeing her when we hooked up. He never mentioned her," Felicity argues, reaching for the menu and skimming over the drink list. I'm sure he didn't have time to mention that piece of info, you know between ramming his tongue down her throat and his dick in her pussy.

Joey fucking Trudeau. I can't believe she dated him. What the fuck? The guy is as douche-y as a douche nozzle. Of course he'd cheat on her. He screwed every girl in school, not giving one shit he was usually in a relationship at the time. "Harper dated Joey?" I ask, trying to confirm this tidbit of detail.

"I guess. Rumor has it they were talking marriage," she shrugs, not looking up from the wine list.

"And you screwed him?"

Her eyes finally meet mine. I expect to see guilt or something, but I find no trace anywhere. "I didn't know they were dating. He came into the bar I was hanging out in and started flirting with me. Next thing I know we're in the bathroom going at it when the owner walks in. Did you know Mara ran straight to Harper and told her?" she asks, her eyes wide with shock.

"You don't say?" I reply, dryly. "Mara's still around?"

"She owns this bar with her husband, Brent," Felicity adds absently, checking her nails. Of course she'd recommend the same place where she was caught screwing a taken man.

"So Harper and Joey obviously broke up?" I ask, not even the least bit concerned I'm using Felicity to gain a little intel.

"Obviously, he was bored. No happy man cheats on his girlfriend. He complained all night about his girl working crazy hours and some shit. Something about trying to get her business off the ground."

What a fucking dick. "And he couldn't deal with her making something of herself and working hard to make her business successful?" I'm super annoyed right now, wishing Joey Trudeau would walk through the door so I could put my fist through his nose. The guy was always the biggest tool in school. I can't even begin to wonder what Harper saw in him.

"I guess," she says, rolling her eyes. "Anyway, enough about Joey and Harper. Let's talk about us!" She practically jumps up and down in her seat.

"There is no us," I remind her as the waitress approaches.

"What can I get you?"

"I'll have a Bud Light bottle," I say, already knowing it's a one-beer limit for me tonight. One beer to be polite, and then I'm out of here.

"And I'll take a Sex on the Beach," she croons, throwing in a giggle for good measure. Something tells me if I offered, there'd definitely be some sex later. But there's no way in hell I'm offering.

Not happening.

I wouldn't even touch that with someone else's dick.

"So, what have you been up to since graduation?" I ask as my beer is placed in front of me. I'm not super curious, but needed something else to talk about besides Harper and her ex.

"Well, I went off to New York for a while. I worked on Broadway for a bit, starring in a few shows. At the beginning of the year, I was just getting burnt out, ya know?" she asks, flipping her hair. "I missed home, so I moved back."

"Broadway, huh? That's pretty impressive," I reply, chugging half my beer in one gulp.

"It was soooo amazing," she bustles. "And New York was a dream come true," she adds, her eyes bright with excitement. I try to recall phone conversations with my mom, and I don't recall her ever mentioning Felicity and Broadway. Not that I would have retained the intel anyway. I was usually halfway around the world when I'd get a few minutes to talk.

"Good for you," I reply, drinking another big gulp.

"And how about you? Are you seeing anyone?" she asks, not very subtly.

"I'm not, but also not really interested right now. I just got home from the military and am taking over my family business."

"But what if the right girl comes along? I mean, then you won't be able to deny the chemistry," she adds, leaning forward and pressing her chest together. The grin she gives me is hopeful and alluring, but does nothing for the male parts of my brain.

Now if we want to talk about male parts, let's go back to that spinning class from hell, where I had to stare at Harper's perfect ass for thirty minutes. Talk about a boner-inducing nightmare. I was afraid I was going to injure myself when I got off the bike. I spent half the class hard as stone and wishing I could throw her down on the mat and pound her like nails.

And now I'm getting hard again...

"Well, I should head out," I say, adjusting my pants and sliding my beer bottle to the front of the table.

"What? You can't go yet! We've only had one drink," she pouts, jutting out her bottom lip like a toddler.

"'Fraid so. I have an early day tomorrow." I don't, but I don't need her to know that.

"Fine," she whines, her voice like nails on a chalkboard. "I guess it's okay since I'll be seeing you at eight tomorrow morning!"

"Yep," I reply, sliding from the bench seat. "See you in the morning."

Felicity springs out of the booth, throwing her arms around my shoulders and plastering her fake tits to my chest. "I'm so glad you're home, Lath," she whispers just before placing her lips to my cheek. She had just painted them a dark shade of pink, so there's no doubt in my mind I now have a lip mark to match.

A throat clears over my shoulder and I turn to find Freedom. She's glaring, but not at me – at Felicity. "Out slumming it tonight, Latham?" she asks me, but doesn't take her narrowed eyes off the woman who's still plastered to my chest.

"Oh, zip it, Free. We were just having a drink, for ol' times' sake," Felicity retorts, her arms still tangled around me.

"Mmhmm, I bet. Watch out, Latham. Rumor has it, this one has crabs," Free whispers just loud enough for half the bar to hear.

Felicity gasps. "That's not true!"

Free shrugs her shoulders. "That's what I heard," she says, turning her back to us and walking over to the bar. She slides onto the empty barstool to the right of Harper, who's talking to Mara on her left. Harper looks freshly showered, her damp hair pulled up on top of her head in one of those messy bun things. Her face has minimal makeup, and if I do say so myself, she looks probably more beautiful right now than ever before.

Felicity is babbling beside me, probably trying to convince me she doesn't have something itchy between her legs, but I completely tune her out. Instead, my attention is focused solely on the beauty at the bar, pretending to ignore me. But I saw the way she watched me out of the corner of her eye. She's wearing a blue fitted tee and a pair of shorts that should be deemed illegal to wear outside of the home.

Not that I don't enjoy them.

Hell, I think I'm enjoying them a little too much, if the sudden tightness in my pants is any indication.

Every dick in the joint is suddenly focused on the trio of women at the bar, or more accurately, at the pair of seemingly endless legs on the woman in the middle.

Jealousy rears its ugly green head, and I don't like it.

"Ladies," I say, sliding in between Harper and Free, essentially blocking the view of her from the rest of the assholes in the place.

"Satan," Harper replies without even glancing my way.

"Aww, Harp, are you still upset your brother had to come fix your car?" I tease, reaching over her shoulder and grabbing a handful of popcorn. When she finally glances my way, an evil glare on her beautiful face, I offer her a smirk and a wink. Nothing gets Harper's blood boiling like that deadly combination of male ego. I say deadly because several times she's tried to maim me or threatened to cut off an appendage.

"You're such a dick," she grumbles, repeatedly stabbing me with her blue eye daggers.

"You want my what?" I can't help it. I say it just to see if flames will actually shoot out of her ears.

"I want to cut off your dick."

Leaning forward once more, I inhale her sexy, sugary, clean from the shower scent. "Sounds kinky. I'm not usually into BDSM, but for you," I stop, glance down and take a long look at her exposed legs, "I'd be willing to give it a try." Standing up straight, I take her beer bottle and bring it to my lips. "But I'm tying you up, love. I like to be in charge in the bedroom."

Her face flushes. Damn, if that isn't the sexiest thing I've ever seen. But it's quickly followed by her ears turning bright red in rage with the smoke I was wondering about earlier, billowing from her ears. "I'd rather tie you to a tree and let the wildlife feed on your decaying carcass."

"This is so much better than porn," Free says to Mara, who gives her a nod and smirk. "You two should just do it already. This beating around the bush, I hate you thing is fun, but I think you're drawing it out too long. Let's get to the sex."

"I'd rather have sex with a porcupine," Harper retorts, reaching for her beer bottle, but coming up empty. She turns my way and glares, earning a wide smile from me as I bring the beer to my lips and finish it off. "I hate you."

"So you've said. Repeatedly," I remind her, setting her empty bottle down on the bar and waving over the bartender. He looks familiar, and it only takes me a few seconds to figure out that it's Brent Tanner, Mara's husband. "Hey, man," I say to my former classmate, extending my hand.

"Hey, Latham. Finally home from the Army?" he asks after shaking my hand. He reaches down into the cooler and pulls out another beer, popping off the top, and setting it in front of Harper.

"Home for good," I confirm. I also realize I'm still wedged between Harper and Free and have my chest plastered to her. I also realize she doesn't move, so I don't either.

"Are you buying me another?" I hear over my shoulder and find Felicity standing behind me. She reaches out her hands, latches on to my arm, and pulls me back, essentially cutting off my connection with Harper.

Turning to Brent, who gives me a knowing look, I tell him to grab a round for everyone. While he does, the girls go back to ignoring me, but not really ignoring me, and I go back to trying to extract my body from Felicity's talons. Finally, when I finish my beer, I set the empty on the counter and wave off another.

"Leaving?" Brent asks.

"Yep. Big day tomorrow."

"Doctor's office opens at eight. I'm sure they can give you something for the itch," my redheaded minx announces loudly to the bar.

Not letting her have the final word, I reply, "Maybe next time you'll disclose all of your STDs before you maul me in the men's bathroom and give me crabs."

She gasps as I throw her a wink, turn, and head toward the exit.

"Bye, Lath! I'll see you tomorrow," Felicity hollers.

I throw a wave over my shoulder without turning around and push through the door. Before I'm completely out of sight, I glance back, enjoying one last look of those long legs and short shorts. It'll be those images that accompany me to bed later tonight. I'll even pretend she's using those legs for good and not trying to strangle me with them.

Smiling, I open my truck door, slide the key in the ignition, and give it a crank. My ears instantly start to bleed when Britney Spears blasts through the speakers at full volume. "Fuck!" I holler, my fingers fumbling with the knob. Once I'm bathed in silence, I can't help but laugh. Funny, she'd pick "...Baby One More Time" to play as her form of torture.

Good call.

However, one thing she may not realize: one time will never be enough. I'll always want more.

Chapter 7

Harper

IT'S A BEAUTIFUL DAY. I mean picture perfect, sun is shining high in the sky, you can taste the salt on the ocean breeze day. My favorite kinda day.

Free is opening the shop for me, which gives me an extra two hours this morning to run my errands. I've already stopped at the bank, the post office, and am heading to the market to grab a few things to stock in the fridge for my lunches and snacks. Just opposite the market is the bakery that opened a handful of years back by a fellow Rockland Falls alumni. Jasmine Clifton had her grand opening of Sugar and Spice nearly five years ago. She was a couple of years younger than I was in school, but I remember her as the person we all went to for the best bake sale treats.

Her window catches my attention immediately. There are three gorgeous, intricate wedding cakes on display of all shapes and sizes. Since we don't have any hotels, nor resorts for things like destination weddings, the ones that do happen in town are usually on the smaller side, at one of the many small churches or maybe even on the beach. There's nothing more beautiful than a beachside wedding.

My stomach growls as I stare at the detail on the three cakes. One is pure, bright white with a softer off-white lace overlay. It's simple, classic, and stunning. The second cake is tall with brightly colored flowers flowing from the top tier and down the sides like a beautifully flowing stream. The third cake is small, with only two fat tiers, but the intricate sugar sand and seashells sets it completely apart from the others. Anyone having a beach wedding would *want* this cake at their reception.

I have no idea how long I stand there and stare, but I don't care. The cakes are stunning, but I bet they taste even better. I mean, it is almost lunchtime, and I have yet to eat. The sign in front of the cakes draws my attention. *Cake samples available for bride/groom.*

I bet they have chocolate.

"Whatcha doin'?" a voice whispers in my ear, making me jump a foot in the air.

"Jesus, Latham, creeper much?" I ask, turning his way and holding a hand to my racing heart.

"Not my fault you were lusting over the cake and didn't hear me approach." He shrugs his wide shoulders, his blue Douglas Hardware polo molded to his impressive arms and chest, but what really draws my attention right now is his throat. It's thick and dusted with a coarse matting of dark hair. It makes me want to lick it, and I've never wanted to lick a neck before.

Until now.

"Don't you have babies to scare?" I ask, giving him my back and turning to face the yummy cakes.

"'Fraid not, sweetness. I have nothing but free time and no one to torture but you."

"Lucky me," I grumble without turning back to face him.

I see his shadow fall over the window and feel the heat radiating from his body as he steps up behind me. And I can smell him. It's a combination of musky soap and fresh cut wood. It surprises me how much I actually really like the scent. I like it so much I actually sway his way, just the slightest, but of course, he notices, offering me that stupid cocky smirk, reflecting in the window, I want to punch right off his face. And then kiss his full lips. The combination makes my body tingle.

Stupid, traitorous body.

"I bet that's chocolate cake," he whispers. The bastard knows my weakness.

"Who cares?" I ask, though my voice holds no conviction.

Latham chuckles. "I bet you do. If memory serves me correctly, you would do *anything* for chocolate cake."

"That was one time in fifth grade," I argue, crossing my arms over my chest.

Stepping into my personal space, he practically plasters his body to mine. His breath tickles my neck as he asks, "What was it that you did again?"

Not one to back down, even though I really could use a little distance between us so I can think, I reply with a sweet smile. "I duct taped Nicholas Leitz to the swingset."

"And why did you do that?"

Closing my eyes, I sigh in resignation. "So I could have the last piece of chocolate cake."

"It was his birthday, Harper!"

"I know!" I bellow, making him laugh. The next thing I know, we're both laughing right there on the sidewalk. The way his entire face lights up when he smiles makes me forget for just a few seconds that I hate him. We both stare at the cakes, neither one of us really saying anything else.

Suddenly, he grabs my hand and pulls me toward the door. "Come on."

"Where are we going?" I ask, even though I already know the answer.

The bell chimes as we enter the cool bakery, the scent of sugar and cinnamon permeating the air. My mouth instantly starts to water. "Holy mother of all things chocolate, do you see this?" I ask, my feet carrying me to the display case. Chocolate scones, s'mores brownies, double chocolate fudge, and Bavarian cream chocolate iced donuts. I don't care if I have to spin for two hours every night for the rest of my life, I'd do just about anything for that donut.

"Can I help you?" Jasmine asks as she comes from the back area. "Oh, hey, Harper! How are you?"

"I'm so good right now, Jasmine. Can I get one of those donuts?" I ask, drool probably hanging from my chin as she giggles and retrieves a wax paper square for my breakfast. Or lunch, I guess, since it's closer to noon than breakfast time.

That's also when I notice the free samples on the counter. Fudge. Samples. I barely even chew as I reach for the first piece and slide it into my mouth, the rich sweetness hitting my tongue and setting my senses ablaze. "Holy shit," I mumble with my mouth full.

"My little muffin-bottom loves chocolate, doesn't she?" Latham coos in a sugary sweet voice, drawing my attention, as well as Jasmine's.

"Excuse me?" I ask, whipping around to face him and giving him my trademark death stare. Oh, my mouth's still full, by the way.

"Hi, Jasmine, I'm not sure if you remember me. Latham Douglas," he says, extending his hand over the counter.

"Oh, Latham, of course! How have you been? Are you back in town?"

"I am, thanks. I just couldn't stay away from my little pookie any longer," he says, grabbing my hand.

I swallow hard over the fudge and give him a look. What the fuck is he talking about?

"Wait, are you...are you guys together?" Jasmine asks, her face alive with excitement.

Before I can say "Fuck no!" Latham opens his big-ass mouth. "We are!"

"Fuck," I grumble, trying to pry my hand from his grip.

"And...we're getting married!" he announces to God and the only woman within hearing distance.

"Shut up!" she screams, clapping her hands with excitement.

"Yeah, shut up," I mutter, my mouth hanging open.

"So, I thought we'd stop in and try some of those cake samples you posted about in the display," Latham says, bringing my hand to his mouth and placing tender kisses along my knuckles.

I can't breathe.

"Absolutely! Do you have a date set yet?" she asks, glancing between my new fiancé and me.

"Not yet, Jasmine. It's a fairly new development."

"Really new," I whisper, watching as his lips continue to dance on my skin.

"I'm so excited! Let me go grab some samples. Meet me over at that table in the corner," she hollers as she turns and retreats to the back room.

"What the fuck is wrong with you?" I growl, ripping my hand from his and hitting him across the shoulder. The very hard, unforgiving shoulder. My hand throbs, but I'm not about to give him the satisfaction that his stupid muscles injured my hand.

"What? I thought you'd be happy. Now you get chocolate cake," he reasons, leading me to the table.

I plop down hard in the chair and rub my throbbing temples. "You could have just bought me some chocolate, Latham. You didn't have to tell her we were getting married, you big, dumb idiot!"

He sits down across from me. "Oh, well, it seemed like a good idea at the time."

"At what time did a fake engagement seem like a good idea, Latham?"

He just smirks. "It's okay to admit you're a little excited at the thought of being my betrothed."

"I'd rather streak naked through the town square on Sunday morning, right after church."

"I wouldn't mind seeing that, actually," Latham says, leaning back in the chair, his big long legs extended out casually before him so that the front two legs lift off the floor.

"You'll never see it. Ever," I growl, kicking my foot out and pushing against the chair. Latham teeters for a second before realization sets in. He falls backward, going down hard, his back and the chair hitting the floor with a loud, wood-splitting crunch.

"Oh my word, are you okay?" Jasmine comes running in, a platter of cake samples in her hand.

"He's fine," I reply with a nonchalant wave, not even looking over at my stupid fake fiancé as he climbs off the floor. Jasmine sets the platter down and goes to Latham, trying to help him off the floor. "Is this chocolate?" I ask, diving into the first cake sample without a care in the world.

"It is," Jasmine replies, a little out of sorts. I can feel her eyes as she glances from Latham to me, probably trying to determine how I can be so unconcerned at my fiancé being laid out on the floor. That thought makes me giggle.

"Something funny?" he whispers in my ear, his hot breath tickling my earlobe. I admit I shiver. Just a little.

"Are you okay, dimple bottom?" I ask, chewing my first chocolate cake sample and offering him a victorious grin.

"I'm fine, sweet cheeks. Falling more in love with you every second of every day," he coos, stroking one of his big fingers down my jaw. His words finally register: love.

And suddenly, I'm choking on my cake.

Latham starts pounding on my back as I gasp and swallow my mouthful.

"Oh my God, are you okay?" Jasmine comes over holding her hands to her mouth. "I hope the pieces weren't cut too big," she adds, glancing down at the platter.

"No," I gasp, wiping away the tears that developed, "it's fine. They're fine. I just got so...choked up on my...love for Latham." His name comes out a whisper.

"See, she's fine. We just can't contain our love," Latham flaps, offering Jasmine a wide smile. It's a charismatic one that makes women everywhere giggle like schoolgirls.

And cue the giggle in three...two...one...

Jasmine giggles. "Let's have a seat. I usually have more flavors to sample, but since you've just stopped in, I don't have a full variety. But this is a good start," she says, handing Latham the match to the sample I already tried. "This is double chocolate cake with a mocha and French vanilla icing."

I watch as Latham brings it to his mouth. I can't take it anymore. I need it. So, I reach out and take the cake and shove it in my mouth. He laughs, while Jasmine looks at me like I'm a monster. No, Latham is the cake-eating monster. This was his brilliant idea, so I get all the cake.

"Good?" he asks, licking the bits of cake and icing left on his fingers.

"So good." Yes, my mouth is full when I say it.

"Wow, okay," Jasmine says, her wide eyes full of shock. "I guess you like that one. This one," she says, pushing a sample toward each of us, "is a banana cream cake with white chocolate fudge icing." I shove the sample into my mouth whole. "It's fabulous with fresh bananas layered with milk chocolate fudge."

"Jesus, Latham, did you taste this?" I ask, glancing at my pseudo-fiancé. He has yet to eat his sample, but is intensely watching me devour mine. He slowly takes a bite, a drop of white chocolate icing dotting his upper lip. I want to lick it.

I'm sure that's the icing talking...

"It's delicious, giggle lips."

"What else do you have?" I ask, glancing down lovingly at the succulent little samples of cake.

"My goodness, you do love your sweets. I'd do anything to have your metabolism," Jasmine says, sliding a third sample in front of me.

"Oh, it's starting to catch up with her, isn't that right, gingersnap?"

"What do you mean?" I ask, glaring at him across the table, savoring the sweet strawberry cake piece.

"Oh, it's nothing, angel cakes. I don't care at all that you've put on a little weight," he assures me, the cake in my mouth suddenly turning dry and heavy.

"Weight? But Harper still looks as amazing as ever," Jasmine says with an uncomfortable chuckle.

"She does," Latham assures. "I just can't help but notice how much she's been eating lately. And she's putting it on in the middle. It makes me wonder if maybe..." he says, looking down at my stomach.

I glance down, trying to figure out what in the hell he's talking about, when suddenly, Jasmine bursts with excitement. "Oh my God, she's pregnant!"

"What?" I wheeze, gulping down the sawdust cake.

"Well, I don't know for sure, but there are signs," Latham says casually, taking a healthy bite of strawberry cake. "Wow, this one is delicious. It might be my favorite. What do you think, Mama?"

I stare at him, wide-eyed and too shocked to speak. Whatever I attempt to say comes out a squeak. The rest of the tasting continues, and I barely participate. I'm stuck on the fact I'm apparently engaged and suddenly pregnant. It's not the engagement that has me speechless, but the nonexistent pregnancy. I've always wanted a baby, and abruptly, the thought of actually having one seems almost...real.

Except I haven't had sex in more than six months.

Pretty sure a baby at this point would be a miracle.

"This is so exciting," Jasmine sings, and I don't dispute her claim.

Well, not really her claim.

Latham's.

He's sitting over there, all cocky and proud, and wearing a smirk while he boosts about how amazing the cake samples are. I'm sitting here, pissed as hell as he ruined this cake-infused moment, and now worried I'm carrying a few extra pounds in the waist area. Just goes to show how low he'd stoop to have the final say.

Or the property.

He's getting in my head, and I can't have that. I need to stand strong and not wobble under his brand of meanness. I can outsmart anything Mr. Latham Douglas throws at me. I mean, he used cake to his benefit today and look where that got me? Engaged and apparently pregnant.

Asshole.

He may have won this round, but he won't win the war.

I can't help but giggle as I click enter, confirming my order for first thing Friday morning. The express two-day shipping costs a small fortune, but it'll be worth it. Except, I won't be able to see the look on his face when he opens it.

Pity.

I'll just settle for the satisfaction of knowing I got him way better than his stupid cake/fake wedding/surprise baby joke yesterday. Which, by the way, took me a while to convince Jasmine that I wasn't knocked up with Satan's spawn. The engagement? Well, I left that fight to deal with another day.

Now, I'm standing at my fancy new laptop, a wide smile on my face, and ready to flip the open sign for the day. The sun is shining, the weather is perfect late-July weather on the beach, and I have a date for Saturday night.

Yes, you hear me right.

A date.

It happened last night when I was leaving the gym. I had to run an extra mile and row my ass off to burn the calories from yesterday morning's cake-fest. Do I regret it? Not for a second. I could have done with a little less Latham, but the cake was amazing, so sometimes, you have to take the bad with the good.

Anyway, back to my date. When I was finished working out, freshly showered, and heading to the small beverage counter for a smoothie, one of the regulars stopped me and bought my drink. We chatted for a few minutes, and that's when Skyler asked me out. At first, I wasn't sure if I wanted to accept his invitation. I mean he's a little older than me (not a big deal, really) and is recently divorced (also, not a huge deal either), but for some reason, I hesitated.

Am I ready to date? It *has* been half a year since I was in a relationship with the spineless bastard known as Joey Trudeau. It wouldn't hurt me to go out and enjoy a drink or meal with someone of the opposite sex who isn't family. Although, I have to admit, I'm not sure Skyler is the right guy for my return visit into dating.

That's when I saw Latham.

He was standing in the gym, just over Skyler's shoulder, and he was talking to one of the barely legal gym bunnies who show up every day in itsy bitsy workout attire and take selfies on all the equipment. All the guys drool all over them, and apparently, Latham is no different.

So, I glanced back at Skyler, his mustache starting to turn gray at the lip, and say yes.

And now I have a date on Saturday night, and I won't think about Latham at all.

My email dings with a notification, which turns out to be my order confirmation for my Latham gift. This is me, not thinking about him. To be fair, I vowed not to give him a thought on Saturday. I didn't say anything about today. As I peruse over my order confirmation, a smile spreads across my face.

This is going to be the best *gift* ever!

Chapter 8

Latham

COME FRIDAY MORNING, I REALIZE I have a problem. A big one.

Namely, Harper Grayson.

And the fact she increased her bid on the property between us.

I guess, technically, that's two problems.

The first one creeps up right about the time I go to sleep. And wake up. And shower. And hear someone humming one of those stupid-ass boy band songs she's so fond of. Basically, she's a big problem I can't seem to eradicate from my mind. It's like she pitched a fucking tent in my head and is in it for the long run. Speaking of tents, I seem to be pitching one regularly too. Every time I think about her, things start to happen in my pants.

That second problem is the reason I'm at work early on Friday morning. I put in a call to my realtor, Pete, who said I've made the best offer I could and that it was a waiting game. Two offers on the table, and it was up to Mrs. Morton to decide which way she wanted to go. Of course, it wouldn't hurt to grease the wheels a little, if you know what I mean. That's why I'll be stopping by Mrs. Morton's place this weekend to see if there's anything I can *help* with around the house. You know, maintenance shit. She only has granddaughters, so I'm sure she'd appreciate a big strong man stopping by to help her mow her grass or mend the fence. Plus, Mom's making me one of her famous carrot cakes to take with me.

No one can resist Mom's carrot cake.

That deal is as good as mine.

So, by the time lunch rolls around, I'm in a damn good mood. Even dealing with Felicity can't dampen this day. She prances around, flirting with the customers in a way that would make my grandpa spit nails, and always finds herself "busy" when it comes time to actually check out the customers. But today, not even her constant touches get under my skin.

Today, is a good fucking day.

"Latham, you have a package!" Felicity hollers from the front counter. I've slipped into the office to get started on the payroll, something else that won't even dampen my good mood.

I get up and head up front, wishing Dale hadn't taken the first lunch break today. Felicity's there, a wide smile spread across her pink lips, as she waves a cylinder in front of my face. It's about a foot long and has no distinguishing markings to tell what it is.

"What's that?" I ask, reaching for the package.

"I'm not sure, but it has your name on it," she replies, stepping forward and placing the cylinder against my chest, running her nails along my pec as she goes.

"Thanks," I grumble, stepping around her claws and setting the package on the counter.

There's no company name on the return label, just a PO Box address. Most of our shipments come to the back door, and I don't have anything outstanding that I'm waiting on. It must be a sample. We get them occasionally from distributors and companies hoping we'll carry their product.

I slice through the tape and apply a little pressure to the plastic lid. It's not easy to get it to move, but once it does, it pops open.

It. Fucking. Pops. Open.

And I'm showered in something tiny.

I blink, my ears ringing from the noise the canister made when the lid blew, and realize I have spots in my vision. It's like there's shit stuck to my eyeballs.

"Oh my God!" Felicity exclaims, laughing hysterically behind me.

"What the fuck," I grumble, swiping at my eyes and finding my hands covered in tiny pink flecks of...

Glitter.

"You've been glitter-bombed! That's the best gag ever," she continues, cackling and carrying on. "It's pink too! You should see your hair." Turning around, I glance her way, only to have her burst out into a fresh wave of laughter. "Holy shitballs, it's in your beard too!"

"What the hell is this shit?" I ask, running my hands over my face and seeing little pink particles rain all over the counter and floor.

"It's a glitter bomb. Haven't you heard of them?" she asks, earning a growl in response from me. "So anyway, you send an anonymous glitter bomb to someone and it explodes, raining glitter all over the place. That stuff is horrible to clean up," she adds, making no movement to retrieve a broom.

"That's just fucking great," I grumble.

"Oh, it was great," she says as I shake out my hair. "It's stuck everywhere. I think you have it in your ears."

"I need a shower," I state, wondering how long it'll be before Dale returns so I can slip upstairs and clean up.

"Oh, a shower won't help much. Glitter is like little pieces of hell that glue themselves to everything and anything. You'll be picking that stuff out of your hair and clothes for weeks," she adds with another giggle. "Who did you piss off?"

"What?" I ask, turning to face her.

"What?"

"What did you mean about pissing someone off?" I ask.

"A glitter bomb. They advertise as the best way to payback someone you hate. Glitter is a nightmare."

Hate.

Fuck me.

That little devil.

"I'll be back," I yell, as I round the counter and head toward the door.

"Where are you going?" Felicity hollers.

"To buy a thong." I fly out the door and stomp down the block.

As soon as I reach her door, I take a few deep, calming breaths before I give the glass door a tug. It opens easily, the little bell above announcing my arrival. Free is standing at the counter and glances up, instantly bursting into huge fits of laughter. "Are you trying out for a music video? That's pretty badass, Latham."

"Where is she?"

"Who would you be referring to?" Free asks, an ornery smile on her bright red lips.

"Don't play coy with me, Freedom Rayne," I state as I approach the counter.

"I would never, Latham Douglas," she mirrors, fighting another smile. As I approach the counter, her laughter fills the room once more. "Holy shit, it's so much better up close."

"Ha, ha, laugh now," I grumble, leaning on the counter, fighting my own urge to smile. I don't know why being covered in pink glitter would make me want to grin, but for some reason, it does.

"Oh, Latham, I didn't realize pink was your color."

I turn to the right and see the woman responsible for my new style coming out of a closet door off to the side. Her arms are loaded with boxes, her hair pulled up in a tight ponytail that reveals the long, slender column of her neck. Suddenly, all I want to do is lick and suck on that tender skin.

"I suppose you wouldn't know anything about this?" I ask, turning to face her as she approaches the counter, setting the boxes beside me.

"About your festive new pink look? I wouldn't know a thing about it," she coos, batting her eyelashes and smiling sweetly. But it's the glimmer of evil in her eyes that gives her away.

"Nothing, huh? Okay," I state, standing up tall like I'm going to leave. "I guess I have nothing else to do but this..." And I start shaking off like a dog.

"Latham! Stop! You're getting glitter everywhere!" Harper screeches, putting her hands up to block the flying glitter.

When I stop, I just stare down into her stunning blue eyes. They're wide with laughter, and maybe a little irritation. "You made a mess," she grumbles, refusing to look away.

"You should see my store." Then I take a step forward, invading her personal space. Harper's eyes widen just a little bit in alarm, but she doesn't back down. Instead, my little tomcat juts her chin up high and places her hands on her hips in a defiant manner. It's so fucking hot.

"I'm sure Felicity would be more than happy to clean up your mess." The way she says my employee's name makes me want to crack a smile. It's like something left a horrible taste in her mouth.

"It's funny, she seems to always be busy doing something else when it comes time to...work."

Harper shrugs. "Then, I guess you'll be cleaning it yourself." She steps forward until we're chest to chest, and I pray she can't feel my growing erection in my pants. "I would tell you to shower, but I hear glitter is hell to get off the skin. Especially, the hair," she adds, bringing her hand up and running her palm along my stubbled jawline.

Electricity zips through my blood at the contact. Her eyes darken, and suddenly, all I can think about is kissing her.

"I'll go get a broom," Free says, but neither of us turn to acknowledge her statement. We continue to stare at each other, contemplating our next moves. If it were up to me, my next one would be to take her in that supply closet, strip off all her clothes, and devour her entire body with my tongue.

"That wasn't very nice," I tell her, referring to the glitter gift.

"You called me fat," she replies, her hand still resting on my jaw.

"I would never."

"You insinuated it. Half the town probably thinks I'm carrying Satan's spawn right now."

"You'd be so lucky," I retort, earning a snort and eye roll. I take a step forward, pressing her firmly against the counter. There's nowhere for her to go, and she knows it. Her eyes widen more, but her tongue gives her away. It snakes out and wets her bottom lip.

All I can think about is kissing those full, lush lips. "But Harper?" I ask, bringing my own hand up and cupping the back of her neck.

She makes a noise, but doesn't actually say a word. Instead, she shivers against my body as I press my aching cock into her stomach. "I haven't fucked you, Sweetheart. Yet." I lean down, keeping eye contact until the last possible second. I slide my lips along her jawline, another shudder sweeping through her body. Fuck, do I love the way she responds to my touch. "But I will."

Memorizing the way she feels, smells, and tastes, I let my lips glide along her tender flesh for too long, yet not nearly long enough. The bell above the door chimes, making us both jump apart like guilty teenagers. Reluctantly, I pull away, dropping my hand. Her eyes are glazed, her mouth slightly opened, her breathing a bit erratic.

Fuck me, I want one more taste of those damn lips.

But before I can pull her into my arms, she transforms into businesswoman Harper, steeling her back and pulling down the front of her shirt. Her eyes narrow as she glares tiny little daggers at me. I want to crack a smile, but my dick doesn't think this is too funny right now.

"Good day, Mr. Douglas," she says curtly.

"Yes, I should get back to the store. I have a...mess to clean up."

That gets a tiny smile. "Well, enjoy your pink glitter."

"Turnabout is fair play, Miss Grayson. Just remember that," I state as I turn my back to her, coming face-to-face with the new customer for the first time.

My mom.

"Latham?"

"Hey, Mom." Talk about uncomfortable.

"What are you doing here? Bothering poor Harper, I see," Mom teases, a look in her eye I don't want to dissect.

"I received a gift from poor Harper a few minutes ago." Harper snorts behind me. "I just stopped by to say thank you."

"Does this gift have anything to do with the fact that you look like you've spent the last three days straight at a strip club?" Mom asks, smiling widely, sweeping her hand across my shoulder and sending little sparkles of pink flying everywhere.

"I heard he was trying out for a boy band," Harper chimes in, humor laced in her face.

"I do love a good boy band," I mumble, heading toward the door.

"What can I do for you today, Kitty?" Harper says, her voice all sugary sweet for my mother.

"Well, remember that blue nighty I purchased last week? I'd love to get the same one in pink. Bud just loves that lighter shade against my pale skin," I hear my mom say, making me stop dead in my tracks.

"Mother?" I holler over my shoulder.

"Yes, Latham?"

"Maybe, next time, wait until I'm out of earshot before talking about lingerie and my dad."

"Noted, Son. Enjoy your afternoon! I know we will," she hollers. And with my boner effectively squashed (probably for a very long time), I head back to my own store, the sounds of Harper and my mother giggling following me even after I step out onto the sidewalk.

I make my way down the block, swinging open my own business door, and head straight to the back staircase. I completely ignore Felicity (who hasn't made one move to clean up the glitter) and Dale (who's looking at me like my body was taken over by aliens) and take the stairs two at a time. I'm in desperate need of a shower and probably hypnosis, because as much as I try to push it from my mind, I just can't stop thinking about the moment my lips touched her skin.

Or the way her eyes lit up right before that moment.

Or the way my body fired to life for the first time in...ages.

Harper is definitely dangerous, and not just to the business.

To my heart.

***

"You play poker?" I hear over my shoulder as I throw a couple of frozen pizzas into my cart. When I turn around, I find Jensen Grayson standing behind me, a friendly smile on his face.

"You don't spend half your military career on foreign soil and not play poker," I answer, offering my own smile and my hand for him to shake.

"Good to see you, Latham. I stopped by the hardware store for a few things a week or so back and your old man told me you were returning to take over. He seemed pretty excited to have you back."

"I'm pretty excited to be back. Believe it or not, I was starting to miss this crazy town," I confess.

"Crazy is right. And speaking of crazy, I heard you had some issues earlier today with pink glitter," Jensen says, a wide smile on his face.

"You understand what I'm dealing with here, right? She's certifiable."

Harper's younger brother laughs. "Oh, definitely, and for some reason, she has her eyes set on you."

"Goodie," I grumble. "How long do you think before she gets bored and bugs someone else?"

"Well, let's see," Jensen says, glancing up and acting like he's counting. "Never?"

I can't help but chuckle. "That sounds about right."

"Anyway, all I have is a poker peace offering. Tomorrow night, seven at my house. Beer, some food, and best of all, we can take Samuel's money," he adds, slapping his hands together and rubbing them anxiously.

"Count me in. Text me your address and what you want me to bring," I say, pulling out my phone and adding him as a new contact.

"You can bring something snacky. I'm making Rhenn bring all the beer, since he's the new guy."

"New guy? What am I?"

"You're *not* the new guy. You were born and raised here, just took a few years to gallivant around the world. He's the man who's practically shacking up with my little sister, therefore he brings the beer," he states, clipping his phone back on his belt when my contact is all set.

"New guy, huh? Marissa getting married?"

"Not yet, but it'll happen. I can feel it," Jensen says as he grabs his own frozen pizza from the freezer. "His name is Rhenn, and he's actually a pretty decent guy. I still plan on making him buy my beer for as long as I can finagle it though," he adds with a laugh.

"Will she be there? I haven't seen your little sister in probably a decade," I ask, throwing a few bags of frozen vegetables and potatoes in my cart.

"Nah, it's usually just guys. I invited my buddy, Garrett Levitt, so there will be five of us."

"Sounds like fun. I'll see you tomorrow."

"See ya, Latham," he says, turning and heading the opposite direction.

Jensen was two years behind me in school, and even though I didn't hang out with him or Garrett, I knew them. Hell, everyone knows everyone in Rockland Falls. Small town, and all that. He was on the JV football team, while I was on Varsity, so we often found ourselves at the same place at the same time. Plus, I loved to torture his sister, so there's that.

I think a night of playing poker, drinking a few beers, and hanging out with guys who aren't wearing the same socks they've worn for a week is a positive thing. Poker night already has more going for it than what I'm used to. No, it's not all smelly and gross overseas, but at times, we're lucky to have five seconds to change our fucking socks when we're in a hot zone. Sleep was another commodity I'm used to stealing whenever I could, keep moving whenever I couldn't.

After I finish my grocery shopping, I head back to my tiny apartment above the hardware store. I really should ask Pete to find me a few available houses to look at. I was pretty good at saving the wages I made, and now have a decent little nest egg to fall back on. Getting a loan for a mortgage shouldn't be too difficult, even with the expansion I have planned for the business.

When the groceries are put away and the oven is preheating, I turn on the television and pop the top off a beer. They're talking preseason football on *Sports Center*, but I don't pay much attention to it. I haven't been able to really follow sports in a few years. Hell, I haven't been able to do much of anything except work for a few years. That's why this next phase in my life is so important to me. Not only does it give me something positive to focus my attention on, but it's also helping my family. Dad's ready to step back, even though he's barely sixty. His health hasn't been the best lately, and that's why I need to make sure I'm here – at home. Where I belong.

Now if I could do something about the *other* problem holding my attention. She's about five ten, with blue eyes and red hair. She's hotter than a chili pepper in Texas, and as feisty as a rattlesnake. But do you know what? I've always been drawn to her like a moth to a flame. That's probably a very accurate analogy too, considering she'd love nothing more than to burn me alive at the drop of a hat.

But Harper still threatens the plans I have for Douglas Hardware. Beautiful, sassy Harper, with skin so soft it's like touching pure silk and a smile so captivating it kept me company many nights in foreign countries over the last decade and a half. She's already increased her bid, which will keep her in the running where Mrs. Morton is concerned. That's why I'm pulling out the big guns tomorrow and stopping by for a visit. By the time I'm done with Mrs. Morton, she'll be wondering Harper who?

That building is as good as mine.

Chapter 9

Harper

I HAVE A FRESHLY BAKED French vanilla and caramel cheesecake sitting in the front seat and a smile on my face. No, I didn't make the creamy, rich dessert, but Marissa did. I only had to promise to oversee the family bed and breakfast tomorrow so she and Rhenn can go sailing.

Easy peasy.

Plus, Marissa will make sure to take care of all the meal prep before she goes, so my job is literally the easiest ever. Check out a few guests, throw in a couple loads of laundry, and make a bed or two. Done. It's not like I have big Sunday afternoon plans anyway.

That reminds me of my Saturday night plans.

My date.

With Skyler.

I mean, he seems nice. How bad can dinner at the Mexican restaurant in town be? I love their grilled shrimp enchilada, so that's always a plus. Right now, I need to focus on the task at hand:

seduce Mrs. Morton with delicious cheesecake so she sells the building to me.

Easy peasy lemon squeezy.

I really should have probably had a shot of Jack before coming over here. Why am I so nervous? I've known Mrs. Morton my entire life. Just because she's judgmental and curt, grumpy on a good day, doesn't mean I can't enjoy a few minutes of early afternoon time with her. Just as I turn onto her street, a big black Chevy truck pulls away from the curb in front of her house, heading in the opposite direction.

What. The. Hell. Is. He. Doing. There?

And then it hits me.

"Slimy rat bastard," I holler as he drives away from me, heading in the opposite direction. This pretty much confirms my suspicions Latham is the other bidder on the building between his store and mine.

I throw my car in park and turn the key, angry Latham beat me to the punch. What else could he be doing here? Stopping by for a friendly afternoon visit? Hell no. He had ulterior motives.

Like me.

Grabbing the cheesecake from the front seat, I paste on my friendliest smile and head up the walk. The yard is freshly trimmed, the bushes manicured perfectly, and the flowers in full bloom. Definitely one of my brother's jobs, I grin fondly, thinking about all the hard work and dedication my younger brother, Jensen, puts into his landscaping business.

When I approach the wooden door, I raise my hand to knock, only to have the door open before I can. "Can I help you?" Mrs. Morton asks as if she has no idea who I am.

"Good afternoon, Mrs. Morton, I'm Harper Grayson. You may remember me. I am friends with your granddaughter, Mandy." My smile is so wide, it's starting to hurt my face.

"Oh, yes, of course," she grumbles, stepping out onto the front porch. "You were the one who convinced my sweet little Mandy to sneak out of her house in high school, only to be picked up by the sheriff later that night after curfew."

Well, hell. Of all my accomplishments and accolades, *that's* what she remembers of me?

"Umm, yeah, sometimes we all do silly things when we're younger," I try to reason, starting to feel a little hot under the collar where Mrs. Morton is concerned. "Anyway," I start again, pasting back on that smile, "I was in the neighborhood and wanted to drop off this homemade cheesecake! It's French vanilla and caramel," I beam.

She glances down at it, looking it over with a critical eye, before taking the dessert from my hand. "Thank you, dear. I do enjoy a good cheesecake," she says, dropping the dish on the porch swing with a thump. I watch as the cheesecake smashes onto the clear plastic cover that helps keep it fresh.

"You're welcome," I reply, waving my hand casually, glancing down at the poor, mangled dessert. "By the way, your yard looks amazing! You obviously take exceptional care of it," I boost, not above getting in a few positive comments about my brother.

"Yes, well, this nice young man stopped by earlier and helped me. I usually have your brother take care it, but he's been so busy lately."

Wait, what?

"Yes, he is very sought-after this time of year, but what do you mean nice young man?" My blood runs cold.

Mrs. Morton beams widely, a smile I've probably never seen grace her face in all the years I've known her. "That handsome Latham Douglas. He stopped by to lend me a helping hand a while ago. Brought me some of his momma's delicious baked goods, and then offered to trim my grass, hedge the shrubs, and water and prune the gardens. He's just such a delight, that sweet boy," she croons, gushing over the Devil himself.

"Yeah, he's something," I mumble.

"He even had all the tools and items in the back of his truck. I don't have any of that stuff anymore, since I just hire someone to do it. Ever since Stanley passed away and my old bones don't work the way they used to."

"I'm sorry for your loss," I say, trying to think back to when Stanley Morton passed.

She waves a dismissive hand. "Ehh, it's been two decades. He's in a much better place." Mrs. Morton glances down at the dessert. "One where the neighbors don't bring you mangled cheesecake."

"No...but it wasn't..." I close my eyes and take a deep breath.

"Thank you for stopping by, Harley," Mrs. Morton says, turning toward her door, leaving the cheesecake on the swing.

"It's Harper."

"What?" she asks loudly when she reaches the screened door.

"Nothing," I mumble. "Enjoy your day, Mrs. Morton."

She doesn't respond, just opens the door and steps through, leaving me dumbfounded on the front porch. What the hell just happened? And what in the world did she do to the poor cheesecake? I turn to head back to my car, feeling majorly defeated and played. Before I hit the bottom of the stairs, I turn back to the swing and swipe the cheesecake. It may not be pretty anymore, but it's still cheesecake, and you don't waste it!

I stomp back to my car, even more frustrated and determined to win this bid. Latham thinks he can come over here with his sexy smile and strong muscles – Wait. Stop thinking about his attributes, Harper. Anyway, he thinks he can come over here and charm the likes of Mrs. Morton, and well, he has another think coming. Sure, he may have gotten the edge today, but I'm not going down easily or without a fight. He wants to play dirty, I'm ready to play ball.

Dirty ball.

I can't help but snort. Aunt Emma would be all over that sexual innuendo.

With my cheesecake in my lap, I head to my store to plot my next move. Free is there and is always good for a few dirty ideas when it comes to revenge. He may have won this round, but this is war, and the only person coming out victorious on the other side is going to be me.

I pull my car into the restaurant parking lot a few minutes before seven. Skyler wanted to pick me up at my place, but I insisted I just meet him here. I don't know him well enough to actually hand over my home address. That's something I picked up quickly during my time in New York City.

Exhaling deeply and pushing that thought out of my head, I grab my phone and fire off a quick text to Free.

Me:	Just arrived. Wish me luck.
Free:	Did you pack the condoms?
Me:	What? I'm not having sex with him!
Free:	Then why, again, are you going on this date?
Me:	Not all dates lead to sex, Freedom Rayne! What kind of girl are you? *insert shocked emoji*
Free:	The kind that likes to have her hair pulled every now and again, Harper Grayson.
Me:	*giggle snorts*
Free:	Text me when you leave. I'm going to your brother's.
Me:	Samuel's?
Free:	He would be so lucky. No, your other brother's. It's poker night. I ran into Garrett earlier today, and he mentioned he's going to Jensen's to play. I bet your uptight, anal brother will be there too. Bonus if I can make him blush in the first two minutes of my arrival.
Me:	Well, you have fun. Don't take all their money. Jensen has shoes to buy for my nephew.
Free:	I make no promises. *kissy face emoji*

I slip my phone into my purse, swipe on a coat of nude lip gloss, and head to the restaurant. Inside, I'm instantly comforted in the scents of fresh salsa and tortilla chips, and my mouth starts to water. Glancing around the restaurant, I find Skyler standing up in a booth in back, waving to catch my attention. I offer a small smile and slowly make my way to our table. Of course, I know most of the people at the tables along the way, so after a brief greeting to half the restaurant, I finally find myself sliding into the booth.

Skyler is smiling widely – or at least I think he is. Hard to tell sometimes with that Tom Selleck mustache he has going on. "You look lovely," he says, reaching for my hand. When I place it in his, he brings it to his mouth and places his lips on my knuckles.

But all I can think about is it looks like a small squirrel is frolicking on my hand. I try not to snicker (that would be rude), but a little noise slips out. I try to cover it with a fake cough, but then it just sounds like I'm fake coughing. Skyler glances up at me, his smile faltering just a little.

Now I feel like shit.

"So glad you could make it tonight," he says, taking a sip of his water, glancing over my shoulder to the door.

"Thank you for inviting me," I reply, offering him a smile. I grab my menu and give it a look, even though I already know what I'm going to order. It's what I order every time I eat here.

"I'm a little surprised you said yes, actually," he says without looking up from his menu.

"Really?" I ask, setting my menu down on my place setting.

"Totally. You're way out of my league," he adds with a wink and a grin. "And I'm a few years older. I wasn't sure if age mattered."

"How much older?" I ask, curiously. I knew Skyler was a bit older than my thirty-two years, but the way he says it makes me a bit more concerned.

"Well, I have kids," he says in way of answer, taking another drink of his water, so I do the same. "That are in college."

I choke. "College?" I gasp, trying to get the water down my throat and not have it fly across the table and onto Skyler's shirt. "And that would make you..."

"Fifty-three."

"Wow," I say aloud, even though I don't really mean to. "You don't look nearly old enough to have a kid in college." Yet, now that he says it, I can totally see his age in the gentle wrinkles around his eyes and the subtle graying around the temples and mustache.

"Two, actually. Well, in college. One still in high school."

Huh. Age is just a number right?

"So, three kids, then?"

"Yep. How about you?" he asks, glancing at the door over my shoulder once more.

"Oh, no kids for me yet," I answer, glancing back down at my menu.

After we order, the conversation quickly turns to his ex-wife. "She even took the door knobs off the doors. I tell ya, when she cleaned out the house, she wiped it clean."

"Really?" I mean, what else do you say?

Fortunately, our food arrives quickly, and I'm able to distract myself from the small critter on his face by shoveling my food into my mouth. I've always been a big eater, something that didn't bode well for me while in New York.

"It must be good," Skyler says, taking a small bite of his taco...with a fork.

"So good. I love this place," I answer.

"My wife never ate like that," he says, pointing at my plate...with his fork. "She had salads everywhere we went."

"Oh," I reply, glancing down at my half-eaten enchilada with extra sour cream and guacamole.

"But you have a hearty appetite. I can appreciate that," he says, taking another bite of his taco...with his fork. "No wonder you have to work out so much."

I stop my own fork halfway to my mouth and glance across the table. Did he really just comment about my gym activities and eating habits?

"My wife used to cook tacos on Tuesdays. She called it Taco Tuesday," he adds casually, still eating his taco...yep, you guessed it. "She loves Mexican food. Loves this place."

But what really caught my attention was that multiple times this evening, he referred to her as his wife. Not his ex-wife.

"She's in travel. Runs the agency uptown by the coffee shop. Travel Pros. Ever been there?" he asks, looking over at me with curiosity before returning his eyes to the front door. I can't get over the fact he's barely asked anything about me – but I practically know all about his former life with his ex.

"No, I haven't. How long ago did you say you divorced?" I ask, setting my fork down on my plate.

"Three months. Well, she left me three months ago. It's not final yet. I had been hoping for reconciliation, but I caught her on a date last weekend with the lawyer across the street from her office. They were eating here, actually." He glances around the room and a thought hits me. Did he bring me here in hopes of running into his ex and making her jealous?

Just then, the door opens and in walks a couple, their arms thrown around each other in a romantic embrace. Out of the corner of my eye, I see Skyler sit up straight, glaring at the couple who just entered the restaurant. Suddenly, he reaches for my hand again, almost knocking over my water glass.

I should have ordered the margarita. I could use a drink.

He brings it to his mouth, and before I even know what's happening, he's sucking on my finger. Sucking. On. My. Finger! I gasp out of shock. He thinks it's out of excitement. "I'm so glad you came tonight, baby," he says seductively and low.

My favorite enchilada threatens to make a reappearance.

"Excuse me?" I ask, tugging on my hand, but he refuses to let go.

"Later tonight, I'm going to show you what else I love to suck on," he says a bit too loudly for my liking and wiggles his eyebrows. The entire time, the squirrel above his lip brushes against my hand, making me consider just cutting it off to make a quicker escape.

"You know what, I think I should go," I say, pulling my hand back with force and elbowing his glass of water. It topples over, sending cold water and ice into his lap.

"Shit!" he bellows, drawing the attention of everyone in the restaurant, including the couple who just so happened to be walking by our table.

"Skyler?" she asks, shock and anger written all over her face.

"Marge! What a surprise! I didn't know I'd see you tonight," he squeaks, blotting at his wet pants with the napkin, making me want to call bullshit.

I dig into my purse and pull out a twenty, ready to get the hell out of Dodge. Tossing it on the table, I scoot from the booth.

"Wait, don't go, baby."

"I'm not your baby," I tell him adamantly, making a beeline for the door without even a glance back. "Thank you for dinner, but I'll be leaving now."

I don't even hang around to hear the rest of the words he immediately starts to exchange with his wife. Ex-wife. Whatever.

As soon as I get in my car, I fire off a text.

Me: Date a total bust. I need booze.

It only takes her a few seconds to reply.

Free: Poker night. I brought wine. Come play.

She had me at wine. I drop my phone into my cup holder and pull out of the parking lot. Before I merge onto the street, the door of the restaurant flies open and Skyler and Marge spill onto the sidewalk. They're clearly arguing, her hands flying around as she tries to make her point. I turn up the 98 Degrees, blasting "The Hardest Thing," singing along as if I were standing on stage belting out the words alongside Nick, Jeff, Drew, and Justin.

Boy bands are life.

As I pull into my brother's driveway, I note Free's car in the street, along with my brother Samuel's. Rhenn's here too, which means they're probably torturing the poor guy for dating our youngest sister. I should go save him.

Or join the fun.

I don't knock (I never do) and push my way into my younger brother's small house. It's the perfect size for him and my nephew. Two bedrooms with a decent-sized backyard. "Hey," I holler as I enter the living room and head for the kitchen.

"Hey!" they all reply, the sound of poker chips being thrown onto the table.

I walk up to Jensen first, throw my arms over his shoulder and kiss his head. "Don't mind if I crash, do you?" I ask, knowing he'd never say yes.

"Do I have a choice?" he teases, noting I'm already sitting down in the empty chair across from him.

"She could leave and take Freedom with her," Samuel says beside me, glaring at my best friend. She just smiles sweetly in return, tapping the top of the massive pile of chips in front of her.

"You'd miss me, Sammy."

"Samuel," he growls, shooting eye daggers her way. She doesn't seem to mind, though. In fact, I'm one-hundred-percent confident she gets off on ruffling his feathers. It's sort of her thing.

"I see Free's cleaning house again," I state, motioning to the stack of chips in front of her.

"Doesn't she always," Garrett grumbles, his own stack looking fairly small.

"I don't mind the competition," Rhenn says, taking a drink of his beer bottle. His stack of chips is pretty hearty, and so is the stack in front of me.

"Did you know I was coming?" I ask, taking the chip from the top and throwing it in the pile.

Jensen just gives me a look and shakes his head.

"How was the date?" Free asks, picking up the five cards thrown in front of her.

"Date?" Samuel asks, turning to face me. "With who?"

Always the protective big brother.

"A guy from the gym," I reply nonchalantly, picking up my cards and giving them a look. Two kings and a queen. Not bad.

"Does this guy have a name?" Jensen asks, throwing a chip in the middle of the table.

I follow suit, throwing my own to match, and reply, "Don't most people have names?"

"Don't we a wisenheimer. We may need to check this guy out," he adds, asking for two cards.

"No need," I reply, setting two cards down on the table too.

Rhenn is the dealer, so he tosses me two new ones as he makes his way around the table. "There's always a need. We always check out who our sisters date," Jensen says, picking up his two cards.

"You had me checked out?" Rhenn asks, looking up from his hand.

"Hell yes, we did," Samuel says, looking across to the man dating our youngest sister.

"Anyway, you have nothing to worry about. It was one date," I say, throwing more chips down on the table.

"Date?"

That voice.

My body responds instantly.

"Yep, our girl Harper had a date tonight," Free answers in my place.

I glance up and find Latham standing in the doorway, his dark chocolate eyes boring into me. There's an intensity to him tonight, one that has my body buzzing and my mind a little fuzzy. The way he's watching me makes me squirm a little in my seat.

"Did she now?" he says casually, but his jaw is full of tension.

"Hottie from the gym. Big muscles. Bigger dick." Samuel chokes on his beer at Free's brash words, making her giggle.

I feel him towering over me, yet I refuse to look up. I keep my eyes trained on my cards, pretending to think about my next bet. "You're in my seat," Latham says low and huskily.

"I didn't see your name on it," I sass, throwing another chip in the middle when it's my turn. "Call."

Suddenly, I'm moving. Latham lifts me in the air as if I weigh nothing and sets me down on his lap. I freeze as soon as my ass makes contact with his thigh. His very hard, muscular thigh. Like the kind of thigh that makes girls everywhere swoon and turn into crazed sex fiends.

"My seat," he growls in my ear, taking the cards from my hand. "Mine," he adds as he splays his large hand across my lower back, his finger grazing over my ass. Suddenly, I'm not sure if he's talking about the cards, the chips, or...me.

But do you know what I don't do? Move.

I sit right there, my ass snuggled against the best thigh in the world, and watch as Latham commands the table with the hand I set up for him. He wins, of course, and motions for me to rake in his winnings. There's a low hum in the air, and it feels a lot like sexual tension. It's dark and dirty and makes my nipples tight in my bra. It also makes me acutely aware it's the man I despise who makes me feel this way.

I just pray no one else notices.

Chapter 10

Latham

HER ASS.

It's the best thing I've ever seen and is currently pressed against my thigh. Just a few inches off from where my quickly thickening cock is resting. I thought for sure she'd jump up the moment I picked up her from my chair and set her on my leg, but she didn't. She hasn't moved. Not after the hand she won and not after the two that have followed. If anything, she seems to have settled in for the long haul, wiggling that perfect ass against my leg and playing her cards.

She's killing my concentration.

Thank God she's into the whole poker game, trash-talking her best friend and family like a pro. It's quite comical to watch, actually, and a small part of me is pretty fucking grateful her taunts and torments are aimed at someone else for a change.

The front door opens and we all turn to see who the latecomer is. Marissa, Harper's little sister comes in, the sweet scent of cinnamon and sugar following in her wake. "Hey, guys," she hollers as she enters the room and sets a pan on the table. The moment it's out of her hand, Rhenn pulls her into his lap and kisses her as if he hasn't seen her in weeks.

"Gross, stop," Jensen mumbles goodheartedly.

"It's worse than when Mom and Dad used to do it," Harper chimes in, throwing a disgusted face at her little sister.

After several long seconds, Free throws in a catcall, making the scowl lines around Samuel's eyes much more pronounced. I think he even growls before mumbles, "Okay, that's enough."

"I've missed you," Rhenn whispers softly, running his hand up Marissa's cheek and into her hair.

"It's been two hours," Harper teases, wiggling once more on my leg. My dick twitches. She does it again, as if she can't seem to get comfortable. That or she knows the effect she's having on my body and wants to prolong the torture as long as possible.

Probably that.

After another few minutes of wiggling, my pants start to feel dangerously tight. My cock is aching, raring to go in my pants. My imagination starts to run wild, even though I try to think about anything other than the fact I'd love to strip off her capris, pull my cock from my own jeans, and slide her just a little to the left until I'm buried balls deep inside her sweet pussy. My hand grips her hip as she moves again, her legs shifting just a little. When she does, her thighs fall open and her left leg brushes my cock.

Jeezus, I'm going to explode in my pants.

Harper doesn't say a word, but keeps her leg pressed firmly against my cock. There's no way she can't feel the impact she has on my body, no way of hiding the truth, because the truth is I want her.

Bad.

When I turn and look at her, those bright blue eyes are wide with something that makes my blood boil. Need. And I shouldn't get excited at the way she looks, all hot and bothered, probably picturing the same things I'm fantasizing about. Well, that or she's picturing maiming me with a butter knife. You never know with this little minx.

"I'll be back. I need to use the restroom," Harper says, slowly getting up from her perch on my leg, grazing her left hand over my swollen cock as she goes. Oh yeah, she definitely knows what she's doing.

I give her exactly thirty seconds, and then pull my phone from my pocket, pretending to receive a message. Free is dealing the next hand, but I throw mine out to stop her. "Don't deal me in this one. I have to make a quick call," I say, standing up carefully and quickly turning my hips to hide my erection. As I head toward the hallway, I can feel the eyes on the back of my head, probably those of her oldest and most protective brother.

In the hallway, I slip my phone into my pocket. I can hear the water running in the bathroom, which tells me she's about finished. As soon as the door opens, I pounce, pulling her across the hall and into the first open door I come to. I ignore the baseball posters and the Lego creations and press my body into hers, caging her against the wall. My hands thread into her hair, the soft red curls sliding effortlessly between my fingers. Her eyes are still wide, wild with desire.

"What's this I hear about a date?" I whisper, my lips dangerously close to hers.

Her chin rises challengingly and her eyes narrow. "Is that a problem?"

"Fuck yes, it is," I confess, hating she has me this tied up in knots over the prospect of her dating. "Is it serious?" I ask, running my thumb over the shell of her ear and down the column of her neck.

She opens her mouth to speak, but closes it. The wait is killing me. If she tells me it's serious, I'll back away, both figuratively and physically. I'm not about to jump headfirst into some sort of love triangle bullshit. If she's with someone else, then I'm out. I don't play games and I sure as fuck don't share. "No, it's not serious. It was just one date. There won't be a second." Her words are breathless, her body sagging into mine. The first thing I notice is how easily we fit together, like puzzle pieces.

With one hand tangled in her hair, the other hand slides down her side, gripping her hip. Her eyes are wide, yet hungry, probably mirroring my own. She opens her mouth to speak, but I silence her. With my lips.

My kiss is firm, hungry, and full of every ounce of pent-up desire I try to fight when it comes to Harper Grayson. Her sassy little mouth opens immediately, allowing me to sweep my tongue inside and dance with hers. My entire body is on fire, a live wire charged to the max. One little spark and I know we'll explode.

A throat clears behind me, but I ignore it. My hand tightens on her hip, digging into her flesh. She moans against my lips, her body swaying more, grinding against mine. I'm one second away from slamming the door and taking her on the bed when I hear, "I hope Max doesn't see you like this."

The words are like a bucket of ice-cold water thrown over our heads.

Harper gasps and jumps back, only to encounter the wall. My hand instantly goes to her head to see what kind of damage she caused when it slammed against the drywall, but she quickly pushes my hand away. The fire I once saw dance in her eyes is quickly replaced with shock and, unfortunately for me, a bit of embarrassment.

"Max isn't even here," Harper whispers to her older brother, clearing her throat and looking anywhere but at Samuel or me.

"No, but he could have been."

"Stop being a stiff," she grumbles, pushing against my shoulder until I move. My body weeps when it's no longer pressed against her. I miss the feel of her skin, her curves, her lips instantly.

"Is that a mortician joke?" he asks, straightening the tie around his neck. Yes, the man still wears a necktie to play poker.

"It's whatever you want it to be. I'm an adult," she replies, straightening her back and raising her chin.

"You are. You're an adult who's making out with someone in her nephew's bedroom," he says, piercing her with a look. He doesn't even glance my way.

"The only thing I apologize for is that you interrupted," I say, earning a glare from both Harper and Samuel.

"Zip it, Douglas. You got me into this mess."

"No mess, Grayson. At least, not yet," I reply, wiggling my eyebrows in the way that infuriates her. I can practically see the steam rolling from her ears.

Harper turns toward the door. "Thank you, Samuel, for coming to get me. I'm sure it's my turn to deal."

"It is," he replies, spinning on his expensive shoes and heading back out to the dining room.

"That was a mistake. Don't ever kiss me again," she says, her voice stern, yet I catch the hint of uncertainty.

"I can't promise you that, Sweetheart. Especially when you throw yourself at me and kiss me back the way you did."

"I did *not* throw myself at you!"

"But you did kiss me back."

"Lapse of judgment. It won't happen again," she counters, crossing her arms. My eyes immediately shift to her chest, which only makes me think about that kiss once more.

"Stop it!"

"Stop what? I didn't do anything."

"You're staring at me."

"Guilty as charged. Maybe you should stop wearing low-cut tops that make my dick want to come out and play."

Harper gasps. Her eyes also fall to my crotch. "Pig."

As her eyes return to mine, we continue to glare at each other. The sexual tension is so thick, you could cut it with a knife. My body craves hers, and if the way her nipples are poking through her top are any indication, I'd say she craves me too.

But not tonight.

Tonight, I'll let her think about that kiss.

About how good it will be when she lets go.

Because there's one thing I'm as certain about as the sun rising over the Atlantic every morning, it's that my time with Harper isn't over. This attraction isn't going anywhere. I'll have her.

Again.

"I'll let you have your moment, but know it won't be long."

Her voice is wobbly. "Won't be long for what?"

I take a step forward until we're chest to chest. Her breathing hitches when I grab her hip and pull her against me once more so she can feel what she does to me. "Until I've got you pinned against the wall again. Only this time, there'll be nothing between us but air."

Harper's eyes darken into deep blue sapphires, but she doesn't reply. I let go of the hold I have, saddened to break the contact once more. She tries to calm herself, closing her eyes and taking a few deep breaths. Then, she turns and starts to head out the door. When she reaches it, she stops, but doesn't turn around. "Latham?" she whispers.

"Yeah?" I reply, clearing my throat and trying to will my erection into submission.

"Were you really jealous? Of my date?"

Her question catches me off guard, but I won't lie to her. "Yeah. The thought of him touching you made me want to put my fist through the wall."

She finally glances over my shoulder and quietly asks, "Why?"

"Because we have unfinished business." About fourteen years' worth of it.

Her eyes never leave mine, and after a few very long seconds, she finally nods and walks away. She didn't argue with me, which is a miracle all in itself, but she didn't counter my statement. Probably because she knows it's true. We have something to finish. To settle. A discussion that should have happened years ago, but never did. An apology too.

But not tonight.

I don't know when the right time is exactly, but I know it's not when we're surrounded by her family and friends. Soon, though. Because this damn sexual tension between us isn't going away as I had hoped. If anything, it's getting worse. It's like it has merely been simmering on the back burner for all these years, waiting for that little spark to set it ablaze once more.

And tonight?

Tonight, the match was lit.

It's Friday. It's been a crazy-long workweek filled with long hours and even longer nights. Nights filled with images of the woman next door as she kissed me back last Saturday night at her brother's house. It's those images that have me taking longer showers than normal.

Today, I'm dealing with Felicity. She's already broken the printer, and now I'm trying to clean up a paint mess since she didn't close a lid completely before placing the gallon in the mixer. If it were anyone else but her, I'd already have fired her ass. Twice. And that's just today. I'd been on the verge of getting her out of my store just about every day this week.

But my dad won't let me.

By four, I'm tired, hungry (since I skipped part of my lunch to clean the mixer machine), and irritable. I had to throw on an old hardware store T-shirt, since my polo was trashed by the paint, and apparently, I'm a little behind on my laundry. Just my luck this one smells like it's been in the back of my drawer for the past decade. I keep myself busy restocking the shelves by the north wall, as far away from Felicity and her endless chatter as possible. She's set to close with me tonight, which means I'll be doing just about everything, including counting out the register.

The bell chimes over the door, and I opt to keep plugging away at my restock, instead of running over to help the customer. Felicity will holler if she needs me. The customer approaches the counter, and it's a voice I immediately recognize. "Hey, Felicity," Harper says somberly.

"Oh. Hi."

"I need to buy a few building supplies," she says politely.

"Building supplies?" Felicity snorts. "You?"

"Yeah, me. Do you see anyone else around?" Harper barks, her annoyance evident.

"I'm just surprised is all. A supermodel who builds?" Felicity laughs.

"I'm not a supermodel," Harper says softly, and something catches in my throat.

"Oh, that's right. You didn't make it in New York," Felicity retorts. I can practically picture her flipping her hair over her shoulder.

"Can I just purchase this stuff on my list?" Harper asks, the sound of a piece of paper rustling barely audible.

"Sure, sure. I can help," Felicity sasses.

"You are very good at helping. I mean, look how well you *helped* Joey with his zipper in the bathroom of the bar that one time."

And that's my cue.

Felicity is just getting ready to open her mouth, probably to spit off something mean and nasty, when I approach the counter. "I think I can take it from here," I announce, grabbing the slip of paper from Felicity's hand. "Why don't you go finish stocking the stains." It's not a question.

Felicity's eyes narrow as she continues to stare at Harper, who just smiles sweetly back. "Fine," my employee grumbles, flipping her hair over her shoulder again and stalking off to the wall I just left.

"Hey," I say, offering her a small smile. She's fucking gorgeous in her black capri pants and light blue tank top. There's bunching around the neck that falls down her chest, settling between her magnificent boobs. My eyes can't help but drink her in.

"Hi."

That familiar tension is back, so I get to work keying in the material she's purchasing. When I get to two-by-fours and plywood, I glance her way. She gives me a small smile and shrugs. "Doghouse."

"You're building a doghouse?"

"Yep," she replies when I hand her the piece of paper. "I'm not sure which screws would work best, so go ahead and pick some out for me. The lumber I'd like to be green-treated, since it's going to be outside year-round."

Still, I stare. "You're building a doghouse?" I ask again, stupidly.

Harper rolls her eyes. "Yes, dummy, I think we've already established that."

I choose to keep my mouth shut, not wanting to offend her with something sexist, but to be honest with you, we rarely get female customers in here who are building something themselves. Usually, they're stopping by for supplies for their husband. Something about Harper building anything with her hands has me all sorts of excited. It's something I'd love to see.

"Wait here," I tell her as I head over and pick out a box of screws and the sandpaper she needs. I return to the front, aware Felicity is hovering very close, and ask, "Do you need it delivered?"

"No, I have Jensen's truck. Can you just load it up now?"

"I can," I tell her, printing off her material list. She pulls out her debit card, which I immediately swipe to complete her transaction. "Pull down the alley and stop under the south overhang. I'll meet you back there."

Harper grabs her papers and heads out the front door. I don't hang around long enough for Felicity to rejoin me at the counter. I holler I'm heading back to load lumber, and make a beeline for the back door.

The sun is bright in the late-July sky, instantly warming my skin. I pull four green-treated two-by-fours from the pile, check them to make sure they're straight, and set them aside. Jensen's big truck pulls down the alley, stopping exactly where I instructed her to park. She hops out of the dirty work truck, a weirdly seductive contradiction in her work attire. As much as I try to ignore her appearance, my eyes have a mind of their own and drink her in. Her ass looks amazing in those black capris.

"Stop staring, perv," she sasses, rolling her eyes for good measure.

I don't reply, instead choosing just to chuckle as I head over to the plywood. She puts the tailgate down as I throw the first piece over my shoulder and meet her back at the truck. I set it down in the bed, careful to slide it in without hitting the toolbox. It only takes me a few minutes before I have all four sheets loaded in the truck. Then, I head for the two-by-fours I set aside. Picking all four up and throwing them over my shoulder I head for the truck bed, only to find two eyes following me everywhere I go. Except those eyes are focused on my arms.

Just before I move them off my shoulder to slip them into the bed, I say, "Stop staring, perv."

Harper crosses her arms, her eyes narrowing. "I wasn't. I was checking out the boards to make sure you were giving me straight ones."

"Sure you were," I tease, drawing out the first word a little too long. "You were watching my arms. Admit it."

Her chin rises. "I will do no such thing."

"Suit yourself," I state, carefully closing the tailgate. "You're all set."

"Thank you." It seems almost painful for her to say those words.

"No problem."

Then, we're surrounded by awkward silence. Her eyes don't meet mine as she fidgets with her hands, kicking at small rocks in the alley.

"So, you're building a doghouse this weekend," I state, not because I need to verify this information, but because I'm not really ready for her to leave and I'm trying to draw out our time together.

Again, she rolls her eyes. "Seriously?"

"Is Jensen helping?"

"Why would Jensen need to help? Because I'm a woman, I can't build a doghouse?"

"I never said that. Some of these boards are heavy, and I just wanted to see if you needed any help."

"I don't need any help," she replies quickly, heading toward the truck cab. "But if it would make you feel better, I'm going to start tomorrow afternoon after I close the shop. Stop by so you can see how a real woman builds something."

My dick twitches.

"Maybe I will."

"Fine!" she yells, climbing up into the cab and firing the engine. Before she pulls out, she rolls down the window. "Bring the beer. If you're going to sit around and watch me work, the least you could do is buy me a few drinks."

Before I can reply, she rolls up the window and drives out of the alley. I watch until she rounds the corner, disappearing completely from sight. With a smile on my face and a renewed spirit, I head back into the store to finish out the day. Yeah, I may be working on a Saturday, but at least I have something to look forward to after. And if there's anything to look forward to, it's Harper Grayson with power tools.

I just hope she doesn't try to kill me with one.

Chapter 11

Harper

WORK WAS CRAZY BUSY, RIGHT up until the shop closed at two. It took me an extra fifteen minutes to get everything shut down, and even though many of the displays could use a refresh and reorganize, it'll have to wait until Monday. Right now, I have a date with a circular saw and my drill.

As soon as I get home, I throw on a pair of old jeans, a blue tank top, and pair of old Ariat boots from my cowgirl days. It's hotter than Satan's balls outside, but fortunately, there's enough of a breeze off the ocean that makes it somewhat bearable. Snuggles is out with me, running puppy circles around my legs until she takes her chew toy and parks it under the tree. I already moved her water bowl and a bit of food there, so she'll be set for the next few hours while I work.

Jensen stopped by after work last night to help unload his truck and trade vehicles. He set up the sawhorses and got all of my materials in order. He offered to come back by this afternoon to help with Max, but I knew they already had plans to attend a baseball game. There's no need for them to miss it when I'm perfectly capable of building a doghouse. I have a rough idea of how I'm going to build it in my mind, and a sketch on a piece of notebook paper. Jensen is a visual person, so when he stopped by, he doodled while I told him my ideas. Together, we finalized a pretty kick-ass doghouse for my baby girl.

I glance one more time to where she's snoozing under the tree, and get the first piece of plywood positioned on the sawhorses. Before I know it, I have my cut lines chalked out and I'm ready to go.

When I was younger, Dad used to build things. Bookshelves, coffee and end tables, nightstands. Little things like that, and then he'd sell them at the local craft shows. Mom was always in the kitchen with Marissa, and so Jensen and I would find ourselves in the garage with Dad. Samuel was often studying, rarely finding the time to help cut, screw, and stain whatever project Dad was working on. Not me. I loved it. He's the one who taught me everything I know and gave me the confidence to build just about anything I want.

Those storage shelves and display cases at Kiss Me Goodnight?

Built those myself.

Sure, most people look at me, standing five foot ten, weighing barely one hundred and thirty pounds, and wearing perfectly contoured makeup, and think I'm just a pretty face. I'm the girl who went to New York to model. The one who starred in a toothpaste commercial on national television. But I'm more than that, dammit. Yes, I may sell sexy panties and lingerie, but I can also cut just about anything with a jigsaw and figure difficult measurements in my head.

I'm versatile like that.

Two sides in and Snuggles starts to bark. Glancing up, I see her heading to the fence gate, tail wagging in joy. Latham approaches the gate, throws open the latch, and enters the yard like he owns the freaking place. Jerk. My dog doesn't seem to mind the stranger in her yard. Instead of eating him (the way I had hoped), she runs circles around his legs, stands on her back legs, and begs to be petted.

"Traitor," I grumble, grabbing a second sheet of plywood from the stack and jockeying it on the sawhorses.

"Need help?" Latham asks, setting his cooler down on the ground and approaching where I work.

"No." I don't mean it to come out snippy, but it does.

"Okay," he replies, hands in the air in surrender, and backs away. "You clearly know what you're doing. I was just trying to help you move the board."

"I got it." Deep breath. "But thank you for the offer," I tell him, glancing his way again. He's wearing well-worn jeans that hang dangerously low on his narrow hips and a dark green Army T-shirt. It too looks well-worn, the coloring fading just a little bit.

"I'm just going to sit over here where you can't accidentally cut off my hand with your saw. Holler if you need help." Latham grabs his cooler and heads over to the shade tree. My patio furniture is on the deck, so he marches up the stairs, grabs my favorite lounger, and returns to the place my dog was just resting. Snuggles seems particularly happy to have a friend join her under the tree, lying on the ground directly off to his left, where his hand can continually pet her head. He pops off the top on a beer bottle, takes a hearty swig, and sets out to watch me work.

I've never had an audience before.

It's weird.

And a little exciting.

Pushing all thoughts of my voyeur out of my mind, I finish measuring out and cutting the two roof pieces. In fact, I get lost in my work and completely forget about Latham being here. The radio on the deck plays 90's music as I continue to get all of my pieces cut out, softly singing along as I go. The only one left is the base. Needing the third sheet of plywood, I head over to retrieve it, only to be met with another set of hands.

"Before you say anything, I know you can carry it, but since I'm here, I don't mind helping." Latham throws the sheet over his shoulder and carries it over to the sawhorses for me. I don't argue, even though I really want to. My argumentative nature comes out in full force when Latham is involved. I don't know what it is, really, but the man has always had this infuriating ability to get under my skin.

"Thanks," I reply, grabbing the tape measure from my tool belt and marking out my corners.

Latham grabs the chalk line and holds it in place, following my lead. He never pushes me out of the way (like Joey did when he tried helping me make one of the display shelves for the store). Instead, he stands to the side and jumps in exactly where I need, never once taking over the project. Before I know it, we have all the pieces cut, including the two-by-four trim, and are ready to start piecing it together.

"I have to admit, Harper, you're a refreshing contradiction," he says as he pulls another beer out of the cooler and hands it to me, before taking one for himself.

"Why, because I can build my own shit?" I ask, sweating a little (okay, a lot) and enjoying the way the cold beer quenches my thirst.

"Well, yeah. Most women would just go out and buy a plastic doghouse, let alone try to build one themselves," he says, drinking about half his bottle in one gulp.

"Well, I'm not like most women," I retort, setting my bottle aside and reaching for my drill.

"Don't I know it," he mumbles quietly, finishing off his bottle and tossing it in the outdoor recycle bin. When the glass hits what's inside, Snuggles jumps up from her nap under the tree and rushes over to make sure he's okay. I can't help but shake my head at my traitorous dog, though if I were telling the truth, I completely understand why she likes him. Though, I'd never admit that aloud, so I don't say a word.

"Let's get this thing framed up and then I'll throw dinner on the grill," I say, digging out the box of screws Latham picked for me in the hardware store.

"Wow, dinner? Will it be poisoned?" he asks as he continues to pet my dog, the corners of his lips turning upward.

Why am I suddenly really jealous of my dog? I'm sure it has nothing to do with the fact his large hands are rubbing across her belly, my puppy's tongue hanging out of her mouth and her eyes practically rolling back into her head while she gets a rubdown.

Stupid hormones.

Pushing them out of my mind, I grab the sides and start to bring them into position, reaching for one of the clamps. Just as I connect with one, a warm hand wraps around mine, sending bolts of electricity coursing through my body, landing firmly between my legs. My panties are suddenly worthless.

"Let me grab that, Sweetheart," he whispers, towering over my like a giant on steroids. My body starts to react in ways I wish it wouldn't, at least when it comes to the Devil, yet I can't seem to control it.

I don't even call him out on his term of endearment, mostly because I'm not sure actual words would come out of my mouth. My brain is short-circuiting, my throat dry, and my head reeling from his touch. Plus, there's the fact I actually kinda like it when he calls me that.

Wait, what?

No.

No, I don't like it.

I'm no one's sweetheart, especially Latham's.

My mind is at war as we work side by side for the next hour. It's hard to hate him when he's so damn helpful. He assists by cutting the little triangles I use to keep the sides together, holding them in place while I screw. He holds the level, but only checks the accuracy after I've settled on the position. He remains quiet while I work, which is completely un-Latham-like. I even catch him humming along to one of the songs on the radio, but as soon as I call him out on it, he turns cherry-red and refuses to acknowledge me. Before long, the doghouse is completely assembled, and I couldn't be happier with the work.

"Nice job," he says, digging another beer out of the cooler and handing it to me, both of us standing beside the project to admire our handiwork.

"Thanks. I appreciate the help," I reply, taking a drink from the bottle.

"Did you just compliment me? And your brain didn't even explode!"

"Shut up or I'll take it back."

"You can't take it back. No takebacks."

"What is this, third grade? Of course I can take it back!"

Latham takes a step closer. "False!" he yells, rousing my puppy from her slumber once more. "No takebacks, I called it."

"You called it after the takeback, though. That doesn't count."

He steps closer again. "It does count. My rules."

I blink, suddenly realizing how very close he is. He's standing directly in front of me, and I can smell the mixture of sweat and soap on his skin. His chocolate brown eyes are dark with little speckles of gold, and they have me pinned to where I stand. His lips curl into that stupid smirk, and suddenly, kissing him seems like the best idea I've ever had, which is crazy, considering I don't even like the guy.

Okay, so maybe that's not entirely true.

Anyway, I'm point two seconds away from going up on my toes and kissing that smirk right off his face when I feel two paws on my thigh and a cold nose on my hand.

Saved by Snuggles.

I glance down, breaking the contact with our eyes, and pet my dog's head. The moment she's satisfied with some attention, she turns to Latham and demands the same from him. "Yeah, we see you," he says to Snuggles, getting down on one knee and giving her proper attention. Her tongue lops out of her mouth as she stares up at him with lust in her eyes. I'm pretty sure my dog has a crush.

And what's not to like?

He's tall, gorgeous (though I'm not really admitting that out loud), and smells amazing even when he's a little sweaty. So I can see why she's all googly-eyed. "I have an idea," he says, not moving an inch out of my personal space. "You said something about dinner, right?" He barely waits for my head nod response before continuing. "Why don't you go up and get started, and I'll finish cleaning up the mess. I take it you're going to paint it?" he asks, glancing over my shoulder to my nearly finished doghouse. I didn't use good enough wood to stain it; something he definitely would have noticed.

Finally, I take a step back. "Yes. How do you take your steak?"

He seems surprised by the question. "Medium-rare."

"Thank God you didn't say well-done. I just might have to drop your meat on the ground before throwing it on the grill," I tease, though not really. I've never understood someone who wants their meat cooked until it's practically jerky.

Latham chuckles. "I like my meat juicy, tender, and the perfect shade of pink," he replies, making my pulse quicken. His eyes blaze with dark fury, and something tells me he's not at all referring to the slab of meat I'm about to throw on the grill.

Needing to step away and cool off (yes, I'm considering throwing my head in a bucket of cold water), I move and start to head to my back porch. I whistle for Snuggles, but when I glance over my shoulder, she's attached to Latham's leg, completely ignoring my call. When I reach my sliding glass door, the cool air pelts me in the face, helping calm down my overheated skin.

I pull the two steaks from the fridge, thankful I grabbed them from the butcher. My original thought was Jensen and Max would stop by to help, later, after their ball game, but I haven't seen my little brother. I guess when I told him I had this project in the bag, I wasn't expecting him to actually listen. Placing the steaks on the counter, I grab my mallet and give them a few good whacks. Just as I'm swinging, I hear the door slide open.

"Huh, can't say I was expecting someone to beat my meat for me today."

"It helps that I'm picturing it as your face," I reply without looking up from the thick ribeye.

"Good to know you think of me when you have your hands on meat," he says, coming over and turning on my faucet to wash his hands. "I left the house under the tree."

"Thank you. I'm going to paint it tomorrow," I tell him, dropping the mallet in the sink and grabbing the seasoning.

"Can I help?" he asks, coming to stand beside me, resting his hip against the counter. I can feel his eyes following my every move.

"Just grab us each a cold drink," I tell him, heading to the door with the steaks, tongs, and seasoning.

By the time Latham joins me on the porch, I have dinner on the grill and am taking a seat at the patio table. "You have a nice area back here," he says, setting down two cold beers and taking the seat directly across from me.

"Thanks, it's really what sold me on the house."

"You bought it?"

"Last year," I tell him, taking a big pull from the bottle. "I had rented before, but never had any room. Plus, most rentals don't allow pets, and I knew I wanted to adopt a dog."

We both glance over to the doghouse, where Snuggles is sleeping, big paw hanging out of the opening. "I'd say you did well."

"That must have been hard for you to say."

"Why?" he asks, catching me off guard.

"I didn't expect so many compliments today."

"I've always paid you compliments, Sweetheart."

I roll my eyes. "Is telling me my hair is short like a boy's and then snapping my bra a compliment?"

He grins. "The highest of compliments."

"Right. So when you told me my ass looked fat in my cheerleading uniform, that was a good thing?"

"I don't remember. Do you still have that old uniform? Maybe you could put it on and refresh my memory," he replies with a wicked grin and an evil glint in his eyes. "Besides, I do recall you telling everyone in high school you caught me learning how to kiss by making out with the oak tree in my backyard."

I snort, and not even very ladylike. "They called you Woody for days."

"The guys were scared to get undressed in front of me in the locker room," he growls, making me laugh even harder.

"Bet that was awkward," I giggle.

"Awkward doesn't even begin to cover it," he says as I stand up and flip the steaks to sear the other side.

We're both quiet as I get the meal ready. I bring out plates, silverware, napkins, and the sides I had picked up from the deli. "I hope you like spaghetti salad. Max loves it, and I was prepared to have them over tonight," I say as Latham sets the table.

"Max is your nephew, right?"

"Yes," I reply with a smile. "Jensen was married to Ashley Taylor for a few years and had Max."

He takes another drink from his beer, leaning his hip against the railing. "Ashley Taylor? Few years younger than us?"

"That's her. She wasn't very pleasant in school, and she definitely didn't grow out of it. She and Jensen go round and round regularly. I think her goal in life is to make his hell," I reply as I turn the heat down low and prepare to finish cooking the steaks on a low heat.

"It couldn't have all been bad though."

"No, it wasn't. At least not in the beginning. I thought they were done years ago, but then she got pregnant with Max. I think he stuck it out as long as he could, but then it just didn't work anymore."

"Too bad," he says, throwing his empty bottle in the trashcan and grabbing another. "It's always hard when kids are involved. Lark has a two-year-old."

"She does? How is she?" I ask, flipping the steaks one last time.

"She's good. We're heading over there tomorrow to see her and Vivian."

Smiling, I take the meat off the grill and shut off the propane. "Vivian. I love that name."

"She's the spitting image of my sister," he adds fondly.

"And her father?" I ask, as I bring the meat to the table. As soon as I set the plate down, Snuggles wakes up from her nap and comes running. I give her a pointed look. "No begging."

Latham grabs the tongs and sets the first one on my plate before setting the larger one on his. "He isn't in the picture. In fact, I don't know who he is. She won't tell me. Just says it was a thing that happened." He doesn't make eye contact and the tips of his ears turn a bit red. I can tell he doesn't like the fact he doesn't know, or maybe it's that this is something he can't fix. Latham has always been very paternal when it comes to Larkin.

"Well, good for her for making it work."

"She had a lot of help from my mom and dad, but she's a strong woman with a good head on her shoulders," he says cutting into his dinner. I watch as he brings his fork up to his mouth and takes his first bite.

He chews slowly, savoring the taste and cut of good meat. I can't help but watch the way his strong jaw moves, the way his Adam's apple bobs when he swallows. "Damn, that's good."

Pleased, I cut into my own steak and take a bite. His eyes are on me as I chew and swallow, much like mine were on him a few moments ago. "What?" I ask, glancing up and finding him still watching me. "Do I have food on my face?" Yes, I just asked that with a mouthful, but I can't help it.

"Do you always talk with food in your mouth?"

"Yes," I reply, shoveling potato salad into my face. "Always," I confirm while chewing and smiling at the same time.

Latham laughs and shakes his head. "How in the hell did you make it as a model in the city with manners like that?"

He's teasing. I know he is.

But I feel the words clear down to my gut.

I glance down, scooping up a smaller bite. "Easy, you don't eat when you're a model," I reason.

He watches me, clearly wanting to ask more questions, but I don't let him. I change the subject (something I've gotten good at) and steer the conversation to safer topics. Before I know it, the food is almost gone and our bellies are full. Latham stretches back in his seat, patting his belly happily. I don't miss how he takes a small piece of fat and holds it beneath the table to the little begger at his feet. "Seriously, Harper, that was delicious. Thank you."

"You're welcome. Thanks for your help today, even though I didn't really need it," I reply with a smile.

He laughs. "Of course you didn't need it. You're a badass with power tools."

"I am," I reply, offering my own smile.

When I get up and start gathering the empty plates and bowls, Latham jumps to his feet and swats my hands away. "Let me. You cooked and I can clean."

I stand up and make a face. "Clean? You'll help clean?"

"Yes," he replies, taking the stack from my hands and heading toward the back door. "Hasn't anyone ever offered to clean up the mess?"

"No," I answer, realizing that's very much true, with the exception of Marissa. None of the guys I've ever cooked for have ever offered to help clean up the mess. Usually, by the time their bellies are full, they're ready for the next phase of the night (the naked part).

He enters my house like he owns it and heads for the sink. When he sets the pile on the counter, he turns to face me. "Sounds like you've been dating the wrong men. A real man always helps out in the kitchen, especially after a fucking phenomenal meal like that."

Warmth spreads through me at his compliment. Shrugging my shoulders, I flip the water on hot. "It's fine. None of them were sticking around long enough anyway."

He turns and faces me, maneuvering until he's practically pressed against my chest. "A real man helps in the kitchen, Sweetheart. A good man cleans up after. The better man worships his woman right there on the counter and makes her come three ways to Sunday."

All of the oxygen in the room just...evaporates. I can't seem to suck in a breath, especially with his mouth so very close to mine. Very full, very sexy lips. My eyes move from his lips to his eyes, finding them wide and dark and trained directly on me. I have no idea which one of us moves first, but it doesn't matter. What matters is the way his arms wrap around me, caging me and pulling me close at the same time. Our lips meet in the middle, a frenzy of hunger and need.

My hands dive into his hair, gently tugging and pulling as I thread my fingers through his dark locks. He keeps it short, yet with just enough length I can get my hands on it. Each time I tug, his hands tighten on my ass, bringing me closer to his hard body (and boy, do I mean *hard*) until there's no way air could even slip between our bodies. Our tongues dance, our teeth nip, and our lips devour in a slow dance that's days in the making.

Weeks.

Months.

Hell, years.

He lifts me easily in the air, my legs wrapping around his waist. Latham sets me on the counter, positioning himself right where I need him most. The friction is marvelous, yet frustrating at the same time because it's not enough. It may never be enough. I moan in pleasure as he grinds himself against my center, teasing me until I'm practically crawling out of my skin.

More. I definitely need more.

I grip the back of his T-shirt and give it a tug, pulling it free from his waistband. As if sensing my direction, Latham removes his lips from mine just long enough to pull his shirt over his head and discard it on the floor. His chest is something they write songs about. It's hard, muscular, and has a tattoo; enough to ensure women everywhere have wet dreams for days to come.

My hands glide down his pecs, loving the way the light matting of chest hair tickles my palm. His nipples are small and hard and my tongue waters to taste his skin. "I showed you mine, now you show me yours," he whispers in a gravelly voice, cupping my breasts through my tank top.

"Is that how this works?" I tease, reaching down and cupping his balls.

"Only if you want it to," he replies, his brown eyes locking firmly on mine.

My only answer is to reach down and pull my top up and over my head. I'm wearing one of my older satin sets, mostly because I didn't want to get my good stuff all sweaty and gross while outside working, but I can't seem to find an ounce of concern that Latham is seeing an older pair. In fact, if the way his eyes are devouring my breasts is any indication, I'd say he doesn't mind at all that the dark blue material is slightly worn and has a little pilling. "Jeezus, Harper, you're fucking gorgeous," he whispers, staring down at the mounds that spill over the top of the bra.

"You're not so bad yourself," I reply, unable to stop myself from continuing to touch his chest.

I feel him reach around my back to the clasp. "May I?" he asks politely, his eyes on me the entire time.

"I had hoped you would. I mean, it's only fair."

He smirks. "It is." Then, he releases the clasp and frees my breasts.

That's when I hear him gasp. "When the fuck did you get that?" he asks, his voice deep and hoarse.

Glancing down at the small silver ring through my left nipple, I shrug. "A few years back."

"Holy fucking shitballs, I think I just came in my pants." He has yet to remove his eyes from my left breast.

Rolling mine, I reach down and cup his balls. "You've never seen a nipple ring?"

"Never in real life," he says, his eyes finally returning to mine. "May I?"

I can't help but smile. "So polite. I'm not used to this side of Latham Douglas."

"I have manners for days, but you're about to see the end of them. My rope is quickly starting to fray."

"Then you must hurry. Before the rope...frays."

You'd think I granted him access to heaven. His eyes seem to sparkle with excitement as his head dips forward and his tongue comes in contact with my nipple. Okay, so maybe he isn't the only one in danger of coming too quickly. A gasp spills from my lips as he sucks the ring into his mouth, flicking and toying with both the ring and the skin it's attached to.

"Fucking hell, Harper," he groans, lapping at my skin with his magnificent tongue. After I got my piercing, I was told my nipples would be more sensitive with arousal, but holy shit, I've never experienced anything like this before. My entire body is on fire, hungry and driven with desire. Now, I know exactly what he meant when he talked about his rope starting to fray.

I realize all too quickly he could easily make me come, just by sucking on my nipple and playing with the piercing. My pussy is throbbing, completely soaked through my panties, and begging for more. I reach down and try to grab his cock, but the angle is awkward and I can't get a grip.

"Patience, Sweetheart," he whispers against my skin, and I have nothing left to do but relax and enjoy the ride.

The ride, in all actuality, is rather short because before I know it, I feel an orgasm barreling down on me. Latham continues to suck and lick at the pierced nipple, and reaches over to the other with his large hand. He takes the right nipple between his fingers and pinches. Not too hard, but just enough to send a lightning bolt of lust straight to my pussy. I call out as wave after wave of pleasure courses through my body, as I fly high in the sky and slowly free fall back to earth.

As my surroundings start to return to me, I open my eyes, only to come face-to-face with Latham's dark, hungry ones. The look he gives me sends shivers through my body and desire starts to return. Reaching forward, I go for his belt, only to have my hand stopped before it can reach its destination. My eyebrows arch upward and I give him a challenging look. His eyes narrow on me, but he doesn't say a word. Since he's holding my right hand, I reach down with my left and palm his erection through his pants. Latham's nostrils flare, but he doesn't say a word, doesn't move a muscle.

When I try to pull on his zipper, he stops my hand again. "Why not?" I whisper.

"It's not required because of what I just did," he says.

"Latham, I don't do anything I don't want to do. You know that," I add, running my finger down the length of the zipper.

His jaw ticks with tension. "My pants stay on."

"Well, that won't make it very easy, but I'm up for the challenge," I say, spinning him around so his back is to my front.

I press my chest to his warm back, loving the way his skin feels against me, and run my hands down his chest. I have to move my arms under his, but it gives me better access to what he's hiding in his pants. I undo his belt (because he never said I couldn't) and pop open the button. I can tell he's just about to say something, but I silence him by sliding my hand along his lower abdomen and into his underwear. Latham tenses again, his body going completely rigid as my hand comes in contact with hard, warm flesh. Latham hisses as I wrap my hand around his length, palming his thick erection and wishing I could get my mouth on it.

But we'll save that for another day.

Because something tells me Latham Douglas is an addiction I can't afford to have, yet I don't want to walk away.

Not yet.

Not now.

Maybe not ever.

Chapter 12

Latham

THE MOMENT HER HAND WRAPS around my cock, I see stars. Bright, white light that robs me of my ability to think and breathe. All I can think about is the softness of her skin, the firmness of her fingers, the hardness of the nipple ring pressing into my back. Talk about the surprise of a lifetime there. I wasn't kidding when I confessed I almost came in my pants. The sight of Harper's sweet nipples on display, and with a piercing to boot, well, let's just say she was a fantasy come to life.

My fantasy.

She slowly starts to move her hand, up and down the entire length of my cock. I'm so worked up she could probably make me come in under ten seconds, but I don't want to detonate yet. I want to memorize the feel of her body and taste of her skin. I want to draw out this moment for as long as I can. Who the fuck knows when I'll be able to wrap my lips around those perfect nipples or feel her hands around my aching dick again. But I'm fighting a losing battle. There's no way I'll be able to hang on with her stroking me off.

So instead of fighting it, I just let go and feel.

My hips buck as I drive up into her palm. She places her other hand on my abdomen, wraps her legs around me, and starts to pump faster. It's hard to breathe as her hands works me over, her soft skin caressing my cock. My body is already tightening, a familiar tingle starting at my spine. It spreads quickly up my back and races to my balls. I'm seconds away from exploding and there's nothing I can do but stand here and enjoy the ride.

Her hand pumps hard (well, as hard as she can, considering they're confined to my boxer briefs). My cock starts to drip. My hips start to thrust. I imagine what it'll be like to thrust into her sweet pussy. No, that's not happening tonight, but soon. I can feel it. We've been dancing around it for too long to just up and forget about it. Now, I've had a taste, and I need more.

Harper scores her nails down my chest, and my hips drive forward. I'm there, ready to explode with nowhere to go with the mess. As if sensing my problem, she pulls my boxers down and points my cock at my chest. She leans back ever so slightly and cradles my back to her chest. I lean back and explode, coming all over myself. Curse words fly from my lips as her hand tightly caresses my pulsing cock, milking it for everything I have. A shudder sweeps through my body as I sag against the counter, against her. "Fucking hell, woman."

"Mmm," she whispers in my ear, her warm breath tickling me and breathing a whole new life into my body. My cock hasn't even had a chance to soften yet, and suddenly, it's ready to go again. But this time, he wants in her pussy.

That's why I need to go.

As much as I want to fuck Harper, I won't do it tonight. Not when we just sort of met on solid ground. It's not the most stable of land, so I have to be careful not to rock it too much and risk the entire thing collapsing.

Plus, there's the little issue of the building between us. She still wants it, and so do I. We're bidding against each other, and until that issue is resolved, I don't want to sleep with her. Fine, I *want* to sleep with her, but I don't think it's a good idea. Actually, I'm pretty sure it's a horrible idea.

Trying to get my breathing under control, Harper grabs a hand towel from the counter and swipes it over my chest. I take the material in my hand, finishing up the job, and stand on shaky legs. Her legs are still wide and I turn to face her easily enough. My lips find hers, wet and eager, but I keep the kiss from heading into the direction that involves both of us panting with a lot less clothes.

Finally peeling my lips away, I rest my forehead against hers and just breathe her in. My eyes are locked on her crystal blue ones, too many emotions and conflicting thoughts swirling between us. Where in the hell do we go from here? I know where I'd like to go, and that would be to the bedroom down the hall. But that's not happening. Not yet, anyway.

"How about we finish up these dishes?" I ask, taking her by surprise. I think she's expecting that trip to the bedroom too.

"Okay," she says softly, offering me a smile. It's not a glare or one filled with annoyance and mischief I'm accustomed to. It's a genuine, beautiful smile that makes my heart tap dance in my chest, and suddenly, I'm questioning my own decision not to advance this portion of the evening.

I grab the dishcloth, flip on the water, and try to ignore the raging hard-on in my pants. Shouldn't be a problem at all.

Before I head over to my sister's place to meet my family on a beautiful late Sunday morning, I fire up my laptop. I'm smiling as I bring up the program I downloaded for a rainy day. Well, the sun is shining and there's not a cloud in the sky...

But today, it's raining.

I can't wait.

I log into her laptop, careful not to mess with anything but the music program that came standard with her new laptop. I glance through my playlist, looking for the perfect song.

Yes.

That one.

I click upload, adjust the settings, and log out of her system.

Illegal?

Fuck yes.

Do I care?

Not in the least.

I take a few minutes to clean my trail, and shut down my computer.

She's going to hate this.

She's going to hate me.

But I don't stop smiling the entire time I finish getting ready. I grin like a loon the entire trip to my sister's house. I laugh easily the moment my sister asks me if I'm seeing anyone special to put that smile on my face.

No, I'm not seeing anyone.

But she's definitely special.

"Who is she?" Larkin whispers as I help her clean up the lunch dishes.

"Don't worry about it," I tell her, not really wanting to get into it right now. I don't even know what's going on between Harper and me, and I'll be damned if I'm going to spill my guts to my nosey little sister right now.

"Fine, be that way," she whines, stacking the dried dishes back in the cabinet.

My two-year-old niece's giggle filters into the kitchen, putting an instant smile on my sister's face. "How's she doing?"

"Perfect," my sister boasts. "She has a little friend from daycare that she wants to come over and have a playdate."

"Sounds nice. I'm sure she'd get a kick out of an afternoon of playing princesses with her little friend," I confirm, draining out the water and rinsing away the soapsuds.

Larkin smirks. "I think there'd be only one princess in this castle."

I finish and glance at my sister. "What do you mean?"

"It's a prince. Her friend is a boy."

A boy? Hell no. "Not happening," I tell my sister with conviction.

She laughs. "They're two, Latham, not getting married." A growl slips from my throat. "Stop being such a big overprotective uncle right now. Five seconds ago, you were all for this playdate."

"And I still am. If it were a girl."

Larkin rolls her eyes. "You're ridiculous. I think I'm going to invite them over next weekend."

"Do you even know them?" I ask, leaning my hip against the counter.

Again, my bratty little sister rolls her eyes. "Of course I know them, dummy. It's Rockland Falls, not Chicago."

"Who is it? I can do a background check."

"Stop it."

"Who're the parents," I insist, crossing my arms over my chest and offering my best big brother glare, letting her know I mean business.

"Lath."

"Lark."

"Evan Parker."

"Evan Parker?" I repeat, wrapping my head around the fact a name from my past was just thrown in the conversation. Evan was one of my best buds back in grade school. We hung out a lot until I got into sports. Evan was much more of the bookworm type, which is what originally drew us together as friends. I'm a much bigger book nerd than anyone would guess. In fact, even with the ability to play a few sports, I was a big dork in high school.

"Yeah, Evan. He was married for a short period of time, but it didn't last. He raises his son full time now."

"Where's the ex?" I ask, curious about the friend I've long lost touch with.

"A flight attendant, I believe. Travels a lot so he takes care of their son. She has him whenever she's home, but I rarely see her pick him up from daycare." I continue to watch her. "What?"

I shake my head.

"I was talking about a playdate with his son. You're the one making this into a date."

"I didn't say anything about a date. You did." Now, I'm glaring.

"Stop with the big brother act," she replies, narrowing her eyes.

"It's not an act."

For a third time, she rolls her eyes as my niece comes running into the room. "Uncie, come pway!" Vivian yells, throwing herself at my leg and attaching to it like a twenty-pound spider monkey.

And that's how I spend the next hour, crawling around on the floor, wearing a pink tiara and a dozen dangly necklaces. My sister takes pictures, probably to use for blackmail down the road, and my parents laugh, but I don't give a shit. I have the best afternoon with my niece, playing and making her giggle.

When it's finally time for her nap, she throws her tiny arms around my neck, kisses my scruffy cheek, and tells me she "woves me." I never really thought too much about the future (outside of expanding and growing the hardware store), but after spending a little time with Vivian, I'll admit that tiny seed has been planted. My mom just sat there and smiled, probably already picturing another dozen little grandkids running around the house, and for the first time, I don't feel myself starting to sweat at the idea.

Now, it doesn't seem so bad.

Chapter 13

Harper

I HAVE A SHIPMENT COMING this afternoon with a small order of negligées and warmer pajamas, but that doesn't stop me from oversleeping on this hazy Monday morning. Even with my massive amount of work to accomplish, I still turned off my alarm instead of hitting snooze.

There's a small storm cell just off the coast, making everything dark and gloomy – just like my mood. I spent way too much time in my backyard yesterday, thinking about my Saturday, nonetheless. In fact, I haven't stopped thinking about it. All of it. I painted my doghouse, stapled in a soft rug on the floor, and positioned it under the tree so Snuggles has shade all day long.

And yes, tried to eradicate all images of Latham getting me off just by sucking on my nipple ring.

Didn't work. I spent the entire night wet, needy, and having to take care of it myself with the vibrator in my nightstand drawer.

Now, I'm five minutes late to open my shop and didn't have time to grab a caffeinated drink from the café down the street. Thank goodness for my small four-cup coffeepot in the very back of the kitchen cabinet. Let's just hope the creamer in the mini-fridge isn't expired.

I'll just worry about lunch later...

I quickly turn on the lights and flip the open sign, hoping my tardiness hasn't cost me a sale. Though, if I'm being honest, my entire mojo is just off today, so it wouldn't surprise me if I had a line of customers waiting that walked away the moment I didn't open the door.

Yeah, probably not, but still...

I set my purse on the counter and fire up my laptop. While I wait for it to do its thing, I head to the kitchen area to find the coffeepot. Maybe if I'm lucky, I'll stumble across some crackers or something to go with the brick of cheese I stashed in the mini-fridge. Just as I open the cabinet, music rings through the building. It's a loud and twangy song I recall from my childhood. Tammy Wynette starts to sing about standing by her man.

The fuck?!

I race back to the front to locate the source of the obnoxious country song, only to find it blasting from the one thing I wasn't expecting: my laptop. I click on the music icon, something I used for the first time last week. However, I know there was no country music in my library. So where the hell did this song come from?

I start to click frantically. "Zip it, Tammy," I mumble to myself, desperate to get her to stop crying about her man, when finally the song stops. "Thank God."

Except, it starts again.

"What the hell?" I yell to no one, moving the mouse and trying to click on the music app. Nothing works. After several frantic double-clicks, the app finally opens, displaying a lovely photo of the woman singing. I'm sure it's a great song and all, I mean, who doesn't love the fact she's supporting her man through all his *issues*, but come on. Enough is enough. But when I click on the stop, nothing happens.

Nothing. Happens.

Tammy still belts out the lyrics to her iconic song, drowning my shop in her familiar twangy vocals.

"Son of a bitch," I groan, trying everything.

Exit.

Control, Alt, Delete.

Escape.

Exit, exit, exit.

Slam laptop down on the counter.

Okay, I didn't do that one. It's new, after all, but I want to.

Just as I'm about to hurl the brand new laptop into the wall, the bell chimes over the door. "Oh, dear, why are you playing music so loud?" Mrs. Henderson asks, blanching as she tentatively steps inside.

"I'm not. Well, not really. I'm not sure why it's playing this," I tell her (well, I yell at her). "Come on in!"

"What?"

"I said come on in! Is there something I can help you with?"

She starts to glance around, but her attention is elsewhere. It only takes a couple moments before she starts to retreat back to the doorway. "You know, I'll just come back. Another time..." she says as she hightails it out of my shop so fast, you'd think I told her the deli was offering free cheesecake.

Groaning, I glance to where my first customer of the day was once standing, before turning back to the offending device on my counter.

After an hour (yes, a motherfucking hour) of listening to the same song over and over and over and over again, and scaring off another potential customer, I call my big brother. "Hello?"

"I need help."

"Why are you yelling? And can't you step outside or something? Why are you blasting music in my ear," Samuel grumbles.

"I *am* outside! That's the problem! My laptop is blasting Tammy Wynette!"

"I didn't think you liked country music," he states matter-of-factly.

"I don't! Focus, Samuel."

"I don't understand."

"My. Laptop. Is. Playing. Music. And I can't get it to stop."

"Turn it off, Harper. There's a little exit button at the top of the screen. Click it," he says, his voice carrying a tinge of annoyance, as if he's talking to a small child.

"I did! I clicked it a thousand times."

"Then it must not be coming from that app. Do you have any other music apps on there?"

"I don't know," I whine – yes, whine. "Can't you come over and fix it?" He is our resident computer nerd, after all.

"Sorry, I'm unavailable. I can come by around three, after the Sparling funeral."

"Fun," I crack. It's still a little weird my brother is a mortician.

"I have to go. Good luck," he says before hanging up, not giving me enough time to say goodbye.

"Whatever," I snap at no one, setting my phone down on the counter and wishing I had a landline so I could slam the receiver down on the base.

My stomach growls angrily, probably because it's tired of hearing Tammy too, which reminds me I didn't even get to make my morning coffee. Ignoring the song belting from the small speakers, I head to the kitchen area and fire up the coffeepot. It's a small four-cup jobby, and even though I could seriously go for about sixteen cups, this one will have to do in a pinch.

It doesn't take long before the pot is ready and I pour myself a large mug. I check the fridge and find the creamer outdated, confirming the worst. I have nothing to pour into my black coffee. My day officially blows. My coffee's shit and my pretty boutique sounds like a country western bar.

The hours drag on.

Yes, with Tammy crooning on repeat about the importance of standing by her man. Over and over. And over and over... I try to pretend it's not happening, but that doesn't work well. Every time the song ends, a sense of sweet relief washes over me, only to have it dashed away with the start of the song all over again.

"Holy shit," I hear hollered over the music. "What the hell is happening in here?" my best friend says as she enters my shop, her eyes wide with shock.

"Welcome to Hell, population one."

"Seriously, why are you blasting that music?"

"I'm not!"

"What?"

"I'm not! I don't know why it's playing that song."

Free approaches the counter, sets the bag of sandwiches down, and comes around to check out my laptop. I watch as she brings the music app up and does the exact same things I've done all morning. She stares down, clearly thinking, before reaching around the back and unplugging the small speakers, bathing the shop in silence.

"Oh my God," I yell, throwing my arms around her and hugging tightly.

"Why are you still yelling?" she asks quietly.

"I don't know," I grumble.

"What the hell happened?"

"I have no idea," I start, grabbing the bag of sandwiches and pulling out my lunch. "I came in, fired up the laptop, and it started playing that song. What time is it?"

"Just after one. And that one horrible song? Over and over?" she asks incredulous, taking a bite of her own sandwich.

"Yes, it's been horrible. I lost about six sales this morning because no one wants to shop with Tammy Wynette screaming in their ears." I've been listening to that singular song on repeat for almost four hours.

"You don't even like country music," she adds, pointing out what we both already know.

"I know. When I loaded up the library, I can promise you Tammy Wynette wasn't added to either playlist." I have two: one that can play softer music at the shop, and the other with my favorite tunes from all my favorite artists for after I close.

"And the fact you couldn't turn it off? It's like someone played a joke on you," she says just as I take a bite of my sandwich. It turns to dust on my tongue and like puzzle pieces, things start to click together.

"Latham."

"What?"

"Who else would tamper with my laptop? Plus, he's the one who set it up!" I growl, balling up my empty sandwich wrapper and tossing it in the garbage. I start to pace, back and forth between the counter and the front window. I walk four miles in a short amount of time, trying to figure out what to do.

What to do...

Anger grabs hold, balling in the pit of my stomach before coursing recklessly through my blood. I'm at the door before I even realize what's happening. "You're okay?" I ask over my shoulder.

"I'm fine. Go."

That's the only reply I need before I'm out the door and stomping down the block to the hardware store. The moment my feet hit the sidewalk, the rain cuts loose, pouring down so hard that it practically hurts when it hits your skin. I start to run, but it doesn't help. When I reach the front door of Douglas Hardware, I'm soaked through like a drowned rat. Figures...

I rip open the door with aggression, the friendly little bell announcing my arrival when I enter, annoying me further. My sandals squeak as I head to the counter in search of the man whose balls I'd love to squeeze in a vise right now. Only when I reach it, it's not Latham I find, but the older (and friendlier) version of the man I loathe.

"Harper!" he says happily, before taking in my soaked appearance. "Oh, dear, you got caught in the rain."

"Oh, hi, Mr. Douglas," I reply, feeling a tad bit of my annoyance wash away. I mean, it's not his fault his son is a horrible, conniving devil who deserves to have his intestines ripped out with a wooden spoon. "Is Latham around?" I ask, shoving my wet hair from my eyes.

"He's off on Monday afternoons," he says, a hint of laughter in the old man's eyes.

"Great," I mumble, feeling the weight of my anger wash away in defeat.

I turn to head back to the door, leaving a trail of rainwater in my wake, when he speaks again. "I think he's upstairs, dear. You're welcome to go up and have a word with him." The way he says it, with a tinge of mirth in his voice, has me pause. "He's up there alone. It's well insulated and private. You know, in case you have to yell." Now, he does smile.

Steeling my back, I face Latham's father. "Thank you, Mr. Douglas. I'd love a few moments to speak with him." My anger sweeps back in like a mini tornado, ready to pummel and damage whatever stands in its path.

And that path is leading me to Latham.

"Up those stairs back there. He rarely locks the door," Bud says, a small smile on his face as he continues to price whatever new product is in the box without giving me a second glance.

"Thank you," I state as I move around the counter and head toward the stairs. As I ascend quietly, I can hear Bud humming a happy little tune. I keep my movements light, not wanting to tip Latham off to a visitor just yet. I prefer the element of surprise, which is why I find myself gently turning the knob on the door and happy to find it unlocked – as speculated.

I quietly push open the door and step inside the tiny kitchen that opens to a small living room. There's not much room to maneuver, and I can't help but wonder how a man as big as Latham moves around in this itty-bitty apartment. Sound filters from another room, letting me know he is, indeed, home. Before I have a chance to close the door, his words find their way to where I stand. The hairs on the back of my neck stand up as realization sets in.

He's humming.

He's humming Tammy Wynette.

The same song that just so happened to be blasting through my shop for the last four hours.

Yeah, I'm going to kill him.

I grab the door behind me and give it a good, hard slam. The force rattles the walls and can probably be heard by Bud and any of the customers downstairs, but I don't care. All I care about right now is injuring the asshole who messed with my laptop and ensured I had a shit-tastic day.

Stomping my feet with each step I take, I head toward the place where I heard him humming. As I round the corner, I hit a wall. No, not a wall, really. This wall is large and hard and reaches out to grab my arms. I hold out my arms to steady myself and encounter hot, wet flesh.

"Harper?" he asks, but his words barely register. I'm staring at Latham, fresh from a shower and wearing a towel.

Yeah, I know you're picturing it too.

My jaw unhinges, I just know it, but I don't care. My eyes feast on his chiseled torso, the mouthwatering tattoo, his eight-pack abs, and that delicious V at his hips that disappears beneath the towel. And the bulge. Let's not forget about the way the towel practically wraps around his cock like a hug. A hug I wouldn't mind giving it.

With my mouth.

He must sense where my mind is because that big, thick cock jumps beneath the terrycloth and starts to grow. Within a matter of seconds, it tents the towel and points directly at me as if begging to be played with. And I'll be damned if I don't want to wrap my hands around it and give it a few friendly strokes.

Then, I hear him chuckle.

Suddenly, I remember exactly why I'm here and it isn't to play with his magnificent cock. Instead, I should be wrapping my hands around his neck. "See something you like?"

"I see something I'd love to chop off with a plastic knife," I growl, finally returning my eyes to his.

"Sounds kinky, Sweetheart. Did you come over here to help me shower or should we skip the shower and go straight to sex?" he asks, leaning his broad (and still wet) shoulder against the wall and crossing his arms over his chest, casually.

"I came over here to kill you. Do you want your mom to have an open or closed casket?" I snarl, holding my eyes on his sparkling brown ones.

"You're giving me a choice?" he asks, smiling brightly.

"For your mom."

He snorts a laugh. "So what brings you over here in the middle of the day, spunky Harper?"

"Tammy. Wynette." I make sure to throw in a little extra female dramatics and pause between the first and last name.

"Tammy, huh? Isn't she dead?"

"You'll be seeing her very soon. Well, probably not. You're going to hell for your stupid childish pranks."

"Childish?" Yes, his eyes light up with humor. I want to punch him in the face.

"Childish!" I yell, letting my frustration and anger for him get the best of me. "You cost me sales! The music was so fucking loud no one wanted to shop. They all left thinking I was trying to torture them with bad country music!"

"You wouldn't know good music if it hit you upside the head," he chastises. "It's a thousand times better than that boy band bullshit you listen to."

I throw my hands in the air. "You're impossible! And frustrating! And completely...impossible!"

"You said that already. I like to think it's part of my charm," he teases with a wink.

Yes, he winks.

So I punch him in the chest.

"Ouch!" I holler, shaking my hand and infuriating me even further. He laughs, so I slap him across the arm. My palm instantly starts to sting, making my eyes water. Shaking my hand, I glare daggers at the asshole whose hard stupid muscles just injured me.

"Well, stop hitting me, Sweetheart," he chides.

"Stop calling me Sweetheart!" I yell as I launch myself at him.

Suddenly, I'm wrapped in his arms and our mouths are fused together. My legs snake around his waist, the apex of my legs rubbing over his thick erection. The kiss is hungry, passionate, and full of desire. His mouth is everything I want, but more accurately, everything I remember.

Latham's hands rip at my shirt, exposing my heated, wet flesh. I suck on his tongue, drawing a deep growl from his gut that vibrates through my bloodstream and lands between my legs. He turns and pins me against the wall, his large hands gripping at my ass and holding me steady against his body. His tongue sweeps into my mouth at the same time his cock thrusts upward, sliding against my swollen pussy and eradicating a loud gasp from my lungs.

He moves a hand without breaking the connection of our mouths and raises my shirt once more. His hand is hot against my flesh as he pushes it all up and exposes my soaked bra. Thank God I wore one of my favorite red lace bra and panty sets today, not that it matters. I'm pretty sure anything I wear would look the same thrown on the floor.

His mouth rips from mine, and I suck in huge lungsful of sweet oxygen. That is until his hot mouth dips down and grazes across my breasts. My nipples are hard, pebbled against the coarse material, and begging for his mouth. He reads my mind and with one hand, pulls down one of the cups of my bra. With his dark eyes locked on mine, his tongue slips out and swipes across the ring in my nipple at the exact same time he rubs his cock against my center.

"Latham," I gasp, my eyes rolling back in my head at the onslaught of sensation.

"Tell me to stop, Harper. Tell me and I will," he whispers, his voice low and gravelly.

I don't even have to consider it. I know what I want. "Don't stop. Please," I beg.

His eyes turn black as realization sets in. He pauses, holding my gaze for confirmation. Instead of giving him words, I fuse my lips to his, thrusting my tongue into his mouth and tasting him once more. He's a hit to my system, a shot of alcohol on an empty stomach. He affects me in a way no other man ever has.

My back is pressed against the wall, my legs wrapped around his waist, when he pulls my shirt the rest of the way over my head, the wet material slapping against the floor. The moment it's gone, his lips are back on mine, devouring me and leaving me completely breathless. There's something so magical about his kisses that has always made me feel wanted – and not because of my face or my body – because of *me*. Even when he was horrible to me back in school, when we pushed aside all the torture and teasing, I felt like I was the only one he saw.

Especially that night.

That one amazing night.

Latham places his large hand on my breast, cupping it and toying with the metal ring. My body zings with desire, with passion, as I close my eyes and let all those sensations wash over me. "I'm going to set you down and take off your wet pants. If you don't want me to, say the word." His voice is deep and gruff, just the way I remember it.

My eyes meet his. "Hurry up, Latham." My words hold a bite, a demand.

Things happen quickly after that. He sets me on the floor and before I can shimmy out of my wet work pants, he has his hands on the closure, unbuttoning them and sliding them down my legs. My sandals are gone too, and suddenly, I'm standing in nothing but my red lace panty set. "Fucking hell," he groans, his eyes feasting on my body. "Do you always wear this beneath your clothes?" he asks, standing completely still and devouring me with his eyes.

"Who else is going to ensure the product I sell is comfortable, sexy, and worth the cost?"

"So fucking sexy," he whispers, wrapping his hand around my hip and bringing me flush against his body. "For the rest of my life, every time I see you, I'll be imagining what sexy little surprise you're wearing beneath your clothes."

His hand slides around to my backside, cupping my bare ass cheek. I can feel his erection sandwiched between us, feel every jolt of electricity that zips through my body as my nipples drag against the lace bra. My entire body is on fire, and if I don't feel him inside me soon, I think I might explode. "Latham?"

"Yeah?" he whispers.

"Lose the towel."

His eyes burn bright as he reaches down and drops the towel. His erection – then, impressive for an eighteen-year-old boy, is nothing compared to the man he grew to be. Thirty-two-year-old Latham is all man, from his rock-hard, chiseled body, to his thick, long cock. He's the one fantasies are made from, and right now, he's a walking dream come true.

Without removing my eyes from his cock, I shimmy out of my panties – they're soaked and useless anyway. He reaches around and unclasps my bra, leaving us both completely naked. We both stare, drinking in the sight of the other's body, as if committing it to memory. I have a perfect recollection of that one night so many years ago, but it pales in comparison to how I feel right now.

His mouth descends on mine once more, hot and hungry and full of need. I'm backed against the wall, his arms wrapping around me and pulling me against him. He lifts at the same time I jump, my legs finding a comfortable place around his trim hips. It also lines his cock up perfectly for where I ache. My body hums with anticipation as he slides against me, coating himself in my wetness.

Then he moves, his dick lining up and pushing inside. My body stretches to accommodate him, almost to the point of pain, reminding me it has been a while. Well, that and the fact Latham is much bigger than my last three boyfriends.

When he's fully seated, we both still and exhale a long, deep breath. Then, as if something lights the fuse, we move. He pulls back, his hands gripping my ass, and slams forward, sending my body into hypersensitive overdrive. I feel everything: his hands, his cock, his breathing. And now, I feel his lips, as he finally leans forward and kisses me. It's a hard, determined kiss, full of pent-up desire and maybe even a little frustration. We're like oil and gasoline, never mixing well, but dangerously explosive when they finally meet.

He continues to press me firmly into the wall, while his masterful cock brings me closer and closer to release with each thrust of his hips. I can feel my body climbing higher as an orgasm barrels down on me. Using the wall as leverage, Latham reaches around and cups my breast. When I'm least expecting it, he pushes upward and pinches my nipple ring. The double sensation has me calling out, I'm not even sure what. My brain sort of liquefies with each thrust of his hips, each tug of my ring. It's too much, yet not enough at the same time.

When he stills completely, I realize my eyes are closed. They open to find his piercing me, searching my face as if memorizing this look, this moment. My heart does something in my chest I don't like. Him. I don't like him. Yes, I'm currently having sex with him, but that's because he's hot. Other than that, he's infuriating and impossible. He rigs my laptop to play stupid country music on repeat, and then has the audacity to show up in a towel when I confront him.

Okay, fine, maybe I'm the one who showed up – unannounced – but whatever... I forgot where I was going with this.

"This won't happen again," I tell him, holding his gaze and giving him my best I-mean-business look.

He smirks and swirls his hips, making my eyes almost roll back in my head. "Oh, Sweetheart, this most certainly *will* happen again."

"So cocky," I grumble, moving my own hips in search of a little friction. When he's holding me against the wall, my legs wrapped around him, there's not much I can do to initiate continuing our sex-capades.

"You want my what?"

"Shut up," I gasp when he pushes so far inside me I feel his hipbones jab my thighs.

"And..."

Rolling my eyes, I keep my mouth shut, pressing my chest into his in search of sweet contact.

"Say it," he whispers, leaning forward and running his nose along my jaw. He holds me completely still, my body so taut with desire I think I might actually explode if he doesn't move soon.

"No." I'm holding out just a little longer.

And then he bends down, raises me up just enough to keep the tip of his cock inside of me, and sucks my nipple ring into his mouth. "Say it," he growls against my flesh, his tongue toying with the bead and lapping at my nipple.

I open my mouth, but nothing comes out. My head falls back against the wall as pleasure races through me, desperately searching for the finish line. A song spills from my lips as he licks and sucks, licks and sucks. My internal muscles flex against the head of his cock, begging for more. He knows I'm close, yet refuses to give me exactly what I want – what I *need*.

"Say it, Harper."

I gasp as he tugs on the ring with his teeth. An invisible line strung from my breast to my pussy pulls tight. I can't take anymore. I'm desperate, and he knows it. "Fuck me, Latham. Now."

He growls, his mouth vibrating around my nipple. "Fuck yes. It would be my pleasure," he roars as he grips my ass hard and thrusts upward, sucking hard on my ring. The combination sends me soaring, flying over the edge of pleasure and freefalling into pure bliss. Latham is right there, grabbing at his own release with each powerful thrust of his hips. My body latches on tight, refusing to let go, as wave after wave of pleasure courses through my body.

A moan spills from his lips as he brings them to mine and sweeps his tongue into my mouth. His body begins to slow as he releases himself inside me, mimicking his movements with his tongue. When his body finally stills, we sag together, sweaty and sated, against the wall. He continues to hold me up, but I'm not sure how. I'm deadweight at the moment. There's no way my legs would hold me if he put me down.

But he doesn't.

Instead, he turns toward the open door behind us and climbs onto the made bed. Even though it's not even two in the afternoon, my eyes are heavy and my body ripples with exhaustion. I don't even argue when he snuggles against me, his warm, hard body actually quite soft and comfortable. My neck moves to the crook of his arm as he gently shifts us into position. His cock (did I mention how large and magnificent it is?) falls free from my body. At first I don't even register the wetness. In fact, my brain function is nil, so I don't quite register it at all. It isn't until he speaks that the force of what we just did hits me.

"Uhh, Harper?"

"Mmmm," I mumble, trying to ignore his words and snuggle into his embrace.

"Sweetheart, wake up. I didn't use a condom." His words are like an electric jolt to the system. My eyes fly open and I turn to look at his concerned face. "I'm sorry, I've never forgotten before."

"I'm on the pill," I tell him, thinking back to my last annual exam and testing. "I had a test at the beginning of the year when I broke up with Joey. I know I'm clean."

The vein at his temple pulses. "I fucking hate you had to get tested because your boyfriend couldn't keep his dick in his pants."

I shrug, worming my way back into the comfort of his body. "He's a stupid mistake. I don't want to talk about him," I reply through my yawn.

Latham wraps his arms around my shoulder, holding me close. "I'm clean too. I was tested in the Army, and it's been a while since I was with someone."

That piques my interest. "Define a while," I coax.

He sighs, his warm breath fanning against my forehead. "About a year and a half."

"Really?" I ask, a bit shocked by this revelation. I mean, Latham is hot – when he's not running his mouth – and clearly knows what he's doing in the bedroom department. Or wall department, would be more accurate.

"Yeah, I didn't date much in the military. I was gone too much for that shit. I had a short-term girlfriend for a while, but during my last deployment, we ended it. It was too hard on her to be back in the U.S., while I was off on some foreign soil I could barely talk about. Plus, the time zone difference made communicating difficult. We decided on ending things by email."

I don't know why, but that makes me laugh. "I'm sure that was hard on both of you," I add with a yawn.

"I'll show you something hard later. First, rest." He kisses my forehead and sets his stubbly jaw against me.

I can hear minimal noise from downstairs, and even though Bud said it was well-insulated, a part of me is praying like hell Latham's dad and whoever else was downstairs didn't just hear him pound me into the drywall like a nail.

I really should get up. I should find my clothes and head back to my store. Free is there, sure, but she's not expecting me to be gone for half the afternoon – especially for the reason I'm not there. In fact, she's probably starting to get a little worried I killed him and am trying to dispose of the body. She'd be the first one to help shovel (best friends are awesome like that).

That reminds me… "I hate Tammy Wynette."

"No one hates Tammy Wynette." His voice is deep and gruff with exhaustion.

"Well, when you have to listen to the same song on repeat for four hours, you might change your tune."

"I thought after five minutes you'd be beating down my door."

I exhale. "I'll admit, I didn't think it was you for a while. Not till Free showed up. She's the one who walked over and unplugged the external speakers."

Latham snorts a laugh. "Sorry, not sorry. You deserved it."

"Payback's a bitch, Latham Douglas," I whisper, as I wrap my arm around his bare chest and drift off to sleep.

Chapter 14

Latham

I SNEAK BACK INTO MY apartment, using the back entrance from the alley so I don't have to deal with my dad, and set the bags down on the counter. Though I'm anxious to get back in bed with Sleeping Beauty, I head to the bathroom to hit the head. Just as I'm starting to zip up, I hear a thump in my room. I pause for a second and listen, not hearing another noise. Maybe I just imagined it...

Washing my hands, I hear the door smacking the wall across the way. I barely have time to dry the water from my hands. As I open the door, I encounter Harper's back, making a break for the front door.

"Going somewhere?" I ask, leaning my hip against the doorway and watching the way her luscious backside moves in her black pants.

She startles, whipping around and facing me. "Oh, I thought you left."

"Which is what you were doing, apparently," I state, shoving my hands into my pockets to keep from reaching for her. My cock is already hard and ready for round two.

"I have to go back to work," she states, crossing her arms over her chest. My mouth starts to water.

"You were sneaking out."

"Was not!"

"Were too. You were slipping away again, but this time, I wasn't sleeping." Her eyes widen in recollection. Direct hit.

"You were the one to leave first," she sputters, stammering for a rebuttal. She hates being wrong or called out. My little pistol has to be right, all the time.

"I went to get dinner," I answer, grabbing my shirt and pulling it over my head.

Her eyes instantly drop to my bare chest. "What are you doing?" she whispers.

"I'm going to show you exactly why you don't sneak out of someone's house." I shove my shorts down to my ankles and kick off my tennis shoes. Her eyes follow my every move, especially when I push my boxer briefs toward the floor. "Turn around." Her eyes are wide and her jaw drops, but she doesn't hesitate. Harper slowly turns around at my command.

I take in the sight of her ass before grabbing the hem of her shirt and gently pulling it over her head. It's dry, which tells me she threw it in the dryer for a few minutes before getting dressed. Tossing it on the floor beside me, I realize it looks just as good on the floor the second time as it did the first. Reaching around, I unbutton her work pants and give them a little push as well. "Where are your panties, Sweetheart?" I whisper in her ear, making her entire body shiver.

"I... I don't know. I didn't see them when I was getting ready." I can hear the excitement, the anticipation in her voice.

"So there's a red lace thong in this apartment somewhere? Do you have any idea how hot that is?" She shrugs her response as I unclasp her bra. My hands are slow and deliberate as I slide them down her arms, removing the last scrap of material from her body.

When I step forward, pressing my hard, hot body against hers, I feel goose bumps pepper her soft skin. She shifts her ass, rubbing it against my swollen cock, short-circuiting my brain (the big one, not the small one making all my current decisions). I run my nose against her shoulder and up her neck, inhaling the scent of jasmine and vanilla as I go. She smells so fucking good.

"I'm going to fuck you. Do I need to suit up?" I murmur, running my tongue against the pulse point in her neck.

"What?" she gasps, arching into my body.

"Condom, Harper. Do I need a condom?"

"No. Just do it."

"It?" I ask with a whisper, running both of my hands down her arms.

"Me, jackass. Just fuck me already," she growls, wiggling her ass against my cock once more.

"My pleasure," I agree as I align myself with her wet pussy. I'm fully seated in one thrust, her tightness wrapping around me and refusing to let go.

This. This right here. This is the best fucking feeling ever. Her body wrapped around me like a glove, so fucking hot and wet I practically lose my mind with desire. My movements are precise and hard, a reminder of how good we are together and why you don't sneak out of my bed while I'm not there. "If you would have left, you would be missing out on this epic orgasm, Sweetheart," I remind just before thrusting hard into her body. Her palms are flat against the wall as she braces for impact.

"Awfully cocky, aren't we?"

"It's more of a promise," I tell her. "You do want to come, don't you? Or should I just stop now?" I ask, slowly retreating from her body.

"No! Don't stop," she hollers, pushing back against me and taking me all the way in once more. "Just...don't stop." Her words are a gasp, a plea.

"Never." And I don't. I thrust my hips and dip my legs, hitting exactly where she wants. She's purring against the wall, grinding back against me. I can tell the moment she starts to come. Her body grips my cock and my name falls from her sweet lips. It sends me barreling into my own abyss of pleasure as my release slams into my spine and pulses through my body. I don't even register what I'm saying, but I know words are spilling from my lips. For all I know, I'm proposing marriage. I don't care. Just as long as I get this, *her*, for the rest of my life.

Harper sags against the wall, my body enveloping her as I lean forward and kiss her neck. I could seriously kiss her neck all day, every day. "And that, Sweetheart, is why you don't sneak out in the middle of the night."

She snorts. "It's almost six in the evening, Latham. Not the middle of the night." She pauses and stills. "Shit! I have to close up the store."

"Free already did," I tell her, kissing down her upper spine.

"When did you talk to her?" she asks, glancing over her shoulder.

"I stopped in after I grabbed the sandwiches. It was just after five, so I wanted to make sure she was all right."

Harper glances over her shoulder. "What did you tell her?"

"That you were currently napping, but would check in with her later."

She groans and closes her eyes. "Great, she knows we had sex."

"That's a definite possibility. She wouldn't stop smiling and commenting about post-sex naptime."

"Uhhhhh," she groans, her internal muscles tightening around my growing erection.

"Don't moan like that, Sweetheart, or you'll find yourself flat on your back on the hardwood floor."

I pull out just a few inches and slowly slide back in. "I have to go," she gasps, pushing back against me once more.

Reaching around, I gently tug on her nipple ring, loving the way her nipple pebbles against my touch. "You're free to go anytime you want," I remind her, making my strokes a little more precise.

She looks back over her shoulder one more time, leaning forward until her ass is pressed firmly against my waist. I grip her hips and drive in hard, evoking another long moan of pleasure. "Well, maybe after just one more..."

Chapter 15

Harper

"THERE'S MY BABY," I COO as I enter my house, Snuggles happily wagging her stubby little tail, tongue hanging down her chin. She jumps on her hind legs, anxious to receive her first rubdown of the evening.

"If it isn't the ugliest mutt in town," Latham says behind me, entering my house and essentially stealing my dog's attention. Snuggles takes one look at our visitor and jumps with excitement. She practically pees down her leg as he takes a knee and pets her.

"Deserter," I mumble, tossing my keys and purse on the table. "You see I'm home, I'm fine. You can leave."

"No can do, Sweetheart. I bought sandwiches, remember?"

"That was an hour ago," I remind him, heading into the kitchen.

Snuggles' nails clip on the hardwood floor, the light jingle of her tags filling the small kitchen. I open the fridge and find a pound of hamburger and some of Mom's homemade egg noodles. Digging the rest of the ingredients out of the cupboard, I get to work on one of my favorite easy peasy comfort dishes.

I toss the hamburger in the skillet to brown and place a pot of water beside it to boil. "Something I can help with?" he asks behind me. When I glance back, he's leaning casually against the doorjamb, tight black T-shirt molded to his impressive upper body. It's almost as magnificent as the bottom half.

"I don't think so. It'll just take about twenty minutes to mix this all together."

He doesn't say a word, but comes over and has a seat at the small bar for two. I barely even know he's there while I brown the hamburger and put the noodles in the boiling water. Once both are done, I drain the water and then add the meat to the pot. A large can of cream of mushroom soup, some milk, Velveeta cheese, and salt and pepper are thrown in too, and I start to stir it together until it's rich and creamy. When I'm satisfied with the results, I grab two plates from the cabinet and dish up dinner.

Latham glances down at the contents before grabbing the fork beside the plate. He takes a hearty forkful and shovels it into his mouth. That wonderful, yet infuriating mouth that brought me so much pleasure earlier, yet smarts off and makes me angrier than a bull in a cage. "This is delicious," he says as I take a small bite.

"Thanks."

"Is this one of your mom's recipes?"

"Nope, actually, it's one of mine."

He glances over and raises and eyebrow. "Yeah?"

"Yeah, when I first moved in by myself, I would experiment with different ingredients. I learned a lot at home with Mom, but it's hard to make huge homemade meals when you're cooking for one. So, I started trying new things and quickly learned you could put cream of mushroom soup in just about anything and make it taste fantastic," I say with a shrug. "This is one of the very first things I created, though I'm sure it's not completely original, but it's still one of my favorites." He doesn't answer, which has me glancing his way. "What?"

"You're amazing." His eyes are locked on mine, and even though I look for it, I don't find a single hint of humor or mocking.

I don't say anything, just dig back in to my meal. It doesn't take long before our plates are clean (he had seconds). When I try to stand up, he sets his hand on my arm. "Let me."

I keep my mouth shut, but stay seated as Latham picks up our plates and rinses them off. He maneuvers around my kitchen effortlessly, and a bit too comfortably for my liking. He grabs the pot and brings it to the counter, glancing my way when he gets there. I point to the cabinet to the right, where he pulls out a plastic container and scoops the rest of the dinner inside. Then, without being prompted, he places all of the dirty dishes in the dishwasher. When his task is completed, he crosses his arms and leans against the counter the way he did the other night.

"Can I ask you something?" His eyes are on mine and I can feel the seriousness in his question.

"Sure."

"Why'd you leave?"

"You weren't there. I needed to get back to work."

He shakes his head. "That's not what I'm talking about, and you know it."

I open my mouth, but close it quickly. I take a second to collect my thoughts before I speak. Glancing down, I run my hand over the slightly raised texture on my countertop. "I got scared."

"Of me?"

I quickly look back up, my eyes connecting with his brown ones. "No, never. I was scared of how...comfortable I felt."

"I wasn't exactly expecting you to be gone when I woke up in the morning."

"It was a little hard to get home early in the morning without a car and wearing a prom dress."

Latham's smile is small. "How'd you get home?"

"I called Jensen. He had his learner's permit and hopped in Mom's car before she woke up. He didn't ask one question, even though I know he wanted to. I'm sure he knew I was with you, considering, you know."

"Considering I was your last minute prom date?"

I feel my face start to blush. "Yeah, considering that. I still can't believe Jake Rodgers backed out on me. Who does that one day before prom?"

"He was the biggest douche in school. Well, besides Joey," he quips, smirking those perfect lips my way.

"That he was. Especially when he told half the basketball team he was only taking me to sleep with me after. When I confronted him, he tried to deny it, but it was written all over his face. Then, the next day, he dumped me, saying I was a stick in the mud. Because I wouldn't sleep with him."

"Little did he know..."

I look up, trying to gauge his sincerity. "Is that why you took me? To sleep with me?"

"That never even crossed my mind."

"Then why did you?"

"Because you wanted to go. Because your date dropped you the day before the dance. Because I didn't have a date, nor plans to go, but it felt like the right thing to do. And because you were the most beautiful girl in school, and I couldn't believe you agreed to let me take you, even after I told the school you had genital warts."

"That was you?" I bellow, not expecting that horrible twist.

Latham laughs. "You didn't know? Shit, Harper, that had my name written all over it."

"I hate you," I mumble.

"So you've said, many times."

We're both staring, wondering what the other is thinking. "Thank you for taking me. And for defending me when Jake tried to start shit at the dance." He doesn't reply, just nods his head. "And... I'm sorry about after. About leaving without saying a word. That was rude of me, and I apologize."

His brown eyes are intense, but don't waver from mine. "I just figured it was because I sucked in bed." He smiles afterward, but I can tell he's serious.

I don't stop the bark of laughter. "Sucked? I recall the only sucking being done was with my mouth," I quip, flashing a quick grin.

Now, he laughs. "Yeah, that was a pleasant treat. The whole damn thing was pretty fucking spectacular. At least it was for me. You know, being my first time and all."

I smile. "I still don't believe that."

"True story, Sweetheart. First time touching a boob."

Now, I'm laughing. "You did have a look on your face – part amazement, part fear."

He joins in the laughter. "I didn't want to mess up. And I didn't want to explode before I even got between your legs. That was my biggest fear."

My neck starts to heat and the blush spreads up my face. "Well, you didn't have anything to worry about, did you?"

His eyes are shining with mirth. "I guess not."

"I always thought guys weren't supposed to last five seconds their first time."

"I guess I'm the exception," he replies with a smirk. "That, or I just had so much practice emptying the pipes in the shower that I built up a little teenage stamina."

I'm caught between trying to roll my eyes and laugh. "I don't know about that. Even though you weren't bad then, your moves have definitely improved," I applaud, throwing him a wink and making him bark out a laugh.

We continue to watch each other for a long moment that turns into a solid minute. So many things unspoken pass between us, things that happened when we were kids, yet define us as adults. He's not that bad of a guy, actually. Even though I want to hurt him half the time, I want to enjoy him too. I'm torn, which is why I keep my ass in the seat instead of walking around the counter and kissing that smile right off his face.

"I should go," he says, clapping his hands together.

Hopping off the stool, I follow him to the front door. See, this is when the awkwardness sets in. I mean, am I supposed to hug him goodbye? High five? Bro back slap?

The decision is taken out of my hands when he stops at the door and pulls me into his arms. I open my mouth to ask what he's doing (even though I already know what he's doing), when his lips press to my own. It doesn't hold any of the urgency his earlier kiss held, but it's mind-spinning just the same. His lips urge mine open, and he dips his tongue inside. It's sweet and sensual, especially when his hands come up and cup my face. I'm ready to wrap my legs around his waist and climb him like a tree, but I don't have the opportunity.

Latham places a chaste kiss on my lips and backs away. "Thank you for dinner," he whispers, still cupping my face.

"You're welcome."

He places one more kiss on my swollen lips. "Good night, Sweetheart. Lock up behind me."

"Hey, Latham?" I holler before he slips completely out the door. He turns and faces me. "I'm gonna need that thong back too."

His face breaks out in a wide, gorgeous smile. "Ain't gonna happen."

And then he's gone.

It's Wednesday and I have yet to see Latham since he left my house Monday night. I even casually strolled by the hardware store yesterday morning, in hopes of spying him through the storefront window, and then spent the next hour chastising myself for being a stupid girl.

I'm not a stupid girl.

Not anymore.

After closing up the store, I head to my office to grab my gym bag. Spin class starts at six, and since I missed Monday's session (thanks to Latham and his sexcapades), I'm in desperate need of some physical fitness that doesn't involve riding a dick like a bucking bronco. Though that was much more enjoyable.

The drive over to the gym is short, and it only takes me a few minutes to change in the locker room. When I head out, I run into Rhenn coming out of one of the rooms.

"Hey, Cowboy!" I greet with a wave.

"Hey, sweetheart," he replies with a wide smile. It's funny, he's called me that since the night I met him, yet I don't get that flutter of excitement in the pit of my stomach the way I do when the nickname rolls off Latham's tongue. "Catching a class?"

"Yeah, spinning starts in a few minutes. What are you doing?" I ask, glancing over his shoulder and seeing a handful of guys and a few girls come out of the room.

"I started a few karate classes on Wednesday nights. Last week, I was talking to the owner, who mentioned the local karate instructor retired months back and no one has replaced him. He offered me the room a few nights a week, and I couldn't pass it up." Excitement twinkles in his ocean blue eyes.

"That's great! I'm sure Marissa is happy to have you around," I say with a smile, bumping my shoulder into his.

His own grin is easy. "Nowhere else I'd rather be."

"Glad you're sticking around, Cowboy," I say, pulling him into my arms. "You make her happy."

"She makes me happy," Rhenn replies, not even caring he sounds like a sappy woman.

"Rhenn." The deep timber of his voice sends tingles of awareness down my spine. I don't have to turn around to know who's standing behind me. I can *feel* his presence.

"Hey, Latham, good to see you," Rhenn replies, releasing me and sticking out his hand for the third party in the hallway to shake. My body tingles with anticipation at his nearness.

"Sweetheart," he whispers in my ear as he releases Rhenn's hand. I can't stop the shiver.

"Well, I should probably head back inside. My next class will be starting shortly," Rhenn adds, turning toward the door. "Oh, will we see you Sunday?"

"I'll be there," I confirm.

"What happens Sunday?" Latham asks, leaning against the wall casually.

"Mary Ann's brother and his family are coming up for the weekend. We're having a family dinner at the bed and breakfast at noon. You should come," Rhenn says to Latham, his invitation making my heart hammer in my chest. Do I want Latham there, interacting with my family?

"Maybe," he shrugs, not committing.

"Well, if you're not doing anything, stop by. They're pretty great people, and Marissa has enough food planned to feed an army." With a quick wave, Rhenn slips back into the room, leaving Latham and I alone in the hall.

After a few tense seconds of awkward silence, I turn to head to my spin class. "Harper." Glancing over my shoulder, my eyes meet his. "You're gonna be late."

"Well, maybe if you would zip it and let me go, I wouldn't be," I retort.

The corner of his mouth twitches and laughter fills his eyes. "See you after class," he says, slowly walking backward to the main room where weights clank together and music pumps through the speakers.

"You're not joining me?" I ask, walking backward myself to my class.

"Oh, I'll be joining you. Later." With a wink, he turns and walks away, disappearing around the corner and getting lost in the sea of gym-goers.

And now, I'm left with spinning, when my body craves another workout. Oh well, I guess I do have something to look forward to.

Later.

Chapter 16

Latham

I'M WHISTLING AS I HEAD up to my apartment to make the call. My realtor called a few minutes ago, but I was finishing up with a customer and had to ignore the ringing. Now, I've got a few minutes to return his call and use the bathroom.

"Pete Benson."

"Pete, it's Latham. How's it going?" I ask, pacing my small living room and kitchen.

"Well, Latham. I heard from Mrs. Morton. She said her son is coming home this weekend, and she'll be discussing both offers with him. She'll have an answer for me Monday."

Monday. I'll know the fate of the empty building between my hardware store and Harper's panty haven in just four short days. "Anything I can do to ensure I get it?" I ask, instantly feeling guilty.

"Turn on the Latham Douglas charm, man. Stop by and schmooze her or whatever. Just make sure it's your offer she picks when she makes her decision," Pete says.

Sighing, I scrub my hand over my face, feeling the several days' old scruff. Usually, in the summer, I hate it, but I guess when summer is at home versus on foreign soil in a shithole, it doesn't seem to bother me too much. "Yeah, I hear ya."

After signing off, I pace my small living area, wishing I had more room to stretch my long legs. I haven't been in too much of a hurry, but maybe it's time to start looking for my own place to live. The small apartment above the store has been convenient as hell, but I wouldn't mind a yard. And maybe a dog.

At that thought, my mind instantly wanders to Snuggles, that ugly-ass mutt who has somehow wormed her wrinkly way into my heart. Damn dog.

And damn the owner.

She has definitely worked her voodoo magic on me too.

There's no time to try to figure it out now. There's still several hours left in the day, and I've got to make a visit to Mrs. Morton in hopes of convincing her to sell the building to me. Guilt tinges the back of my neck and works its way down my spine. My chest aches at the thought of somehow deceiving Harper, but in honesty, she's deceiving me too. At least she is if she knows I'm the one she's in the bidding war with. Harper's fiery side won't let her sit back and not act, which is why I don't think she knows it's me.

Again, the guilt slides through my chest.

I have to push it away, though. This is business, plain and simple. If this were anyone else, it wouldn't matter. I'd do whatever was needed to ensure she signed her building over to me.

Clearly I'm thinking about a certain redhead a little too much because I can smell her succulent, sweet scent. Knowing my break is over, I head down the short hall to the bathroom to take care of personal business before going back to the store to deal with Felicity. She hasn't done anything all day but file her nails, but that's okay. She seems to fuck up whatever task I give her anyway. The sooner I can convince Dad to give her the boot, the better. I've already had to upgrade our back-up computer system since she has somehow crashed the computer and deleted our entire inventory in a matter of two days.

Flipping open the lid and seat, I pull my cock from my pants to piss. As soon as I get a steady stream flowing, I hear what sounds like...splatter. Glancing down, I realize there's something covering the toilet bowl. Unable to stop the flow of urine, I jump back, trying to avoid the piss raining down on my boots and pant legs.

"What the fuck?" I holler, failing to keep the flow angled to the bowl and now peeing all over my damn floor. "Son of a..."

Finally, I stop pissing all over myself, and the floor, and just stand there. I'm so shocked, I don't even know what to do. I mean, yeah, I need to clean up the piss – and change my boots and pants. I quickly tuck my dick back in my pants and zip up, reaching for the faucet and wash my hands. Thank God the bathroom is small as shit and I don't have to go far.

I stick my hands in the warm water and start to scrub, trying to figure out how in the hell Saran Wrap wound up on my toilet.

And then it hits me.

"Harper," I growl.

My motions start to get jerky as I finish washing my hands and rip the hand towel off the towel bar. How in the hell did she get in here without my knowledge? I should have known the moment I smelled her that it wasn't a hallucination. She had somehow gotten into the upstairs apartment. Since I keep the outside door locked at all times, the only way to get in was the entry from inside the hardware store. That means I have a traitor in the mix.

My dad.

Speaking of dear ol' Dad, I hear his voice as he walks through the apartment. "Latham?"

"In here," I grumble, tossing the hand towel on the sink.

A shadow falls over the floor as he fills the doorway. "Ummm..."

"Don't ask," I snip, retrieving a towel from the shelf and the cleaning supplies from the cabinet.

"You do know that goes *in* the toilet, right?" Dad asks, his question laced with humor. "Your mom will be so disappointed the potty training didn't stick. Should I get the Cheerios?"

"Laugh it up, ol' man. This is your fault anyway," I tell him, bending down and soaking up the majority of the urine.

"My fault? How do you figure? I'm not the one who peed all over the floor," he says, his eyes dancing with humor. "Or on your pants." This time, he can't contain his laughter.

"You let the enemy in, didn't you? You were the only one who would have granted entrance to the pretty little devil and turned his back while she Saran Wrapped my toilet." Lord knows Felicity wouldn't have allowed her upstairs.

"Harper did this? You sure?" He coughs to cover his laugh.

"Oh, I'm sure. This has her name written all over it," I mumble, removing the nasty plastic wrap and spraying the hell out of the toilet and floor with a Clorox cleaner.

"I don't believe it. Not that sweet girl next door."

"She's horrible." *She's not.* "A menace." *Who's hot.*

"And you're sweet on her." The old man's voice is sugar sweet.

I can't even deny it, because I am. Always have been.

"Anyway, I should head back downstairs. As soon as you change your pants, you better get down there too. When I was coming upstairs, Felicity was fixing the printer," Dad says, shaking his head.

"What's wrong with the printer?" I ask, crouched down on the floor and trying not to kneel in the piss.

He turns to go but gives me one last glance. "Nothing...before she started fixing it."

"Son of a bitch," I mumble, shaking my head. "I'd rather stay up here with the piss."

My dad's laughter carries through the apartment as he heads back downstairs. I'm left to finish cleaning my mess and probably an even bigger one down in the store when I'm done. After that, I have to figure out how to deal with the redheaded vixen down the block. There's no doubt in my mind she's the one who Saran Wrapped my toilet seat. Total juvenile move, but do you know what?

It's going to be damn fun getting even.

Even though I'm headed down to fix my now-broken printer, there's a smile on my face. I have an idea. A big sparkly one.

The familiar bell over the door rings, announcing my arrival. She closes in about fifteen minutes so I know she'll be distracted. I only need a few seconds to steal her keys and execute my retaliation. Harper's leaning over the counter, writing something on a slip of paper. My groin instantly starts to tighten when I see her formfitting top in a deep purple color that plunges in the front, revealing mounds of creamy flesh. I can already picture the sexy bra she's wearing underneath, pushing those amazing tits together for my viewing pleasure.

"Stop staring, perv."

I snicker and casually stroll up to the counter, taking in her long legs in black shorts that hit mid-thigh. I'm rock-hard, my earlier plan for vengeance thrown out the window. I'd much rather throw her down on the floor or bend her over the counter and fuck the hell out of her.

"Why are you looking at me like that?" she asks, her voice deep and husky.

"I was just thinking about how amazing you'd look bent over the counter, your smooth ass bearing my handprint on display."

There's a quick intake of breath before she clears her throat. "Not happening, buddy."

"No?" I ask, my eyes meeting hers for the first time since I arrived. The desire is clearly there, written all over her gorgeous face.

"No." Harper lifts her chin and crosses her arms over her chest, as she often does when she's ready for verbal sparring.

"Pity," I reply, my eyes dropping down and slowly perusing her from head to toe.

Silence fills the room, well besides the soft 90's pop music coming from the laptop. "Everything running okay?" I ask, glancing down at the laptop and spying her purse on the shelf right below it. Just where I expected to find it.

She stands up straighter and narrows her eyes. "It's working fine. *Now*. What did you do this time?"

Leaning my hip against the counter, I reply, "I didn't do anything. I'm here merely to check on the machine I installed. You know, being all neighborly."

Harper rolls her eyes so wide I'm sure she glanced at her brain. "Neighborly. Is that what we're calling it these days?"

"Yep, neighborly. Last time, I remember you being very neighborly. Care to go another round, Harper?" My cock weeps yes.

A blush sweeps up her neck and stains her cheeks. I love getting her all riled up and flustered. "No," she stammers, her eyes wide. "I'm working."

"Pity," I concede.

Just as I'm about to come up with some way to get her to move from behind the counter so I can access her keys, the shop door opens and a delivery man walks in. "Hey, Harper, sorry I'm late today. Big deliveries to the bookstore and a mix-up at the warehouse. I've been behind all day."

"No worries, Alan," she says, heading to meet the friendly man in the brown uniform. As she rounds the corner, she glares my way. "Don't touch anything."

Holding up my hands, I quick reply, "I wouldn't dare."

Yeah, she doesn't believe me. With another eye roll, she heads to the front door to sign for her package and I slip behind the counter and grab her keys. It only takes me a second to double click the unlock button and another second to set the keys back in her purse, but I know my time is up. She's signing her name and will turn around before I can return to my side of the counter. So, I reach for the laptop and click a few keys, verifying her backup is updating properly.

"What are you doing?" she practically growls when she turns and starts to head my way.

"Just making sure everything is running properly. Sometimes, with new systems, you have to make minor tweaks to your programs," I answer with a casual shrug.

She meets me around the counter and hip-checks me out of the way. "Like you *tweaked* my music player to blast that God-awful song?" she asks, moving the mouse and looking over her laptop screen.

"I have no idea what you're talking about." Her familiar scent wraps around me, making my cock painfully hard. I shove my hands into my jean pockets to keep from reaching for her. She's a nanosecond away from being thrown over my shoulder and hauled off to the nearest mattress, and she doesn't even know it.

Knowing time is running short to accomplish my task, I turn and head toward the door. "Well, it's been great, Harper, but I must be going."

She watches me, her eyes full of skepticism and annoyance, and doesn't say anything as I head out the door, whistling Tammy Wynette. I can practically feel the steam rolling from her ears as I push the door and head out into the late afternoon July sun.

She's going to hate this...

Chapter 17

Harper

I WATCH HIM GO. PARTIALLY because he looks amazing in worn jeans that hang dangerously low on his trim hips, but also because I don't trust him. No way in hell did he just come over to say hi. Or be *neighborly*, as he suggested. Glancing around, I check to see if anything is out of place. I spy the laptop and note the back-up program he was looking at still open, but nothing seems disrupted.

Besides, he's not stupid enough to mess with me right before my eyes.

Right?

Sighing loudly, I push Latham's visit out of my mind and start to shut down the store. As soon as I head to the front door to lock it, it pushes open, a frazzled Adrian Harkins flying inside. "I need help!"

"What's wrong?" I ask, glancing over her petite shoulder to see if someone is following her.

"Mac is coming home in a few hours, and I know you're closing, but I need something that says 'You've been overseas for five months, and I've really missed you. Let's have a baby.' Do you have anything that says that?" she asks, her blue eyes wide with excitement and hope.

"I have plenty that says that," I tell her honestly, locking the door and escorting her toward my bridal section. "Are you looking for classic and sexy or dangerous and sultry?"

"Dangerous. Definitely dangerous. I haven't seen him in over five months, and his plane lands at eight tonight. I want to be naked by eight oh five."

"Well, then let's get you ready to greet your husband, though you may want to wait to get naked until you're home. I'm sure all of the other soldiers and spouses would appreciate it," I tell her with a laugh, leading her through the store to the more risqué section.

She spends a few minutes browsing the selection, but when her eyes land on the black bustier and thong set, I know she's sold. "That will look amazing with your tanned skin."

"You think?" she asks, holding up the bustier and glancing in the mirror.

Leaning in, I whisper, "You'll have him panting like a dog and making a baby in no time."

Her eyes twinkle with glee. "I want this one."

I dig in the small stack for her size, guesstimating her at a thirty-four C. "Let's try this on real quick," I say, grabbing a medium panty and escorting her to the changing room. Adrian checks her watch, her eyes frantic with nerves, and dips into the curtained room. "What about stockings? You're wearing a skirt. Those will be a delightful treat," I holler through the curtain, sorting through the black nylons and finding her size.

"Do you think?" she asks, the sound of zipper teeth sliding and clothes dropping filling the room.

"Definitely. Let me know when you're ready to be snapped in back." With nylons and a garter belt in hand, I meet her at the curtain and wait for my cue.

"Ready."

I slip inside and help fasten the tiny black snaps. I give her privacy and avoid looking in the mirror, but notice the way the black material hugs her torso beautifully. It's a perfect fit. "Here, put these on too," I tell her, handing off the garter and nylons.

"You don't think it'll be too much?" she asks, concern flitting through her ocean eyes.

I grab her arms and give them a gentle squeeze. "He'll die. Trust me." With a wink, I slip out of the room and head to the counter to start ringing her up.

A few minutes later, Adrian joins me at the counter, her hands nervously running down her sides. "I can't believe I'm wearing this."

"You're going to bring him to his knees," I reassure.

Adrian glances at her watch and panics. "Oh my God, his plane is landing in two and a half hours. I have to pick up his parents at their house and drive to the airport."

"You've got this, Adrian," I tell her as she hands me her credit card without even waiting for the total.

"Eighty-five sixteen," I tell her, handing over a small bag for her to place the undergarments she arrived in.

"Wait, that's not right," she says as I swipe the card.

"The garter belt is on me," I tell her with a wink.

"You don't have to..."

Handing her back her card and tearing off the slip of paper to sign, I reply with a warm smile, "I know. Now go make a baby."

Her eyes hold unshed tears as she offers me another smile. "Thank you."

I have to fight my own tears as I reply, "You're welcome. Now go. And tell me how he liked his surprise!" I add before she flies out the door.

"I will!"

And then she's gone, leaving me with a smile and a sadness in my heart.

Mac was coming home to someone special. How did Latham feel when he got back last month, no one there to pick him up from the airport? He didn't even tell his parents he was coming home, just showed up on their doorstep. I'm sure it was a wonderful surprise, but how did he feel watching all of the others receive hugs and kisses from their loved ones, while he headed off to the nearest bus stop terminal for a ride to Rockland Falls.

Suddenly, I want to hug him.

And kiss him.

And welcome him home properly.

My fingers fly through the familiar motions as I close out the register and back up the system. The lights are off and my purse is sitting on the counter as I wait for the final steps to complete. As soon as it does, I shut it down, lock the laptop in the filing cabinet, and make a break for the front door. With my keys in my hand, I set the security system and lock up.

Outside, I pass a few familiar faces as I head next door to drop my deposit off in the night drop off box. Then, I'm racing across the street to my car. Using the key fob, I open my door and start the engine. The air is off – weird, since I thought I had it on this morning – but instead of turning it back on, I decide to let the warm breeze flow through my car. With all the windows down, I head home to take care of Snuggles and take a quick shower.

My happy puppy greets me as soon as I slip inside the house, the air conditioning a welcome reprieve from the heat outside. I bend down and give her a quick pet behind the ears before leading her to the back door. She runs off, anxious to do her business, while I head back inside to take a quick shower.

I don't wash my hair, but shave and exfoliate all of the important areas. When I'm smooth and clean, I jump out of the shower, anxious to head over to Latham's. I smother lotion over every square inch of my body, the rich scents of jasmine and vanilla wrapping around me. I touch up my makeup, darkening my eyes in that sultry way I used to do daily, but now save for special occasions.

Then, I head for my dresser. I already know which one I want. After spending a few minutes with Adrian and feeling the anticipation she was experiencing, I dig out my own black bustier and matching thong set. Mine is an older style, though, with deep red piping and a black lace overlay. Carefully, I snap the back and glance in the mirror. It dips dangerously low, showcasing my cleavage and pushing my breasts together magnificently. The lace thong is sexy, enticing, and bold. Perfect.

I snap the garter belt into place and roll on a pair of stockings. Then, I return to my closet and find my dark blue sundress. It's shorter than the others and will barely hide the stockings that hit just above mid-thigh. It too will be perfect. Keeping my hair up, I retwist it into a knot, letting only a few tendrils hang around my face.

Taking one last look in the mirror, I slip on my too-high strappy sandals, swipe dark gloss over my lips, and head out of my room. I make a quick pit stop at the back door and call Snuggles. She's not too happy to be coming in from outside, but when I produce a treat from the cabinet, she hightails it out of her doghouse and trots up the back steps like her tail is on fire. It wags furiously as she sits like a good girl and shakes for her treat. After a few more minutes of showering her with affection, I fill her food and water bowls, and make sure she's settled for the evening.

Then, I head back to my car.

It's only a few blocks from downtown where my business is, and even though I try to keep the windows open to enjoy the early evening breeze, it's just too hot outside, or maybe I'm a little too nervous. Too sweaty. So I roll up the windows and crank on the air. As soon as I do, I hear a poof sound, and it's suddenly raining.

Not liquid, though.

This is sparkly particles of hell flying through the air and landing everywhere.

Everywhere.

Glitter.

So. Much. Glitter.

I stop at the stop sign, spitting the sliver sparkles from my mouth and glance around. My entire car is covered in it. My dress. My arms. My face.

Dirty rotten bastard, son of the devil, asshole jerk!

He's. So. Fucking. Dead.

Flicking it from my eyelashes, I slam on the gas, catapulting through the intersection and racing toward his apartment. My heart is pounding furiously, much like my fists will be shortly. I'm going to kill him, no doubt. This is how it's going to happen. I always knew it would be murdering Latham that would get me thrown in the pokey, but I never thought it would happen while I was covered in glitter. There's no way in hell I can cover all the sparkly evidence now, but that's okay. Leave a trail. I don't care anymore.

The asshole is going down.

I pull up in front of the hardware store, the closed sign hanging in the window. There's no way he'll hear me pounding on the front door if he's upstairs, so I drive around the back, parking haphazardly in the alley by the back door. I fly out of my seat, raining glitter as I go, stomping up the stairs like I'm storming the castle. I reach the landing and pound, my knuckles hurting under the hard wrap against wood.

Finally, after a handful of very tense seconds, the door opens and Latham stands before me, all gorgeous and cocky. His lips quirk upward as he tries not to smile, sending my blood boiling to volcanic levels. Then his eyes drop down and his smirk falters. His eyes darken and his breathing hitches. My own heart gallops in my chest as he devours me with his eyes, the evidence of his arousal thick in his pants.

"Well, good evening, Sweetheart. You're looking awfully *sparkly* tonight." He never takes his eyes off my thighs, and I see red.

I launch myself at him, ready to scratch out his eyeballs. The force of my leap causes him to stumble, but he rights himself quickly, catching me in his big, stupid arms. I hate the way my body responds to his nearness, his touch. Instead of beating the shit out of him, I find myself wrapped around him like a taco shell, my mouth plastered to his.

The kiss is full of hunger, urgency, desire. My hands slide effortlessly through his hair, gripping and pulling at the dark strands as he kneads the globes of my ass with strong fingers. No doubt, leaving marks, but I don't care. I *want* him to mark me. My back presses into the wall and the door slams, yet he never removes his mouth from mine. He cages me against the drywall, framing my face with his hands. I feel the hard press of his cock between my legs, an ache forming deep in my body. An ache only Latham can quench.

His hands go to my face and the force of his mouth lightens. "You're so fucking gorgeous," he whispers, placing soft, opened-mouthed kisses on my jaw and neck.

"I hate you."

"I know," he whispers, flexing his hips and grinding his erection into my center. Our collective moans are a mix of pleasure and frustration. I *need* him. So bad.

His hands move from my ass to my thighs. "Did you do this for me?" he asks as his fingers graze gently along the black lace trim of the stockings.

"No. I did it for me," I reply, raising my chin and meeting his eyes. He knows I'm lying.

One of his hands slips between my legs, tracing the tie of the garter belt and finding wet panties. "You're like a present I can't wait to unwrap." His finger slips under the material and presses into my clit.

A rush of breath stills in my throat, and I see stars. Then, suddenly, we're moving. "Where are we going?" I ask, my voice not sounding like my own.

His hand sweeps down my jaw and cradles my chin. "To the shower. I don't want you to get that glitter shit all over my bed. Then you're putting this outfit back on so I can fuck you in it."

Chapter 18

Latham

I KNEW SHE'D BE PISSED; that was a given. But I wasn't expecting the fireball of lust to slam into my gut the moment I saw her. She's completely covered in glitter, and I know from recent experience that shit isn't coming off very easily. Desire mixes with my need to touch her, which is why I'm stalking off to the shower like my life depends on it.

Inside the small room, I let her slide down my body and reach for the shower knobs. It's a small water heater and won't stay hot for long, but that's all the more reason to hurry up and get to phase two of my new plan: sex. It wasn't even on the radar as I placed the glitter bomb in her driver's side air vent, nor when I heard her pounding up my steps. But when I saw her in that dress? That fucking short dress that barely covered the stockings she tried to hide underneath? I was a fucking goner.

She reaches down to grab the hem of the dark material, but I stop her hand. "Allow me." My fingers tingle with anticipation as I hold her wide gaze and slowly lift. Not wanting to miss a second of this reveal, I look down and watch as inch by glorious inch, I start to uncover smooth skin. And black lace.

The stockings are held by a garter belt that already has my cock raging with need. The tiniest strip of lace covers her gorgeous pussy, and something tells me there's nothing to the backside. I'll have to check that out soon. As the dress continues to inch up, I find only a sliver of her abdomen before spying more black. I groan in anticipation. My hands are hurried as I pull the dress the rest of the way up and over her head, tossing it somewhere in the room and raining sliver glitter over everything in the process.

And there she is.

The most beautiful creature I've ever seen.

Wearing a black and red bustier and garter belt.

I almost come in my pants.

Scrubbing my hands over my face, I continue to memorize every square inch of her delectable body. "Holy shit," I whisper, drinking my fill of the vision before me.

Harper shakes her head, sending more particles from hell all over my bathroom floor. My cock is so hard it's painful, but there's no way in hell I'm missing this moment. Stepping forward, I reach for her waist and pull her against me so she can feel exactly what she does to my body. With my index finger, I gently run it from the hollow of her throat down to the cleavage pushed up and out by the bustier. Dipping my head down, my tongue follows the same path. She gasps and sways my direction, the hard beat of her heart pounding in her chest.

"You wore this for me." It wasn't a question but a statement.

"And if I did?" she asks, her blue eyes wide with anticipation.

"Then you will be rewarded." I nip at the tender flesh of her breast. "Multiples." A flick of my tongue into the cup of her top hits pay dirt when it meets hard nipple and a ring. "So many you lose count."

She shivers against me.

Reaching behind my neck, I pull my shirt up and over my head and let it fly over my shoulder. Harper's long fingers frantically work my belt, trying to get to the button beneath. I kick off my boots, sending a silent prayer upstairs that I wore my slip-on ones to work today. When the belt is released and the button unfastened, she dives for my zipper. The bite of the teeth pounds through the small room and sends my blood flowing to my cock.

Before she can grip the waist and push them down, I kneel before her and grab an ankle. These shoes are dangerously high, little straps wrapping around her delicate ankles. "These will go back on later too," I inform her before unclasping the buckle and tossing the shoe. The second one follows. Quickly.

As soon as I stand back up, her hands dive into my waist and my pants are pushed to my knees. My dick is practically weeping in my pants, begging to be released from its confines and touched. Then her hands move into my boxer briefs and wrap around my shaft. Pleasure and pain courses through my blood, stealing my breath and vision. "Fuck," I ground out, biting back the release that is dangerously close.

"Oh, I plan on that too," she sasses, a smirk on her gorgeous face.

I rip off my socks, unsnap the little buttons at her lower back, and help remove the rest of her outfit. When we're both completely naked, she grabs my cock and pulls me toward the shower. I go very willingly.

Inside, the hot water pounds at my back, covering our bodies. Mouths fuse together, tongues battle, and hands grasp. We're a heated frenzy of lust and desire, recklessly teetering on the edge of sanity. She strokes my cock, a deep growl rips from my gut. My hand reaches for her pussy, my fingers sliding between the wet folds easily. Two fingers plunge inside her warm heat and she gasps, causing my balls to tighten painfully.

"I'm going to eat this pussy later, Harper," I inform, letting her know there's no room for argument. My mouth craves her taste, her release. Her eyes are wide and wild, her hand gripping my shaft and working it over hard. I'm almost to the point of losing control. She almost has me ready to come, just by grabbing my cock.

I reach for her hips and lift, her legs wrapping around my waist. I drive into her tight body in one fluid motion, my body elated with satisfaction. Until the need for more overcomes the immediate sensation of being home.

Home.

I push that thought out of my head as her hands wrap around my neck and she grinds against me. I pull her up and then bring her back down again. Hard. Her body is tight with the need to come, my own anxious to follow suit. It only takes a handful of pumps before she's there, coming on my cock and milking it for all it's worth. My release follows immediately. My spine tingles and my pelvis thrusts. My balls ache as I come hard inside her sweet, tight body.

My legs wobble, but I don't set her down. I hold her in my arms and touch every inch of her body with my hand. The other helps anchor us to the wall and keeps us from falling. Her lips are soft and pliant as I take them with my own in a gentle kiss that promises more to come.

Her legs start to slide, so I gingerly set her down. Her hair is up, yet matted to her face as the water cascades down every inch of her sparkly body. Without saying a word, I remove the clip and pins from her hair, watching as it falls around her shoulders. Glitter falls everywhere. I guide her back until the water is hitting the top of her head, making sure it's completely saturated. Then I grab my shampoo and squirt a healthy glob in my palm. I've never done this before, and as I lather up the soap in my hands, it makes me happy I've saved yet another first for Harper.

As my fingers start to work into her hair, her eyes flutter closed and her mouth gapes open. A soft moan slides effortlessly from her lips as I use my fingertips to scrub her scalp, hoping I can remove as much of the glitter as possible. I already know it'll take several washes to get it all off her scalp. The sadistic side of me hopes she gets all worked up and pissed every time she combs her hair and sees the sparkle. Maybe she'll think of me.

And probably want to cut off my balls.

I rinse away the suds, careful not to get any in her eyes. As soon as it's free of soap, I grab the washcloth and throw some shower gel in the middle. I don't have any conditioner, or any of that fancy, fruity shit girls like to rub on their skin, but the fact that she's going to smell like my soap – like *me* – has me all sorts of pleased with myself.

With the washcloth, I slowly start to wipe the sparkles from her body. I start at the neck and gently rub my way down. When I reach her nipples, I carefully run the cloth over the piercing, my cock already perking up for round two. My eyes find hers, dark and hungry, as I lean forward, letting the water wash away the soap, and pull the nipple ring into my mouth.

Harper hisses before saying, "God, I love it when you do that." Her hands grip my head, afraid I'm going to move away too quickly.

With the washcloth in one hand, I keep cleaning away the glitter, secretly loving the way my scent clings to her delicate skin. When I finish washing the sparkles away, I drop the cloth, keeping my mouth on her delectable nipple. "When I shut off the water, you're going to go to my bedroom, redress in the bustier, garter, and shoes." I toy with the ring with my tongue.

She inhales harshly, but sasses, "You're not the boss of me."

I suck on the ring. Hard. Her body convulses with desire. "I beg to differ, Sweetheart." Shutting off the water, I turn her around and swat her ass.

Harper gasps. "What the hell was that for?"

"For lying to me," I state, reaching for a towel for her body, then a second for her hair.

"I didn't lie," she retorts, straightening her back and raising her chin.

I gently grasp the sides of her face and place a tender kiss on her lips. "You did. The moment you told me you didn't wear that outfit for me."

Her eyes flair, but she doesn't argue. I watch, dripping wet and yet to grab my own towel, as she steps out of the shower and runs the material over her body. When she's completely dry, she glances over her shoulder and drops the towel on the floor. Before she can take a step away, I reach for her arm and pull her back, not hard enough to hurt her. Her warm, dry body slams into my hot, wet one. My cock is already getting hard and ready for round two. I place another sweet kiss on her lips, loving the way she mewls in my arms. Then, I let her go to head back to my room, smacking her on her amazing ass one more time.

"What the hell was that for?" she gasps, turning dark eyes on me.

I throw her a smirk and reach for a fresh towel. "Because you liked it so much when I did it the first time."

Her eyes narrow, but she doesn't respond. Yeah, she liked that little bite of pain when I smacked her ass. I'll have to remember that later, when she's on all fours and I'm taking her from behind. My cock jumps with anticipation, and my eyes watch as she heads out of the room, a little extra shake to her hips and my handprint on her ass.

My Harper likes to play.

And I'm definitely up for some games.

"I should go," Harper yawns, her head resting on my shoulder as we watch a late-night talk show.

"You should stay." It's already after ten.

"I need to let Snuggles out one more time before bed," she adds, yet to make one move for her clothes. We're currently sitting on the couch, me in a pair of basketball shorts and her in my T-shirt.

"Why don't we go get her and bring her back here?" I offer before I even realize the insinuation. The fact I imply she's spending the night isn't lost on me, and probably not her either. "You can pack an overnight bag too."

Her blue eyes search my face, probably trying to figure out what that means. "Don't overthink it. I'm not saying you're moving in, just I wouldn't mind having you in my bed tonight." My hand wanders down to her ass, slipping easily under my tee and stroking the smarted flesh. She doesn't flinch, but I know it must be tender from earlier. I learned a few solid slaps on her ass sends my girl into a frenzy – especially when she's riding my dick.

"Then I'd have to take her home in the morning before work. I can't take her to the shop. She's not so gentle with delicates."

"Then she can stay with me. Dale is on tomorrow and he loves dogs. She'll be able to go out with me when I'm in the lumberyard. It'll be fun." And as soon as I say the words, I realize I mean them. I kinda want that ugly mutt hanging out with me.

"You're joking, right? Fun? She's still a puppy. She likes to chew and bark and jump."

"Come on, Mom. Let us have a playdate."

Her eyes narrow as she watches me. "Fine, but when she's driving you nuts by noon, you're not bringing her over to me. You have her all day," she reminds, as if that would be a hardship.

"Fine," I reply, clapping my hands together in victory. "Let's go get her," I add leaning closer to her ear. "Then, we'll come back here and I'll fuck you until you're boneless and exhausted."

She shivers and her eyes dilate. It's the only indication she gives that my words have any effect on her. "Let's see if you can keep up, buddy," she sasses, hopping up off the couch and strutting over to her clothes to dress.

I throw on a T-shirt and sandals, anxious to go retrieve her stuff and her dog. As we're heading out the door, her cell phone rings. "Hmm, it's awfully late for Jensen to call," she says as she brings it to her ear. "Hello?"

As we reach the bottom of the stairs, I notice the way her car is haphazardly parked in the alley. I also notice the paper slipped under windshield wiper. My face breaks out in an immediate grin, especially because I realize this little twist is going to piss her off. And if there's one thing I love, it's a pissed-off Harper Grayson.

"Seriously? Why is she being so difficult? It's not like this hasn't been planned for weeks." I glance her way and reach for the ticket, holding it up so she can see. Her face goes from shock to anger as she mouths, "You're paying for that," at me. "Yes, I'm here. Bring him by after work. We'll go for pizza and then I'll feed him ice cream and cookies until he passes out in a sugar coma." Harper smiles at whatever response her brother gives. "Perfect. See you tomorrow."

Then, she hangs up and points her phone at me as if it were a weapon. "Seriously, you're paying that ticket."

"Why am I paying for it?" I ask, reaching out for her keys.

"Because you're the reason I left my car in the alley like this."

"I didn't tell you to illegally park. This isn't my fault."

"Totally your fault. Why are you grabbing my keys? I'm driving."

"Not happening, Harper. There's no way I'm stuffing myself in your tiny sparkly car. I'll move it and we'll take my truck," I say, climbing into the driver's seat, noticing the glitter fucking everywhere. "Besides, I've seen how you park." Her eyes flare with anger as I shut the door and pull her car over to one of the many parking spots behind the hardware store.

"You're cleaning that too, by the way," she states as I swipe all the sparkles from my backside, trying not to grin as I meet her at my truck.

"What?" I ask, losing the battle to not laugh.

"You're an asshole." Her eyes flare as I meet her at the passenger door. "You're vacuuming my car. First thing in the morning," she sasses, grabbing the door handle and getting ready to jump in.

"What did Jensen want?" I ask, helping her into the double cab.

"Oh, his ex is being a twit again. They've been planning his buddy Parker's bachelor party for weeks. Ashley was supposed to keep Max tomorrow night, even though it's Jensen's weekend. Now, she's causing problems, saying she wants to take him out of town for the weekend if she keeps him tomorrow. Mom is working tomorrow night, and even though she'd keep him, it's harder on her to run the bed and breakfast while it's full and take care of Max. Rhenn and Marissa already have a night out planned, so that leaves me."

"And Samuel."

"No one wants their kid babysat by Samuel. He'd probably have them studying human anatomy or reading Shakespeare by the end of the night," she says as I pull onto the main road.

"So, you're watching Max."

"Cool Aunt Harper's got this. We'll go have pizza and stay up way past his bedtime." I can hear the excitement in her voice, and a piece of me yearns to experience that.

"What if awesome friend Latham comes too?" I ask, keeping my eyes on the road, but watching her body language in my peripheral.

She shrugs. "That would be all right too."

Not what I was expecting. I was ready for a fight, but she seemed way too accommodating to my self-invite. "How about I pick you both up at six?"

"We could meet you there," she suggests.

"Well, I will have your dog, so I could stop by and drop her off. Pick you and the little guy up and take you for pizza." Seems logical.

Harper thinks about it for a few seconds before agreeing. "You can't stay the night, though."

"Can't handle me two nights in a row, huh? That's fine. You'll need your rest."

I can practically feel her rolling her eyes in the seat next to me. "Whatever. I don't want to confuse him as to who you are and why you're sleeping in Aunt Harper's bed."

Makes sense, but that still doesn't stop the tinge of longing from bursting in my chest. There's something about going to bed beside Harper and waking up next to her that has all sorts of weird hope and elation taking root in my chest. I never really saw myself as a family man, but the concept holds a bit of merit. Especially if the woman in the picture is Harper.

I don't say anything else as I pull in her driveway. Before I can help her out, she's already climbing from the truck cab and leading me toward the door. I can hear doggy nails on the hardwood floor before she even has the screen door open, and I'm surprised at how excited I am to see the ugly mutt.

As soon as she's through the door, Harper crouches down and lets Snuggles rain puppy kisses all over her face. Then, as if flipping the switch, the dog sees me standing behind her. She instantly jumps up, her little legs slipping on the floor as she barrels toward me. Her tongue hangs out and in her excitement to get to me, I see a trail of wetness on the floor.

"Gross, Snuggles!" Harper bellows as she watches her dog pee a little from excitement.

"Huh, someone must have Saran Wrapped her toilet seat too." Bending down, I let the dog lick and sniff me as I rub that magical spot behind her ears. "Let's go outside," I tell the pup, even though she probably doesn't have to go much now.

"You're cleaning that up," Harper chastises, standing up and placing her hands firmly on her hips.

"I'm practically a pro at cleaning up pee off the floor anyway," I holler, heading to the back door. "Go pack a bag. I'll take care of getting Snuggles ready for our road trip." By the time Harper returns with an overnight bag, I have the piss cleaned up and the dog food, bowls, and leash in a bag. "Ready?"

She glances around, sees the bag of dog supplies and her anxious puppy at my feet, and offers a smile. "Ready."

With that, we're off to our little sleepover.

Like a family.

Which makes my heart sing.

Chapter 19

Harper

I CAN SMELL THE COFFEE the moment I step out of the bathroom. Forgetting all about the towel wrapped around my head, I follow my nose through the tiny apartment. Latham is leaning against the counter, his work jeans hanging dangerously low on his hips and looking totally doable in a well-worn Douglas Hardware T-shirt and work boots. Snuggles clearly thinks so too, since she's sitting at his feet, practically panting with excitement.

"Morning," he says, his voice deep and rich. It's like a direct line to my panties.

"Good morning," I reply, taking the towel off my head and meeting him at the coffeepot. He pours a cup for me and passes the milk and sugar. "Thanks," I say before taking my first sip.

"Your phone was ringing a few minutes ago," he says, nodding toward the counter where both of our phones are charging.

Not a lot of people call me before seven in the morning, so my heart rate kicks up a few beats per minute with worry. When I see the name on the screen, a different form of worry slides down my spine. "It was Mandy, my realtor. I wonder what she wanted so early in the morning?" I question aloud, watching to gauge his reaction.

"Not sure, but you should probably call her back," he says, shoving his hands into his pockets and leaning against the counter, giving nothing away.

"Hey, Mandy, it's Harper. Sorry I missed your call."

"It's okay. Sorry to call so early, but I was heading to the gym and trying to get a few things crossed off my list."

"No worries. What's up?"

"I heard from my aunt. She's making her final decision on the bids Monday. She promised to call me as soon as she decides which one she's going with."

"Really? She didn't say which way she's leaning or who the other is?" I glance over my shoulder to Latham, but find him crouching on the worn linoleum, giving Snuggles a little rubdown. I can tell he's listening, though. I can practically see his ear turned my way and tuned in.

"No, sorry. I tried to get it out of her, but she refused. My uncle is coming down this weekend and is supposed to help her make the decision. So whatever you're going to do, do it fast."

"What does that mean?" I ask, looking out the window at Main Street below.

"Kiss up to her. She loves flowers and cheap red wine. Anything to help you get a leg up over the competition."

"Good idea," I reply, glancing back over my shoulder at Latham. This time, he's looking right at me, and I swear he can hear both sides of the conversation and not just mine.

"I'll talk to you as soon as I know more," she says before signing off.

I hang up the phone and turn back to the kitchen. "Everything all right?" he asks, his gait still casual as he leans against the counter and sips hot coffee.

"Fine," I reply, shoving my phone into the pocket of my capris.

He watches me for several seconds before asking, "Are you in the market for real estate? I thought you owned your home?"

This is where I have a choice. I can tell him about the building next door and call him out on being the other bidder, or I could give him an opening to come clean himself. While option one could potentially result in my twisting his balls until he cries for his mama, it's option two that I go with. "No, no home. I do own my home, and have the monthly mortgage payment to prove it. I've been considering...investing."

Latham nods. "Investing in real estate is a good idea, if you've got the capital. There are plenty of good homes in the area you could get for cheap, flip, and sell for profit."

Not exactly what I was going for. Do I just come out and ask about the building next door? See if the other bidder is, in fact, Latham? Before I can ask, his phone rings. He takes the call, disappearing into the bedroom, my dog hot on his heels. I want to follow, eavesdrop by the doorway, but I don't. As much as I really want to, I don't snoop on his conversation.

Instead, I head into the bathroom and flip on the hair dryer. I mentally run through my day, which will end with a pizza date with Latham and my nephew. Free will be coming in this afternoon and on Saturday, so I'm hoping to slip out for a little bit and pay a quick visit to Mrs. Morton. Flowers and cheap red wine, huh? I think I can manage that. Then, I'll have time to go home and meet my brother with Max, and wait for Latham to pick us up.

Satisfied with my afternoon plans, I flip off the dryer and set it on top of my bag. Latham steps up to the doorway, leaning against the aged, scarred wood. "That was Dad. The delivery truck we were expecting later this morning is arriving early. I've got to go down and get ready to unload a shipment of lumber. You're welcome to stay until you need to open your store."

I glance his way, abandoning my makeup bag. "I'm going to head over and get a few things done before I open."

He nods. "Okay. I'm taking Killer down with me. She can hang with Dad while I'm on the forklift."

My eyebrows quip upward. "Killer?"

"Way cooler than Snuggles. At least with a badass name like Killer, no one will make fun of her ugly face," he teases, the corded muscles in his arms flexing as he pushes off the door frame.

"You can't just rename my dog!"

"Sure I can. She likes Killer better, anyway. Don't you, Killer?" he asks, dropping down to one knee and giving her a pet behind the ears. Snuggles' eyes roll around in her head, and I'm pretty sure she'd agree with just about any name he gave her, as long as he continued to rub her down like that.

"You're impossible," I mumble.

"Give Mama a kiss, Killer. Tell her you'll see her later, after you spend the day with me and Grandpa Bud."

My heart slams against my chest, beating so loudly, I'm sure everyone within a one-block radius can hear. Mama? Sure, I've called myself that. The vet has referred to me as her Mama, but Grandpa Bud? What does that make Latham? Just the very idea of sharing my dog with him, of being tied to him in a way that leaves us both...parents, has my mind all over the place and my breathing erratic.

"Breathe, Sweetheart," he says, standing before me. I didn't even see him stand up. Strong arms wrap around my neck as he pulls me into his chest. He smells like woodsy soap and coffee, and I find myself sniffing his shirt a little longer than I should. "We'll see you in a bit."

Latham plants a quick, hard kiss on my lips, leaving me full of anticipation and yearning, and heads out the door, my dog happily trotting behind. I'm left wondering what in the hell just happened?

Without me even realizing, Latham Douglas, jerk extraordinaire, has wormed his way into my heart. He's stolen my sanity and my dog, and effortlessly, positioned himself right smack dab in the middle of my life. Do I need him? Probably not. I don't need any man. Do I want him?

That's a big hell to the yes.

As I think about the building sitting vacant between his store and my own, I know that right there is the problem.

I shouldn't want him.

But I do.

God help me, I really do.

After Free arrives, I inform her I'm running errands and slip out the back door. My car is still parked beside Latham's truck, a sight that actually makes my heart beat a little faster. There's something so...comforting about having his vehicle next to mine.

Ignoring the longing that tries to settle in my chest, I hop in my car, pleasantly surprised to see much of the glitter particles cleaned up, and head toward the grocery store. It's busier than anticipated for a Friday afternoon, and I get stopped several times with greetings of hello and to talk of the warm summer weather. When I finally have a fresh bouquet of yellow and white blooms and a bottle of red wine (middle of the road in price – I just couldn't see myself buying the four dollar bottle), I head to the counter to pay for my purchases. As the cashier is swiping the wine, I spy a few bags of freshly made caramels. I decide to throw in a few of the sweet treats, hand over the cash, and return to my car.

It only takes me a few minutes to get to Mrs. Morton's place. I pull up in front and park on the street, letting the sun warm my skin as I slide out. My hand is eager as I knock on the door, the sounds of a cheesy daytime soap opera blaring through the closed door.

When the door opens, Mrs. Morton looks just as annoyed this time around as she did last week. "Good afternoon," I coo, cheerfully.

"Whatever you're selling, I'm not buying. Go away. You're interrupting my show," she says, starting to shut the door in my face.

"It's Harper Grayson, Mrs. Morton. I stopped by last week. Do you remember me?" I ask, handing her the flowers, wine, and caramels.

The old woman looks me over carefully with a disapproving eye, leaving me feeling a little out of sorts once more. "Oh, yes, Hailey, I remember."

"Harper, actually," I reply, clearing my throat. "It was such a beautiful day and I was in the neighborhood, I thought I'd drop by for a quick visit."

"In the middle of my show?"

"Oh, well, I do apologize. I wasn't aware your show was on at this time. I just wanted to drop off these gorgeous flowers. I thought they'd look amazing in your picture window," I say, just as I look over and see...flowers.

"Well, a young man stopped by earlier and brought me some. Handpicked them, too," she says, looking down at my store-bought flowers as if there was something wrong with them.

"Oh. Well, that's nice of him. Who is he?" I ask, hoping she'll spill the name and I'd finally have the confirmation I've been seeking.

"Logan. Logan somebody. He's stopped by a few times to say hello. Brought his dog with him today."

The hairs on the back of my neck stand up. "His dog?"

"Yes, ugly little thing. I don't even remember the name. They took my trash out to the curb so I wouldn't miss the garbage man again. Always so helpful, that young man."

"Yeah," I whisper, as rage starts to stab at my gut like tiny little nails. "What was the dog's name?"

"Hmmm, let me see," she says, touching her tiny little chin with her finger. "I don't know that he said. Or maybe I forgot. Who knows?" she says, offering a touch of a smile.

"Well, I won't keep you long, Mrs. Morton. I know your show is on. If you need any more help around here this weekend, let me know."

"Will do, Holly. Thanks for stopping by," she says, turning to head back inside. "Oh, dear?" she asks, stopping me in my tracks.

"Yes?"

Mrs. Morton hands me the candies. "Will you drop these off at the neighbor's house? I detest caramel," she says, taking the wine in one hand and heading off into the house, leaving me standing on the porch. Again.

I growl loudly before turning and stomping down the stairs. This is the second time I've been here, and both times I've been upstaged by Latham. I know it's him, even if she got his name wrong. The ugly dog might have been the biggest clue. Plus, I didn't even get to tell her I was one of the bidders. Now she just thinks I'm some loony person who drops by with random gifts – including caramels, which apparently she doesn't like.

No way is the neighbor getting these.

I unwrap one and shove the whole piece in my mouth, slowly chewing as I fire up my engine and head back to the store. What the hell am I going to do now? I have dinner plans with Lucifer himself in mere hours, and I have to pretend like I don't know he's trying to bid against me for the property between us.

This is what Hell actually feels like.

Well, at least I have caramels...

Chapter 20

Latham

I PULL UP IN FRONT of Harper's house and head around to the passenger seat. I help Killer – AKA Snuggles – out of the seat, who swiftly goes around and sniffs every inch of the front lawn. When she finally finds the patch of grass she's looking for, she squats and takes care of business, while I grab her small bag of items from the back seat. Weird, I'm a little saddened to drop off the pooch. I've kinda become accustomed to having her under my feet all day today.

When she's completed her business, we head up the steps and knock. Harper answers right away, her earlier work outfit replaced with cutoff denim shorts and a black tank top. My cock is ready to play all of a sudden. "There you are! Did you miss me?" she asks the dog, but it doesn't stop me from answering.

"Terribly. It was a long day," I reply, leaning against her doorframe.

Harper rolls her eyes and scratches behind the dog's ears. "Guess what, Snuggles? Max is in the living room. Let's go see Max!" she coos, speaking in that weird baby-talk voice.

The dog takes off, nails clipping hard on the floor, and barrels into the cutest blond-haired, blue-eyed little boy. Max shrieks as the dog licks his face, smiling and laughing as she jumps on his lap. "Hi, Snuggles!" he giggles, trying to pet the happy pup.

"Max, are you hungry?" Harper asks, watching with a fond smile on her face as the dog continues his tongue assault.

"Yes! Pizza!" Max hoots, pushing Snuggles off his lap and jumping up. That's when he spies me in the room.

"This is my friend, Latham. Latham, this is the coolest four-year-old ever, my nephew, Max."

"Pleasure to meet you, Max," I say, crouching down to his level and sticking out my hand. He seems to check me out with a critical eye before sliding his very small hand in my own and giving it a shake. "Do you like pizza?" I ask, his eyes lighting up with excitement.

"Yep!"

"Then, how about we head over to Pizza Castle and have some dinner?" I ask, watching as his head bobbles up and down with enthusiasm.

"Can Snuggles come too?" he asks his aunt, heading toward the front door.

"No, Snuggles can't come with us to a restaurant. They don't allow dogs in places you eat," she tells him, as she grabs her purse and gets ready to lock up.

"That's dumb! Why would they not let dogs come too? Dogs are people too, Aunt Harper!"

"I agree with you one-hundred-percent, little man, but the health department says no." Before she can take the booster seat from the table, I grab it and hold open the door.

"Bye, Snuggles! I'll see you when we get back," the little boy says, waving at the saddened puppy.

"She already went to the bathroom. She'll be fine for an hour or so," I tell Harper as we step outside and secure the door behind us.

"Is that your twuck?" Max asks as he stands on the porch, waiting.

"Sure is," I answer, leading the way to where I parked in the driveway.

"It's big. Like my daddy's twuck." Max smiles a wide grin as I set the booster seat in the back and help him climb up. Harper doesn't say a word, just watches our exchange and climbs in the front seat when Max is secured.

It's a short drive to the pizza joint, but Max talks nonstop the entire trip. I forgot how chatty little ones are. My niece, Vivian, is only two, but she's just as talkative as Max. The only difference is Max's questions actually make more sense, while Viv relies on the classic "Why?" every chance she gets.

"How many?" a server asks as she meets us at the front door, grabbing menus from the bin.

"Three," I state, noticing how easy and comfortable it is to make the proclamation. No, he's not my boy and she's technically not my woman, but for a moment, a tiny sliver of time, it felt right that they were.

I'm not really sure what Harper and I are. We're fucking, yes, but it's more than that. *Deeper* than that. I've always wanted her, even when I was torturing the shit out of her as a kid. Now, I'm enjoying a little more torture, or sparring as some might say, and it feels fucking good. She gives as good as she gets, and I'm not just talking about in bed.

"Are you coming?" her sweet voice breaks through my thoughts.

"Excuse me?" I ask, surprised she'd instantly tease about coming, like she could read my dirty thoughts.

Max's small hand slips in mine and gives me a tug. "Com'on. I want pizza," he demands as he pulls me along behind Harper.

We follow the server to a booth and thank her as she sets our menus down. "I'll be back in a few minutes to get you drinks," she says politely.

"I sit by you," Max informs me, climbing into the booth and sliding against the wall so I can join him.

Harper rolls her eyes and takes the bench across from us. "Figures. You already stole my dog, why not my nephew too," she grumbles as she opens her menu.

"Awww, is Auntie Harper feeling left out?" I tease in a singsong voice.

"Zip it, or you don't get pizza," she instructs, making me bark out a laugh.

"I want cheese," Max informs us, already coloring furiously on the white place mat in front of him.

"Just cheese?" Harper asks, a fond smile on her plump lips.

"And peppers!" he adds without breaking concentration from his masterpiece.

"You got it," she says. "How about you? How do you like it?"

My cock twitches in my pants. I can't help it, I lean forward and whisper just loud enough for only her ears to hear. "On top, bottom, against the wall, reverse cowgirl, which we haven't tried yet, but my personal favorite is to take you from behind so I can touch the base of your spine and watch the way your back arches with each thrust of my hips."

Her eyes are wide with shock, and maybe even a little arousal, and her mouth hangs open. I've stunned her silent. Her blue eyes dart toward her nephew, who's coloring without a care in the world. "I can't believe you said that. We're in the middle of a family restaurant."

I shrug my shoulders as our server returns to take our drink order. We end up adding a family order of cheese breadsticks with marinara sauce and a large pan pizza with green peppers on the whole thing, and sausage and mushrooms added to half. We're both quiet until she returns with our drinks, vowing to return with our breadsticks soon.

"So, I was thinking," she starts, twisting her napkin in her hand and avoiding eye contact.

"About?"

"Sunday. I don't know if you have any plans, but my extended family is coming to town this weekend for a cookout. You might remember Rhenn saying something the other night. Anyway, they'll be here in the morning and are going to do a little sightseeing in the area with Mom, but on Sunday, we're all having lunch at the bed and breakfast. I didn't know if, maybe, you wanted to stop by and eat with us."

I watch her as the nerves take over. She still refuses to look at me, so I decide to wait her out. After the longest minute of my life, she finally glances up and meets my eyes. I smile. "You want me to come meet your family?"

"Not like that," she says, rolling her eyes. But it's *just like that.* She's asking me to come over for lunch, not only with her immediate family, but the clan I've heard a little about from Virginia. "Just lunch."

"Just lunch?" I ask, raising my eyebrows.

She huffs out a deep breath. "Stop looking further into this than it is. It's not like that."

I reach over and place my hand over hers, stopping her from tearing her napkin into tiny pieces. "Oh, that's where you're wrong. It's a big deal. I know it. Did you ever take numbnuts to a family gathering?" I ask, knowing she doesn't need any more indication of who I'm referring to. She shakes her head. "Then it is a big deal," I add, holding her gaze and linking our fingers. "And I'd be honored to come over and hang out with you and your family."

She opens her mouth, but nothing comes out. Instead, she snaps it shut and nods.

"Well, if this doesn't look like one big happy family." The voice instantly grates on my nerves.

"Speaking of numbnuts," I say loudly, keeping my eyes on the woman across from me, making her smile widely.

"What are we, in third grade?" Joey asks.

I finally turn and look his way. He's still several inches shorter than me, probably not much taller than Harper. His dark hair is styled with too much product and his eyebrows weirdly manscaped. "Hey, Joey, how have you been?" I ask, keeping my hand on Harper's.

"I'm excellent. Haven't seen you much since high school. You back home?" he asks, glancing down to where my hand rests.

"Yep, home to stay. Heard you've been hanging out with Felicity," I reply, keeping my smirk at bay and inwardly smiling at myself when my comment hits its mark.

Joey avoids looking at Harper. "No, not really. Haven't seen her around much," he says casually.

"Just in the men's bathroom, right?" I state, loving the way his eyes flare with anger as he glares down at me.

"You should talk, Douglas. I've heard she's working for you," Joey seethes, a cocky smirk on his ugly face.

"*For me.* That's way different than *under me.*"

Harper snickers, causing Joey to turn his glare her way.

"Doesn't matter, anyway," he says, turning his eyes back on me and nodding toward the woman across the table. "Boring as hell in bed, that one," he points to the woman across the table from me, "but I'm sure you already know that." Joey grins wickedly as he reaches down and steals a piece of bread off her plate.

Not wanting to give this fucker an ounce of satisfaction, I slowly bring her hand up to my mouth, keeping my eyes locked on hers the entire time. "Boring? There's nothing boring about this woman, man. She's a firecracker in bed," I say as I place a kiss on her knuckles. Then, glancing back to the asshole, I suggest, "Maybe it was you?"

Joey's eyes darken with rage, but it doesn't scare me any. I've stared down soldiers in foreign countries who were scarier than this piece of shit. "Fuck you," he says harshly.

Now, my eyes turn to stone. "Watch your mouth, Joey. There are ladies and children within earshot. If you can't keep it clean in a family establishment, then I'll have to escort you outside to remind you of how to talk in front of women and children." The harshness and insinuation in my tone leave no room for question, and I take pride in the way he swallows hard.

"You can keep her," he mouths off. "I was done with her anyway." Then, as if he thinks he got in the last word, he turns and stalks off toward a busty brunette in a low cut top.

"Jerk," I state before glancing back across the table. I can't read her expression, as she watches me.

"Sorry about that," she says, her eyes dropping to the table.

"What do you have to be sorry for? You didn't invite him over here to spew his misery," I remind her.

Harper shrugs. "Yeah, but I dated him."

"Well, that's a conversation for another time, Sweetheart. Right now, all we need to worry about is getting some pizza in Max's belly," I state with a smile, glancing down to the coloring kid. He smiles up at me before returning to his drawing rendition of a baseball field. "Do you like baseball?"

"Yeah, it's my favorite! And tomorrow I get to pray with Sawyer again. He said he'd bring me a jersey to wear," Max says with excitement.

I glance over at Harper and give her a questioning look. "Sawyer would be Sawyer Randall, former third baseman for the Rangers. He's also married to my cousin, AJ."

"No shit?" I ask before I can stop the curse word.

"No shit!" Max exclaims.

"That's a bad word," Harper chastises. She looks over to me, her eyes full of humor. "You too. No more bad words."

"Yes, ma'am," I reply with a smile.

Our pizza is delivered, and I quickly help dish up a piece for Max.

"Do you want it cut up or eat it whole?" his aunt asks him.

"Whole like a big boy," he answers with a decisive head nod.

"You got it," I say as I slide a piece in front of him. Once I get one slice on Harper's plate, I place one on my own.

We eat in comfortable silence for several moments, paying absolutely no attention to the eyes I feel watching us from the corner. I go ahead and make sure to touch her often. You know, in case he's still watching. It's not just for show, though. I couldn't stop touching this woman if my life depended on it.

"Hey, Watham?" Max asks, a smear of pizza sauce on his cheek.

"Yeah, buddy?" I ask, using my napkin to clean off his face.

"What's a numbnuts?"

Chapter 21

Harper

AFTER DROPPING MAX OFF WITH his hungover dad on this beautiful Saturday morning, I head in to work. I haven't heard from Latham since dinner last night, but I wasn't expecting to either. He's working today, and the hardware store opens two hours before my own shop. Before he left last night (and after kissing me soundly on the porch the moment we were alone), I promised to text him later with details on lunch tomorrow.

"Please tell me you brought coffee and something sweet," Free says as soon as I step through the front door, carrying the white bag and a tray of coffees.

"Your wish is my command, fair lady," I answer, meeting her at the counter.

"You're the bestest best friend in the whole world," Free gasps before taking a bite of the homemade cinnamon roll I brought from the coffee shop. Their rolls are good, but not as amazing as Marissa's.

"I know," I tell her, depositing my purse under the counter and smiling widely.

"Why do you have that face? What did you do?"

I glance over my cup at my friend. "Me? Nothing," I reply, using my coffee to hide my smile.

"Mmhmmm, I don't believe you. Spill," she says, setting her roll down and taking a drink of her coffee.

"I just dropped off a fresh cup of hot coffee next door," I answer with a shrug.

Free's eyebrows pull together and an evil smile crosses her pretty face. "And this fresh cup of hot coffee is funny...why?"

"The cup of coffee isn't funny at all," I defend, making sure everything is set for the day. Free already had the sales program up and running, as well as the open sign flipped.

"What did you do?" she whispers, her eyes twinkling.

"Nothing. I know he puts just a little sugar in his coffee," I say, leaving my statement open.

"And..." she hedges impatiently.

"And...he won't find any sugar in the break room."

"Because..."

"Because I think someone replaced it with salt." There. Said it.

Free bursts into fits of laughter. "Oh, you're evil. Do you know what you're like when someone messes with your morning coffee?" she asks.

"Yes, I know, which is why I did what I did. A cup of coffee for a cup of coffee," I vow.

"Is this about the spilled coffee thing?"

"YES!"

"He didn't spill it on your samples," she reminds.

"Yes, I know that, but it was practically his fault."

"Why?"

"Because I said so."

That makes her laugh that much more. "I think the real reason you keep doing these little things to each other is because you *like* each other. It's the classic tale of when the little boy likes the little girl and pulls her hair or throws rocks at her."

I stop and think. "I haven't thrown rocks at him yet." Under my breath, I add, "But he has pulled my hair."

"Stop it with the kid games and just admit that you like him. I mean, you are sleeping with him, right?"

I glance her way.

"You're horrible at hiding it. I know the man has an ass you could bounce a quarter off of, for sure, but don't think for one second you're fooling anyone with these little pranks and gags."

"What does his ass have to do with it?" I ask, planting my hands on my hips and facing my best friend.

"Nothing. That was just an added fact. His ass is marvelous."

"It really is," I agree, leaning on the counter and taking a bite of my cinnamon roll. "You should see it naked. Uh-may-zing," I singsong with food in my mouth.

"I knew it!" she bellows victoriously. "I can't believe I'm eating this," Free adds, dropping what's left of her roll back into the container. "I swore off this kinda thing."

"You can't swear off cinnamon rolls. It's sacrilegious," I tell her, finishing the rest of mine in two bites.

"It's the sugars. I'm trying to cut back and eating more natural foods," she informs me before picking back up her breakfast and finishing it off.

"I'm going to move a few displays around. I was thinking of moving the pajamas over by the far wall and moving the body products closer."

"What are you going to put up by the window then?" she asks, tossing everything from our breakfast in the trash.

"I was thinking those new negligées we just got in."

"The old geezers in town will have conniption fits. Let's do it!" she proclaims, meeting me around front and helping me get to work.

A half hour later, I'm neck deep in satin and lace, putting a pretty light pink nightie on my mannequin when I hear the bell over the door. Heavy footfalls follow, and my heart rate spikes, but I don't look up from the task at hand.

"Good morning," Free singsongs from across the room, where she's rearranging the displays of pajamas.

"Morning," Latham's deep voice floats through the air and zaps me between the thighs.

His shadow falls over where I'm working, but it's his scent that catches my attention first. It's rich and clean and so very sexy. It makes me want to throw him down right here on the floor and have my wicked way with him. "Mr. Douglas, to what do I owe this surprise visit?" I ask without releasing the smile that threatens to split my face in two.

"Ahhh, come on, Sweetheart. It's not really a surprise, is it?" he asks. The irritation I expected to hear is void from his voice.

"I'm afraid I have no clue what you mean," I tell him, finally glancing his way and overly exaggerating my eyelash batting.

He laughs. "Sure you don't," he says, reaching down and touching the long pink satin. "This is nice."

"Isn't it?" I ask, looking back at the gorgeous negligée.

His breath tickles the back of my neck as he whispers, "This would look amazing on your delicate skin. I think you should let me buy you one." His lips graze ever so lightly over my suddenly heated flesh.

"I already have one," I whisper.

"You do?" His hands press into my lower back and slide along my hips until he's holding me tightly against him.

"I do. In ivory."

Latham groans in my ear. "Fuck, that's hot. I'll be over at eight tonight. Answer the door wearing that. *Only* that."

I gasp as he nips at the back of my neck, goose bumps rising on my entire body. "What if I already have plans tonight?" I ask, pushing my rear back and against his erection.

"You do have plans. Me."

Before he lets go, he kisses the back of my neck once more. I feel the void of his body against mine immediately. A craving sweeps in like never before. "Oh, thanks for the coffee," he states, his dark eyes alive with mischief.

"You're welcome," I reply, refusing to give anything away.

"Next time you replace the sugar shaker with salt, make sure there are no witnesses to your crime," he informs.

Surprise registers on my face as I complete my Emmy-winning performance. "I have no idea what you're talking about!"

Latham snorts a laugh. "Sure, you don't," he replies, dragging out his words. He throws me a wink and a smile and heads to the door.

"Oh, Latham?" I ask before he can exit. When his eyes connect with mine, I add, "Make it seven. And bring food."

I can see the desire play on his face as he stands a mere ten feet from me. After several heartbeats, he gives me another smile. "See you tonight."

I don't reply with words, just give him a secretive, knowing smile.

"That was so hot," Free mumbles beside me, making me jump.

"What the hell? Where did you come from?"

"From across the room. You didn't see me because you were too busy undressing him and making babies with your eyes."

I roll my eyes. "I was *not* looking at him like that."

"Right," she draws out, but doesn't call me out on my blatant lie any further. Instead, we both get back to work, and before we know it, the displays are perfect and it's just after lunch.

"I'm hungry," I say aloud to no one.

"Me too. Want me to order sandwiches from across the street?" she asks, just as the door opens again. Ever since we rearranged the displays and changed up the front window, we've had several women step in and browse, many making purchases.

"Sounds good," I tell her.

"Oh, look at that thong, Payters! It's crotchless!"

I know that voice.

Glancing up quickly, I find my aunt, Emma, along with her granddaughters, my cousins. "Hey!" I holler, coming around the counter and meeting them at the entrance with a wide smile. "I thought you guys were sightseeing today. What are you doing here?"

"I wanted to see this place that I keep hearing so much about," Emma says. "Oh, look at this. Orvie would love this," she exclaims as she heads over to my more risqué section of the shop.

I'm greeted with hugs by each of my cousins, Jaime, Payton, AJ, Meghan, Lexi, and Abby, as well as their dad's girlfriend, Cindy. They all talk over each other, anxious to catch up on everything that has happened in the last month since our trip to their hometown of Jupiter Bay.

"Seriously, this store is amazing. I'm so glad we were able to get here before you closed," Payton says, making her way over to one of the many displays.

"Well, anytime you want to shop, just let me know. I'll meet you after hours," I tell them as they start to fan out and browse.

"What do you think of this?" I hear behind me and turn to find Cindy, Brian's girlfriend. She's touching the soft satin of the new pink negligée I put in the window.

"I *love* this! I actually bought myself one in ivory," I tell her.

She glances around, making sure her boyfriend's daughters aren't within earshot. "Brian and I are going to surprise everyone with a wedding in a few weeks. I'd love to buy this for our honeymoon," she confides.

My eyes water just a little. "I'm so happy for you," I assure, reaching out and squeezing her arm. "For both of you."

It's been a long time coming that Brian finds happiness again. See, Orval and Emma's daughter married Brian Summer and together, they had six daughters. Unfortunately, when the girls were young, Trisha was diagnosed with ovarian cancer and was unable to beat it. From what I've gathered, Brian hasn't dated much since her passing almost two decades ago, instead devoting all of his time and energy into raising their daughters. Cindy is the first serious relationship he's had since his late wife.

"Thank you," she whispers, glancing around again. "I'm a little nervous to tell them all."

"They're going to be so happy for you, I promise. They love you and already think of you as a mother figure. This marriage will make them all happy, trust me. I've only known them a short time, but they have wonderful things to say about you and the relationship you share with their dad."

Her eyes mist over. "Thank you. We've invited my boys and all of the girls to a cookout in two weeks at our place. We plan to invite you as well. We hope you can all join us."

"We wouldn't miss it," I assure her, pulling her into my arms and giving her a warm hug. "Now, I think this is a beautiful choice. I have the light pink, a soft blue, and the ivory."

"I think I like the pink," she says.

"Me too," I tell her, pulling her size off the shelf. "Now, come back here. I have something that will make him choke on his tongue," I add with a wink, leading her over to the more risqué section. When I find Emma lurking by, I opt for another route. "Come back to the stock room. I have a few extra pieces back there I can show you without prying eyes."

When Cindy chooses a few pieces to try on, I set her up in one of the dressing rooms and tell her I'll be right back. Free is helping Lexi and Payton in the more risqué section, and I quickly spy Meghan, Abby, and Jaime where I didn't expect them: the maternity section.

"Well, I was expecting to see one of you over here, but the other two are a shock," I state quietly. I knew Meghan and her new husband, Nick, were expecting already, but the others are a welcomed surprised.

Abby smiles wide, but whispers, "We just found out and are planning on telling everyone tomorrow at the barbecue."

My own smile matches hers. "I'm so happy for you." I pull her into a hug before turning to my cousin, Jaime. "And you?"

"Three months," she boasts proudly. "We just told everyone last weekend." Jaime pulls out her cell phone and pulls up a picture. Her two-year-old daughter, Amelia, is standing there, wearing an "I'm the big sister" T-shirt and an excited grin.

"Wonderful news," I tell her, pulling her into a hug too.

"And Lexi is too, even though they haven't told anyone." I turn quickly to find Aunt Emma standing behind us.

"How do you know?" Abby asks as we discretely glance over to where her twin sister stands.

"Pssh, Grandma knows everything, Abbers. Especially when things come to *the sex*. I'm practically a master, you know," she says, nodding my way. "Back when I taught Sex Ed to a bunch of high schoolers, they called me the human pregnancy test. I could spot the knocked up girls way before anyone else."

"You taught Sex Ed?" I ask, wondering how in the world I didn't know this.

"Back in the day when a banana was used for more than just good health. Did you know I could roll on a condom blindfolded and with my hands tied behind my back?"

"Uhh..." I start, not really knowing what to say. The mental image that just flashed in my mind isn't pretty.

"It's a talent," she replies with a shrug before turning and walking away to browse.

"Grandma has a colorful past. I'm not exactly sure why we're surprised by any of it, but for some reason, she always shocks us with something wild and crazy," Abby confirms.

"Okay, so..."

"Anyway, I think I'm going to get this," Jaime says, distracting us all from the weirdness that ensued moments prior.

"That's a great choice. The material will work well for a growing midsection," I assure, noting the way the baby doll waist gathers just below the breasts.

"Plus, it's short. Now that I'm out of the first trimester, my libido is revving at max capacity. There won't be much material in the way of me getting what I want," Jaime replies with a smug grin.

"And that would be the construction worker's D," Aunt Emma hollers from across the room, making everyone stop and turn our direction.

"Thank you, Grandma, for clarifying," Jaime quips.

"Her hearing is really good," Abby whispers, letting me know how the older woman was able to hear our conversation all the way across the room.

A giggle slips from my mouth. "There's matching panties on that shelf there," I mention, pointing Jaime toward the stack of satin panties in all sizes.

"Thanks," she replies, heading the few feet away to continue her shopping.

"I like this one," Abby says, pulling the dark red negligée off the rack, her cheeks blushing a matching color.

"That's gorgeous! It'll look amazing with your hair," I say, noting my cousin's long, gorgeous dark hair.

Abby's blush is prominent. "It's like nothing I've ever worn before, to be honest, but I really think Levi will love it."

"Of course he will," I assure. "He's married to a beautiful woman, inside and out." The truth is, Abby reminds me a lot of Marissa. A subtle beauty she doesn't even realize she possesses. But all it takes is the love of a good man to bring out the confidence that's there somewhere. Marissa changed when she met Rhenn, all for the better. He helped her break out of her shell and dotes on her every second of every day. They complement each other so much you can't help but root for them.

"Thanks," she says, a shy smile spreading across her face. "Can I try it on?"

"Of course," I reply, helping make sure she has the right size and steering her toward the unoccupied dressing room.

Cindy comes out a few seconds later, her arms filled with new treasures and a secretive smile on her face. "All set?" I ask, guiding her to the front counter.

"Yep." She places all of her purchases on the counter for me to ring up.

"And, the best part," I start, scanning the barcode with the handheld device, "is you get the family discount."

"Well, you don't have to do that, but I definitely appreciate it," she replies, handing me her credit card once I've finished ringing up her purchases. I carefully wrap them in tissue paper and place them in one of my large logoed bags.

"What did you find?" Lexi asks, coming up beside Cindy and placing her own items on the counter.

"Just a few things," Cindy states, her cheeks tinged with pink.

"Wait, never mind. I don't want to know," Lexi implores, making a gagging face at the thought of her dad enjoying whatever Cindy has in the bag.

"Good, because I'm not telling anyway," Cindy sasses, sticking her credit card back into her wallet and grabbing her bag.

"Did you find everything you were looking for?" I ask Abby's twin sister, Lexi, instantly recalling what Aunt Emma just said about her being pregnant.

"Too much. It's a good thing you're not any closer or I'm liable to go broke in this place," Lexi says, reaching down and sorting through the pieces on the counter. Instantly, I notice a theme. Lexi is definitely the more daring and bolder than her twin sister.

"Well, as I said earlier, anytime you guys want to stop by, just call me. Or if you need anything, I can ship." I start to ring up her items, which consist of a few lace thongs in bold, vibrant colors, a corset in bright pink, and a few bras in equally daring colors. What I wasn't expecting was the long, satin negligée, the same one Latham asked me to wear later. She picked out the soft ivory one with delicate little rosebuds stitched on the bodice. It's stunning, definitely, but not something I'd expect Lexi to choose.

"What do you think?" she asks, her voice a bit uncertain.

"Of this? I think it's beautiful," I reassure.

"I hope Linkin likes it." The nervousness in her voice catches me off guard.

Setting it aside, I reach for her hand. "He's going to forget his own name when he sees you in this," I insist with a gentle squeeze.

"He's never really seen me in something so...simple. I've always worn corsets and little scraps of black lace. Crotchless panties are his favorite," she whispers, and for the first time in the short time I've known my cousin, I watch her blush. "But I have something important to tell him and it's going to be a pretty big surprise. I thought if I were wearing this he might be less shocked by my news. Of course, he'll probably be more surprised I'm wearing this instead of what I normally have on when I'm seducing him into agreeing with me," she says with a slight chuckle.

Suddenly, she stands up straight. "Forget it." She reaches for the delicate nightie. "I can't wear this. He'll know something's up."

I pull the negligée out of her reach. "No way. You definitely need to wear this. Not because you'll shock him or surprise him, but because it's as beautiful as you are, and the thought of him *not* seeing you in it would be a travesty." I squeeze her hand, much like I did Jaime's a bit ago. "Seriously, Lexi, he's going to be so happy when you share your news it won't matter much what you're wearing."

She looks at me from across the counter, a look of shock on her face. Without calling me out, she glances back down at the nightie. "You think?"

"You could wear a burlap sack, and he'd be the happiest man in the world. That guy worships you, and is always talking about more kids."

"But four? I mean, four kids, Harper. I don't know if I can handle four."

"You can, and you will. You're already the best mom to the twins and Stella. What's one more?" I ask with a big smile.

Lexi laughs. "Yeah, what's one more?" With one more glance down, she hands me the ivory nightgown. "I want it. He'll probably die of heart failure before I can even tell him my news when he sees me in this, but I think it'll be a good shock."

"I agree," I tell her as I finish ringing up her purchases.

AJ, Meghan, Payton, Jaime, and Abby all follow. I ring up their new goodies, happy each one found a few new undergarments, pajamas, and some body products to take back to Virginia with them.

We're all standing at the counter, visiting as Emma walks up and slams her hand down. "I'll take these."

I glance down and find a few tags cut off and sitting in a small pile. "Where are the items?" I ask, glancing down to see if she has them in her other hand.

"I'm wearing them!" Aunt Emma proclaims.

"You're wearing them? But you haven't washed them yet," Payton gapes, her mouth hanging open in shock.

"No one has crotch cooties, Payters," Grandma brushes her off.

"No, but they might have crabs!" Lexi bellows.

I glance up. "Umm, no one has crabs. My store is crab-free," I assure, running the scanner over the tags. Glancing at the screen, I'm shocked to see the itemized list that appears. Apparently, I vocalize my surprise.

"What? What'd she buy?" Jaime asks, leaning over the counter and looking at the screen. A gasp fills the store.

"What? What'd she buy?" Meghan mimics Jaime's question.

"Crotchless panties, garter belt, and a bustier!" Jaime roars, making her sisters gasp in shock.

"Grandma!" Abby huffs.

"The bustier is black leather," Emma boasts proudly. "And it's missing the bra cups that hold my girls."

As if on cue, all of us – my cousins, myself, and Free – all glance to Emma's chest. I'm not sure what we're expecting to see. It's not like we're able to see through her shirt, yet we all gaze at her as if her boobs could pop out at any second.

"Your grandpa will be so excited when I get home," Emma adds, coyly. She leans in as if she's about to share a secret, but doesn't keep her voice down as she says, "I always carry my nipple tassels with me. They'll look amazing with this bustier."

A gagging noise sounds over the counter, and I glance up just as Lexi puts her hand over her mouth and takes off to the back for the restroom.

"Way to go, Grandma. You made Lexi throw up with your oversharing," Payton chastises.

"Oh, it's not my crotchless panties that has her sick, Payters. It's the pregnancy," Emma says matter-of-factly.

AJ glances at her sisters. "She's pregnant?"

"Don't look at me! I didn't know," Abby insists, holding her hands up in the air.

A sniffle echoes through the room. "I'm so happy. We're pregnant together. Again," Jaime cries.

"I can't believe four of us are pregnant at the same time," Abby cries, tears streaming down her face.

A throat clears. "Ummm, five." Our eyes all fly to AJ, who stands in the middle of her sisters, trying to hide her smile.

"You're pregnant too?" Meghan asks, unable to fight her own smile.

AJ nods her head frantically. "I just found out this morning."

"And Sawyer?" Jaime asks.

"He was with me when I peed on the stick. He knows."

A massive hug ensues, filled with grabby hands and happy tears. "I can't believe five of the six of you are pregnant. At the same time. Your father is going to be so excited," Cindy adds, hugging each of Brian's daughters. When she gets to Payton, I notice the tears streaming down her face. "Oh, Payton," she whispers, pulling her into her arms and giving her a tight hug.

Payton's sisters all seem to realize what this means. Even though I've only known this side of the family for a few months, I've heard the stories. I know Payton has PCOS, or polycystic ovarian syndrome, and her chances of conceiving are very slim. She went through several rounds of fertility treatment to have her son, Noah, and had a rough time. I can't imagine what she's feeling right now, knowing that all five of her sisters are at various stages of pregnancy, and she's not.

Tears burn my eyes, and I will them away. I'm able to get them under control, but not before one slips out and slides down my cheek. Even Free seems to understand the magnitude of this moment, silent tears slide down her own cheeks.

"It's okay," Payton whispers as the tears fall freely. "I'm so happy for all of you."

"I'm sorry, Payters," Meghan says to their oldest sister.

"I'm not. Am I a little disappointed I won't experience pregnancy with all my sisters? Sure. But I know I'm going home to the family God intended for me to have. Dean and Brielle, and of course, Noah."

Emma steps into the circle and pulls her eldest granddaughter into her arms. "You are, without a doubt, the bravest woman I've ever met. Your life is so full of love, just as God intended it to be. Hold on to that, Payton McIntire. Hold on to them."

They all embrace once more, but Free and I stay where we are, letting them have this moment. I couldn't imagine what Payton must be feeling. Disappointment. Sorrow. Anger. I'm sure it's all there in spades.

"What'd I miss?" Lexi asks, rejoining the group, looking a little green still.

"You're pregnant?" Abby asks her sister. Lexi's eyes go wide, but she doesn't say a word.

"It's okay. We won't say anything," Jaime promises.

"I'm going to tell him when we get home," Lexi whispers, a smile playing on her lips.

She's pulled immediately into a hug, instigated by Payton. The oldest sister looks down at the youngest and says, "AJ's pregnant too."

Lexi's eyes fly to her sister. "You are?"

AJ nods. "Just found out this morning."

Lexi bursts into tears, her hormones clearly getting the best of her. "Five of us?" she whispers, glancing to all of her sisters.

"Five," Payton confirms. "Just as God intended it to be."

Realization seems to hit Lexi in that moment as she turns to the oldest. Without saying a word, she pulls her into a tight hug. The rest of the sisters follow suit.

"Okay, enough of the tears. We have dinner plans tonight down the coast," Payton says, clearing her throat and wiping away any remaining moisture from her eyes.

"Are you sure you don't want to come?" Cindy asks.

The family had invited all of us to drive down the coast for dinner with them. My mom, Brian and Cindy, and Aunt Emma and Uncle Orval are all staying behind to watch all the kids, while all my cousins and their spouses are going to eat. Marissa and Rhenn and Jensen are going, Jensen's son, Max, staying behind with my mom. Samuel's on call this weekend and didn't want to leave town, and I had already made plans with Latham. I'm sure he'd be all for dinner with my family, but my plan for the evening involves very few clothes. That's not exactly conducive to dinner with the family.

The thought of getting Latham naked has me a little flush and squirming where I stand.

"I already have plans, but thank you," I say, praying my cheeks don't betray me.

"We'll see you tomorrow though, right?" Jaime asks.

"I'll be there," I confirm. "Free's coming too," I add, nodding my head to my best friend.

"Great!"

"Well, as much as I hate to leave, we need to get back and get ready for dinner," AJ says.

My cousins all talk over each other as they grab their bags and head toward the door. With quick hugs and waves, they head out the door and pile into the two vehicles parked right out front.

"Phew, that was exhausting," Free says, flipping the open sign to closed.

"No kidding," I confirm, heading back to the counter.

"But at least they bought a ton of stuff," Free says as she makes her way toward one of the tables in slight disarray.

"That they did. Just leave all that until Monday. I'll come in early and straighten it up," I tell her, turning off the register and computer system.

"I won't argue with you there." Free comes back to the counter and helps with our end of business day ritual, turning off the lights and emptying the trash.

Before I knew it, I had everything closed down and was ready to head out. Latham wouldn't arrive for a few hours, but I want to take a soothing bath and shave and moisturize every square inch of my body. And believe it or not, I'm a little worn out from the hour-long shopping visit with my family. I love them to death, but they're definitely a lot to take in.

Waving goodbye to my best friend, I head toward my car, noticing Latham's big truck parked down the alley, behind his hardware store. Three hours until he arrives. Three hours until I open the door, wearing that sexy negligée. Three hours until I get my hands on his amazing body.

I can't wait.

Chapter 22

Latham

MY PALMS ARE ACTUALLY SWEATING with anticipation when I knock on her door. It stands open on the opposite side, letting the evening warmth blow through the screen door. I switch the bag from one hand to the other as I fidget with excitement. The thump of puppy paws and scratching of nails brings a smile to my face, and there's no denying I've fallen for the ugly mutt whose tongue is hanging from her mouth and happily barking to announce my arrival.

"Hey, Killer," I greet just as a vision in ivory comes around the corner.

My heart stops beating.

She's the most gorgeous woman I've ever laid eyes on.

And she's fucking mine.

"Wow," I whisper as she unlocks the screen door and pushes it open. The ivory satin hangs to her bare feet, clinging seductively to every curve of her body. The lace cups hold her amazing tits, slightly pushing them upward, as if offering them up on some silver platter. Two thin spaghetti straps wrap across her delicate shoulders, disappearing behind her back.

Then she turns.

And the back comes into full display.

The straps slide down her back until they reach the soft satin at the base of her spine, her hair cascading in long, loose curls behind her. Desire swirls in my gut, the need to touch her so great, I'm afraid I might die if I don't. "I want to take this off so bad, yet leave it in place at the same time," I state when my eyes finally drink their fill and return to hers.

She pulls the material to the side, exposing her left leg through a slit that runs up the entire length of the negligée to the top of her outer thigh. "I figure this will come in handy," she purrs as she steps closer, running a manicured fingernail down my chest. "You know, if you wanted to leave it on."

My cock twitches and starts to beg. Images of taking Harper while she's still wearing this outfit has me harder than concrete and ready to go. Without breaking eye contact, I set the bag down on the small table and reach for her. My fingers slide effortlessly along the satin at her hip as I gently pull her body into mine. "I'm definitely leaving it on," I answer, bending my head down and running my nose along the long column of her neck.

Snuggles barks and jumps on my leg, letting me know she's not happy to have not been properly greeted yet. "Snuggles, down! You know you don't jump on people," Harper reprimands her dog, yet her tone doesn't stop the dog from wagging her tail in anticipation. In fact, Snuggles completely ignores her mama.

"Down," I tell her, snapping my finger and pointing to the floor. She does as she's told, dropping her nose and gazing up at me with big, sad eyes. Immediately, I take a knee and give the dog the attention she is expecting. Her tail continues to wag as she gives me a wet kiss on the cheek. "You know you're not supposed to jump up like that," I remind the pup, earning another lick on the hand as I rub behind her ears.

When I gaze up at Harper, her eyes are wide. I hop up, and place my hands on her arms. "I'm sorry, I shouldn't have stepped in. It's just we worked on her jumping yesterday when she was in the store with me. I didn't mean to undermine you," I quickly say, glancing back down at the dog. "You need to listen to your mama."

The dog gives me a sheepish look, but leans over and runs her nose against Harper's hand. "It's okay, girl. Why don't you go lay down?"

Snuggles wags her tail, grabs the mangled chew toy she dropped in her haste to get to the door, and heads into the living room for her bed.

"Are you mad?" I ask, pulling her into my arms, the satin sliding effortlessly beneath my hands.

"I should be," she says, looking up from beneath long lashes.

"I didn't mean to overstep, but like I said, I was working with her on not jumping when she was with me at the store, and I just reacted. I really am sorry," I plea.

"How sorry?" she whispers, running her hands up my chest and sliding them around my neck. Her body molds to mine, her sweet voice deep and husky, reminding me of sex.

My cock knocks on my zipper. "Terribly sorry. Horribly sorry. Incredibly, ultra-sorry," I state, wrapping my hands around her waist.

She goes up on her tiptoes, her lips touching my earlobe. "Show me," she says as her nails bite into my flesh.

"I thought you wanted to eat." I can't stop the words from falling from my lips. I'd go a week without food just to have her right here, right now.

"I was hoping *you'd* be the one ready to...eat."

I groan in both pain and pleasure. My cock is painfully hard, my balls so tight I know if she were to touch them, I'd explode like a teenager watching his first fuck flick. My hands grip her waist, my subconscious telling me to loosen the hold, but my cock is in the driver's seat. "I'm definitely a starving man."

Then my lips descend to hers. They're plump and warm and wet, ripe for kissing. I move with a quickness even I didn't realize I possessed, gripping her ass with my hands and lifting. The slit up the side allows the material to move enough for her legs to wrap around me. It's both heaven and hell as heat radiates through my pants, her scent tickling my senses.

My lips aren't gentle. They're bruising, in fact, as I take the kiss from sweet and innocent to hot-as-fuck in about two seconds. I stumble with my left hand, but find the open door. It's closed and locked a moment later, without so much as a misstep in the kiss. Only when the house is secure do we make our way toward her bedroom. I hear Snuggles get up and trot behind us, but block the entrance to the bedroom before she can make her way inside. "Stay." She whimpers a bit, but doesn't follow us as I shut the door.

When I feel the bed hit my knees, only then do I slow the kiss. I lay her on top of the comforter, stretching my body over the top of hers from head to toe. Then, I get to work. Running my nose down the side of her jaw, I inhale her sweet, floral scent. It's part lotion, part shower gel, and all Harper.

She tilts her head, giving me full access to the long column of her neck. I trace it with my tongue, feeling the deep pound of her pulse in her neck. As much as I'd love to continue to nip and suck on her delicate skin, my attention is drawn downward. I dip my tongue into the divot below her throat, and she gasps in response.

I position myself above her, my hands slide easily down her bare arms. She's like a beautiful angel, a halo of auburn hair splayed across the pillow. My cock throbs in my pants, a painful reminder of how bad I want her. No. *Need* her. And I do. I'm quickly realizing I need her. Yes, in my bed, but in my life. My home. A part of my every day. I want to share it all with her, because the thought of not having her by my side is unthinkable.

Because I'm falling in love with her.

"Latham," she gasps, melting against me as I continue to gaze down at the most beautiful woman I've ever seen.

"Yeah?" My voice is deep and hoarse, even to my own ears.

Her blue eyes stare straight into me. "Please fuck me."

Again, I groan and my lips slam down on hers once more. Her mouth immediately opens and my tongue sweeps in. Only, this time, I don't deepen it further. Instead, I return my focus to exploring her body.

With my tongue.

My eyes center on her chest, on her glorious tits. They're covered by a thin layer of ivory satin and lace, the V dropping down seductively between the two. Her chest heaves with anticipation as I run my hands down her waist, gently pulling the material as I go. The chest drops down until her dark nipples peek out of the top, the reflection of her nipple ring flashing in the dimly lit room.

My mouth waters.

Then it descends.

I latch on to one perfect little nipple, then the second – the one that contains the ring. Her back arches and she pushes herself up into my mouth. I could stay here and devour, lick, and suck forever, but I don't want to detour from my objective here: get my mouth on her pussy.

"I'll come back to these," I tell her, toying with the nipple ring with my tongue one last time.

Gently grasping the satin at her hips, I lightly bunch it up at her thighs, exposing tonight's dinner. Her breathing comes out in little pants as I tenderly push her legs apart, settling my body in between. Her flesh glistens, even before I can get my mouth on it. She's so fucking ready, so fucking hot, so fucking mine.

Placing my hands under her thighs, I lower my mouth. My tongue slides along her clit, flooding my veins with fire. I keep my hands under her legs and lower my mouth once more, licking and tasting every part of her. She starts to move against me, riding my tongue. I take the opportunity to slide it inside her wet pussy and feel the moment she contracts around me. She's so close.

I reposition my hands to her ass cheeks, spreading them wide as I devour her. She rocks into me seeking out the friction of my tongue. It doesn't take long before she detonates like a beautiful bomb. She comes so hard, squeezing my tongue and riding wave after wave of pleasure.

I don't wait for her to come down from her high. I need to be inside her so fucking bad, it hurts. Ripping my shirt up and over my head, I toss it in the room and make quick work of unbuttoning my jeans. My boots take a little longer to unlace than I'd like, but with my eyes solely on the vision before me, I'm bound to make a few fumbles. Finally, my feet are bare and I can shove my jeans (boxers and all) down my legs. My cock juts from my body, hard and ready.

My eyes connect with hers once more. They're half-lidded, as if in a sex-haze (one I'm all too proud to have put there), and my heart slams against my chest. I almost confess right then and there – tell her how much I'm falling for her, but I refuse to be one of those jackoffs who says it in the throes of passion. What I do know is that I'd do anything for her.

That's why I have to tell her about the bid.

I have to tell her I'm the guy bidding against her for the vacant building between us. It's the one thing hanging there, like an anvil swinging, ready to slice and dice. She may not understand, but I'll tell her why I did it. I'll explain my family's business is quite possibly going under, and this is our one shot at expanding Douglas Hardware and bringing it back to life. I've seen the numbers. I know small businesses like ours are a dying breed, eaten up by the big box chains, but I refuse to let it go out like that.

I'll explain, and she'll understand.

I know it because my girl has the biggest heart of anyone I know.

Even if she hides it behind her sass and gruff.

Her eyes are wide and her breathing has evened out, but the anticipation is still very much there. "Hang on to the headboard," I instruct as I take my position between her legs. She does as she's told without so much as the slightest hesitation. The movement presses her tits up even higher. "Don't let go, Sweetheart," I tell her as I take my cock in my hand and slide it against her pussy. Her gasp sends shockwaves through my bloodstream, landing heavy in my balls.

"Ready?" I ask, even though I can see the conviction in her eyes. She doesn't answer in words, but nods her head in anticipation and excitement. "Watch," I instruct as I slowly start to push inside. I go slow, ignoring the craving to slam into her warm, tight body. I pull back out until just the head is buried and then painstakingly slowly, push back forward again. Watching my cock slide inside her makes this moment – this feeling – that much greater.

Pulling out one last time, I grip her hips and glance up to her face. Her cheeks are flush and her mouth agape, and I swear I'll never forget this moment as long as I live. A thousand emotions seem to play on her face as I still one last time. Unable to fight the desire to kiss her, I bend down and take her lips with my own. The kiss is slow and tender, full of passion and, yes, love.

I sit back up on my haunches and tell her one last time. "Watch us." She glances down to where we're joined, but I keep my eyes on hers. Her hands tighten on the wood slats and I thrust my hips, filling her completely. Harper's mouth falls open as she moans with pleasure, but she never closes or averts her eyes. She watches as I fill her over and over again.

My pace quickens, my body's desire for release starting to take over. Sliding my hand down her thigh, I hoist her leg up on my hip, opening her up even more. My mouth finds hers, our tongues dancing as I pound into her pussy. I slide my hands up the insides of her arms, loving the way her soft skin peppers with goose bumps. When my hands finally meet hers, I move her hands, linking our fingers together.

This is heaven.

Home.

Her legs tighten around my hips and I can feel her pussy start to squeeze me. It won't be long now, which I'm grateful for, since I'm not sure how long I can hold off my release.

"Latham," she whispers against my lips, her body arching up into me.

I almost say it.

I almost tell her I'm falling head over heels in love with her.

Instead, I squeeze her hands tight and hold on for dear life as my hips begin to thrust. I'm chasing my release, knowing there's no stopping this freight train now. She clamps down on me as her orgasm sweeps in, wild and reckless. My lips claim hers, hard and bruising, and I never let go of her hands. The base of my spine starts to tingle as she clamps down hard on my cock. Bright lights burst behind my eyelids as I come so hard I can't seem to breathe.

When exhaustion sets in and I can no longer hold myself up, I roll to the side, pulling her with me. I bring our joined hands to my chest, not really ready to break that connection yet. She doesn't complain though, just rests her head against my bare chest, right over my heart. I can't help but wonder if she feels how hard it's beating – and not just because of the exertion a few minutes ago.

Because of her.

Just being in my arms.

I also can't help but wonder if all guys turn into wimps when they fall in love...

Needing to clear my head, I lean into her and place a kiss on her forehead. "I need to clean up."

Harper releases my hands, but threads them around my back and wiggles in close. "Just a few more minutes," she says, her voice tinged with sleep and satisfaction.

Who am I to deny her anything?

After a few more minutes, I gently move her body to slide out. I'm quick in the bathroom, anxious to get back to her bed, to wrap my arms around her pliant body. Snatching a clean washcloth out of the cabinet, I wet it with warm water and return to the bedroom. Harper tries to take the cloth from me, but I shake my head. "I got you."

She doesn't speak as I clean her up, running the warm material over her lower body, but I can feel her eyes on me. I toss the cloth into the hamper and slide back into bed. She immediately throws her arm over my waist and snuggles into my chest.

"Are you hungry?" I ask after a few minutes of silence.

"Not quite yet. I kinda like this," she answers, sliding one leg between mine.

I pull her into me and kiss her forehead. "Me too."

Comfortable silence wraps around us as I listen to the sound of her even breathing, though I don't think she's sleeping. So many questions filter through my mind. So many things I want to know about her. I've missed fourteen years of her life, while I was away in the military and she spent part of her time in New York.

Speaking of New York, I've heard a few stories, a few insinuations (mostly on Felicity's part), but Harper seems to be pretty tightlipped about her time there. Did she meet someone, fall in love, and it ended badly? Was she not cut out for the competitive modeling world in New York? Was she safe and taken care of while she was there?

"Can I ask you something?" I finally ask when the scenarios running through my mind start to turn dark.

"Sure."

"Tell me about New York."

I feel her stiffen in my arms and hear her breathing catch. I know something happened; I'm just not sure I really want to know what.

"I went to New York to model. Didn't like it. Came home. End of story," she says, her heart pounding a hard beat against my chest.

Needing to see her eyes, I move until we're facing each other, lifting her chin until we're eye to eye. I can see it there, her panic and fear written all over her beautiful face. "I don't want to push you, Sweetheart. I know something happened. I can see it in your eyes and feel it anytime the topic is brought up. If you don't want to talk about it, that's okay, but I want you to know you can trust me with anything. I'd never do anything to hurt you."

She seems hesitant at first, like trusting me isn't something she's ready for. I get it. She's had a horrible past with a few douches who treated her like shit. I hate that, but I need her to know I'm not them.

Just when I open my mouth to tell her that much, she surprises me and starts talking. "I was eighteen when I first went to New York. I won a modeling gig from a local talent search at the mall right after graduation. It was a weekend gig for a toothpaste company, a large advertising campaign that included billboards, posters, internet PR, and television commercials. I was ecstatic, to say the least. I thought this was my big shot at getting out of Rockland Falls."

She takes a deep breath. I pull her tighter into my embrace, needing to feel her skin against mine and let her know I'm there for her. "Anyway, after the job, a talent scout approached me. She had a few more jobs she thought I'd be perfect for. She talked about lights, cameras, and fame, and promised I'd be on a runway by the end of the year. I ended up signing with her right then and there, came back home and grabbed my stuff, and moved to a tiny little dump of a studio apartment with another girl trying to make it on Broadway.

"It was weird sharing a tiny four-hundred square foot space with a total stranger, but we managed. In fact, Mia and I became good friends. She helped me get a job at a local Starbucks, which is what actually paid the bills, though not very well. I ended up getting a second job as a hostess in a fancy steakhouse restaurant on weekends to offset the cost of living in New York City. Everything was going well, I was able to pay rent and utilities, and do a few small modeling jobs on the side. That money I was able to put back into a savings account, so I had money for any emergencies. It wasn't a lot, but it was something."

Harper averts her eyes, glancing down at my chin. She runs her hand along my jaw, letting my stubble tickle her fingertips. It seems to soothe her, and since I'm a huge fan of her hands anywhere on my body, I let her have the time to explore and touch without saying a word. When she's finally ready, she goes on.

"I was working one Saturday night at the restaurant when he walked in. Keith Glow." She looks at me expectantly, like the name alone is supposed mean something, and yes, I do admit the name is vaguely familiar, I just can't seem to place why.

"I'm sorry, but I haven't exactly kept up with what happens in that circle. How do I know that name?" I ask her, lightly stroking her arm with my thumb.

"Keith Glow. He was the former producer ousted for drugging women." Her words are a whisper, barely audible.

Ahhh, yes, I do remember that story. It was all over the news. Just as I get ready to open my mouth, the puzzle pieces start to click into place and my blood runs cold.

"I was twenty when he introduced himself. He was charming, charismatic, and seemed to really want to help advance my career. Not that I had much of one, at that point, but he seemed so devoted to helping me become a big star."

The tears welling in her eyes do me in. I tighten my hold on her, not just for her, but for me. We both need to feel grounded, the comfort of the other's touch, to know we're both there for each other, despite what bomb she's about to drop on me.

"For the next year, he was able to secure me larger jobs than what my agent was finding. I was attending parties I had dreamed about, meeting people I only knew from the cover of magazines. I was well on my way to making a name for myself, and I had Keith to thank for it."

"No way. I don't buy that for a second. Keith might have opened a few doors, but it was *you* who landed those jobs. It was *you* they fell in love with behind the camera. It was *you* they were signing."

She gives me a wobbly, tearful smile. "I know, but the problem with that industry is it's extremely small. Everyone talks, everyone knows everyone. If someone wants to tank your career, all it would take is just a phone call or two, maybe a couple of photos, and it would be done. You wouldn't even see it coming until it was too late. Until you were the next tabloid cover story and your phones stopped ringing."

Again, she takes a deep breath and reaches for my hand. She holds on for dear life. "I was at a premiere party at some fancy hotel in Paris. I had just finished shooting a clothing spread for a magazine. We had the entire penthouse floor, which included two levels of open space. Keith's wife was there; I had met her several times. She often accompanied him to big parties and such. He brought me a glass of champagne. I didn't think anything about it because he was always doing little things like that. My head started to feel a little fuzzy, and even though I had only had one glass prior, I excused myself to use the restroom. There was a line at the downstairs restroom, so I decided to try to find one upstairs. I knew there were four spread out throughout the penthouse, so I had a good chance of finding one or two upstairs.

"I was having a hard time focusing on the steps. I couldn't seem to make my feet work, but I managed to get upstairs. There were a few people milling around, and a line in the hallway. Suddenly, Keith was there. He told me I wasn't looking so well and asked if I needed to lie down. I don't remember anything after that. Not until I woke up in the master suite."

My jaw hurts from tension, but I don't say a word. So many questions filter through my mind, but I don't ask a single one. I remain quiet and listen. The pain and uncertainty is so evident as she retells a story I'm sure she's never spoken of since it happened.

"He was there, taking pictures of me. My dress was skewed and my breasts hanging out. When I asked him what happened, he said nothing. He was still dressed, and for the most part, so was I, but I knew I had been violated. Maybe not my body, but my personal space, my sense of security, my dignity.

"He dropped the camera back into his pocket and handed me a glass of water. I refused to drink it because something told me *he* was the reason I was in a haze. He just laughed, straightened his tie, and turned toward the doorway. He politely informed me nothing happened and that if I told a soul about this, he would make my life hell. He would sink my career, my reputation, and everything I valued most. He told me no one would believe me, and I would never work in this industry again. But then he went for the final blow. He told me he'd sink my mother's business and make sure the scandal would never die down."

Air seems to thicken as I try to breathe and remain calm. It's hard as fuck to suck oxygen into my lungs at this point, but I don't panic. I don't want to scare her any further than she's already been.

"That's when I left. As soon as I could fly home from Paris, I packed up my car and drove back to Rockland Falls, leaving New York City completely behind. I've never told anyone about what happened." Her words are small, but the meaning is huge. She trusts me enough to share her biggest secret. I want to cry for everything she's been through, everything she's endured.

"You are the bravest woman I've ever met," I tell her, kissing her on the forehead.

"But I'm not. I should have gone to the authorities. I should have fought, but I didn't. I ran."

"You were twenty years old, Sweetheart. No one can fault you for being scared and running away, especially when he threatened your family."

Tears start to fall now. "I didn't care about my career, about modeling anymore. I cared about my mom, my sister. I cared about what this scandal would do to their business. Mom had been through enough when my dad cheated and left. I just couldn't do it to her again."

"Your mom and family are tougher than you think. So are you."

She takes a deep breath. "I know." She remains quiet for a few long seconds, as if gathering her thoughts. "I called them."

"Who?"

"The police department. After the story broke last summer, I called them and told them what had happened to me."

My heart pounds in my chest, tight and hard. "What happened when you called?"

"I wasn't the only one. There were fourteen other women who called, all with similar stories about Keith. They took all of my information and asked me to come to New York City for a formal meeting. I went last fall and gave a complete recount of what happened." She locks eyes on me. "He took a plea deal, in exchange for pleading guilty to invasion of privacy and drugging the women. He'll spend sixteen years behind bars, a year for each woman he violated. There were more, according to the photos he kept, but they never came forward. Without their testimony, they couldn't do anything more."

"You didn't have to testify?"

"Not in court. I was prepared to, but with the plea deal, I think he knew it would be much worse if the jury heard all of our testimonies. And we were all prepared to give them," she assures me.

"I'm proud of you," I reiterate.

"I was a coward."

"No, you weren't. As I mentioned, you were young and scared, and the important part is he can no longer violate anyone else because he's behind bars. And you helped do that."

"I should have done it sooner," she whispers.

Shrugging my shoulders, I reply, "Maybe yes, maybe no. The important thing is you did it." I pull her tightly against me and kiss her forehead. "I'm fucking proud of you."

She releases a shuddered breath. "I've never told a single soul until that phone call and trip back to New York."

I close my eyes, and revel in the feel of her warmth, her skin, her touch. I know it's past time to come clean about the building, which is why I'm going to tell her tomorrow. Maybe after her family cookout, we can come back here – with Snuggles as a buffer – and I can let her know about the bidding war.

And about my feelings.

It's time to tell her.

It's been nearly a decade and a half.

It's time to officially make her mine.

Chapter 23

Harper

I'M PULLING INTO THE DRIVE for my family's bed and breakfast,
the sun shining high in the late morning sky. Latham had to run
home and change, since he didn't bring fresh clothes with him to
my place last night. Not that he wore those clothes for long, mind
you, but he also had to stop by his sister's house and set up a
dollhouse for his niece. If I didn't already promise Mom I'd come
help her get ready for the family gathering today, I would have
gone with him.

But our early Sunday schedules weren't on our side.

No worries, though. Latham should be arriving at the B&B by
eleven thirty.

Am I worried he's meeting my entire family? Maybe just a little.
I mean, he's already met and hung out with my brothers and sister,
but it's the first time he's meeting the extended family – and we all
know how crazy they can be.

Plus, this makes us a little more official, and considering I don't really know the title, I don't know how to react to that. I mean, I guess we're dating, though we've never actual used the term or set any parameters. I guess I'm going to have to just ask him outright. Maybe later today, after the cookout.

I park my car next to my sister's and head inside. I swear I can still smell the fresh paint as I step through the open doorway. The screen door shuts easily and I'm instantly wrapped in familiarity and warmth. I spent a big chunk of my childhood here, right up until I left for New York City. When I moved home, I had felt so...dirty. I needed my own space to lick my wounds and deal with the anger. I went from a small apartment to renting my house for a few years, and worked odd jobs, saving up as much money as I could to be able to afford something better – something for me.

When the house I was renting was put on the market, I snatched it up. It's small, but cozy, and was just right for me. Plus, my stuff was already there, which was a huge advantage. I couldn't imagine packing up and moving after I spent so much time scouring resell shops and garage sales to turn the house into a place of my very own.

Then the next big phase of my life began. Over beers one night with Free and Mara, I realized my dream of owning my own business. I was complaining about the lack of options for intimate items in town, and Mara mentioned the vacant building. Before the end of the night, we had come up with a plan. Sure, I honestly thought it was a pipe dream, but the more I thought about it, the more I wanted it.

It wasn't easy to secure a loan at such a young age, especially after signing papers on my house the year prior. I had to put my house up as collateral, plus have a co-signer. Mom was more than willing to volunteer. After all, she understood going after dreams more than anyone I knew.

That's why I love coming home. Yes, it's the place where I grew up, but it's more than that. It was Mom's dream. She worked hard, started from the bottom, and clawed her way up. Sometimes we went without because the money was needed elsewhere, but do you know what? Looking back now, I know just how much she truly sacrificed. We might not have had the top-of-the-line clothes, but we always had clothes nonetheless. She went without so we didn't have to.

And I'm forever grateful for her sacrifice.

"Hey!" Mom says from the front counter as she helps customers. Their bags are sitting beside them and there's no missing the looks of love they send back and forth. If I had to guess, I'd say anniversary. Early. Probably second or third.

Before I can offer to help them with their bags, Rhenn appears, coming into the main hallway from the kitchen. He's wearing a smile on his face and his hair is a little messy. Something tells me my sister had something to do with that. My sister's boyfriend grabs the bags and heads upstairs, while Mom fills the young couple in on the details of the bed and breakfast and their stay.

I head into the kitchen, where I find my little sister, Marissa. "Hey," I greet before heading to the fridge for a bottle of water.

"Hi!" she answers with a huge smile. There's also no missing the I-was-just-kissed-within-an-inch-of-my-life lips, or the way her ponytail is off center and hanging funny behind her head.

I can't help the smirk that takes over my face. "Have a good morning?"

She blushes instantly. "It was...good," she answers, averting her eyes. Yet the smile still remains.

"Okay, Aunt Emma, but don't come crying to me when Mom busts you making out like teenagers in the kitchen. Or worse... Samuel."

Marissa snorts. "He's seen worse. Did you know he came over last weekend and just walked right into my cottage? Didn't even knock."

"And?"

She blushes deeper red. "Well, let's just say he'll never do that again. I think he's scarred for life."

I bust up laughing. "Kitchen sex?"

Marissa gives me a small nod. "The things Rhenn was doing to me on the counter probably sent our big brother straight to the church." As soon as the words are out of her mouth, we both crack up. Samuel is as straightlaced, and dare I say completely anally retentive, as they come.

"Does he know we're throwing in a little birthday celebration for him today?" I ask. Big brother hates anything that draws attention to him, including celebrating the day he was born.

"Nope, I didn't say a word, and I'm pretty sure Mom didn't either."

"Didn't what?" she asks as she joins us in the kitchen.

"Tell Samuel we're celebrating his birthday," I state, reaching across the counter for one of the fresh cookies Marissa is placing on a platter.

"Of course not. It is better to ask for forgiveness than permission," Mom adds, quoting something my dad used to say. Except, for him, his request for forgiveness fell on deaf ears. His appeal came in the form of mercy for an affair. As soon as Mom found out though, she kicked his cheating ass to the curb. Of course, he wasn't really asking for forgiveness. If he were, he would have fought for his marriage instead of running out, shacking up, and marrying the first bimbo who came his way.

"Speaking of forgiveness," I say, feeling the familiar tightness in my chest return as I think about my time in New York. But after speaking with Latham last night, I knew it was time to come clean with my family. I owe it to them. "I have something to share."

I take a seat across from the island, while Mom and Marissa stop what they're doing and join me. The seriousness on their faces lets me know they understand I'm about to share something big. And I do. I tell them everything about my time in the Big Apple, including the trip back to New York last year. They both cry, of course, being the softhearted women they are. When I finish my piece, I'm engulfed in a tight hug.

"I can't believe you didn't tell us," Marissa sniffles.

"I was scared."

Mom turns me and places her hands on her face. "I'm not happy you didn't tell us, but I understand why. And I'm proud of you for your part in having that horrible man thrown in jail." She pulls me in tight once more. "You are an incredible woman, Harper, and I'm proud to call you my daughter."

I don't speak, just revel in her familiar embrace. Marissa wraps her arms around us too, cocooning me in love and support. The door opens and Rhenn walks in. "Uhh, is everything okay?" he asks hesitantly.

I swipe at the tears that have managed to fall and give him a reassuring smile. "Yes, everything is okay."

He walks over to where I sit and searches my face. "Do I need to kill someone? I know the best ways to hide a body." The look on his face tells me he's deadly serious, even though I think everyone else takes it as a joke. I can read between the lines, though, and I know he's referring to Latham.

"No, not at all. In fact, he's going to be here in just a little bit."

Rhenn continues to watch and eventually must believe me. "Good. I like him."

"Me too!" Marissa chimes in with a smile, returning to her cookie-making post.

"Me three," I whisper, feeling the warmth spread up my neck. I can't believe I just admitted that.

"I'd hate to have to kill him," Rhenn states and comes over to whisper in my ear. "But I would."

I give my sister's boyfriend a reassuring smile. I have no doubt Rhenn would do some serious damage to Latham or anyone who hurt me. He's an incredible friend and a huge support system for my sister. In just a few short months, he has quickly cemented his place in our family.

The next hour is spent getting the food ready for the cookout. Just after eleven, my brothers arrive, with my nephew in tow, as well as the extended family. There's so many of them and the house and yard quickly fill with noise. The few guests who are here are invited outside and mingle with the family. It's a beautiful, perfect last day of July.

And then Latham arrives, and my heart kicks into overdrive.

There's always been something about him. Sure, no one has the ability to crawl under my skin the way he does, but if I'm being honest with myself, it's more than that. Always has been. He's impossibly frustrating, yet is sweet and endearing in all the right ways. He's hard and gruff, but at the same time, tender and sweet. He lets me know he does care with his words and actions.

And I care too.

A lot.

More than I've ever cared about anyone in the past. That's evident in the way I spilled my guts last night about New York, and was comforted in the way he held me so tight, I didn't know where

I ended and he began. It made me realize it *was* possible to find someone who has your best interests at heart and puts you first. Really, I don't need to be first: I need to be loved. I want to be treated as an equal, as a partner, and I didn't realize how badly I craved it until last night.

Until Latham.

My smile is wide as he comes around the corner, immediately intercepted by my brother, Jensen. They start talking right away, smiles on both of their faces, and I can't help but realize how seamlessly he fits into the picture. Into my family. They all love him. Even Samuel, who's standing over by the grill with Nick, shooting big brother daggers at my afternoon date. He does it because he loves me and wants nothing but the best. He glances my way, and I offer him a warm grin, letting him know I've found it.

I'm okay.

Samuel throws me a wink and turns back to our cousin's husband. A few others are pulled into the conversation, which I'm sure is completely stimulating – probably about the importance of life insurance or preplanning your funeral, if I know Samuel.

I can feel his approach before I see him. Not only can I sense his presence, but I can smell his cologne. It's outdoorsy and musky in the sexiest way. "Miss me?" he whispers. He's directly behind me, but doesn't touch me. Yet, his words have me shivering nonetheless.

"Nope," I tease, glancing over my shoulder with a smirk.

"Good. I didn't miss you either," he tells me, though his eyes don't lie. The way they sparkle lets me know his words aren't true.

I turn around and his hand instantly wraps around my hip. "Ready to meet the family?" I ask, all breathy-like. Why am I all breathy?

"In a minute," he replies. Just when I go to ask what the holdup is, he pulls me into his body and plasters his lips on mine. It's a chaste kiss, one that's totally appropriate when surrounded by family, but it causes my breathing to hitch and my mind to spiral anyway. I don't know what it is about his kisses, but they've always done something to me. Even back in school. After prom.

He pulls back slightly, his eyes dark with desire. "Okay, now I'm ready."

"Are you sure, Romeo? I mean, I don't mind meeting you while you're sporting a massive woody, but some of my granddaughters get a little embarrassed. They don't appreciate the beauty and naturalness of the male form like I do," I hear behind me and cringe when I realize Aunt Emma has overheard our conversation.

"Latham, this spunky little spitfire is my Aunt Emma," I say in way of reply, turning to face the petite old woman with an ornery grin.

"It's a pleasure to meet you, Latham," Emma says, pulling Latham down for a big hug. As she does her frail little hands, with the apparent strength of a clamp, reaches down and grabs his ass. Latham jumps in surprise, moving his body in a jerk, but unfortunately, all he does is proceed to thrust his hips forward.

Right into Emma.

He tries to pull back, but Emma seems to latch on with the speed and strength of an agile jungle cat. "Oh, very nice, indeed," she says with a wide smile and a squeeze. After a few uncomfortable seconds (where Latham look like he's going to vomit), she finally pulls back, a cat that ate the canary grin on her face. My aunt glances my way and whispers (very loudly), "Oh, you're a lucky, lucky woman, Harper. Reminds me of my Lexi. Her Linkin's ass is the finest I've ever had my hands on. It reminds me of your uncle's when he was a frisky young man."

"I...wow...thank you?" Yeah, it comes out a question.

Emma reaches over and pats my hand. "No, thank you." Then she saunters away, heading straight to her husband. When she reaches him, she grabs his ass, right there in front of the family, our guests, and God.

"I've never had my ass fondled by a woman approaching ninety," Latham deadpans, his eyes wide with shock.

I can't stop the snort that slips from my mouth. "Let's go meet everyone. I promise no one else will touch your butt," I tell him, reaching for his hand as I pull him toward my cousins and their husbands.

Chapter 24

Latham

BY THE TIME LUNCH IS served, I've been introduced to everyone, including Sawyer Randall, AJ's husband, who used to be a professional baseball player. Harper's nephew, Max, monopolizes as much of his time as possible, including playing catch. I'll admit, I'm starstruck almost as much as the little boy. Twice I've heard him say he's going to be a professional ball player, just like our cousin, Sawyer.

I'm chatting with Linkin and Levi when my phone rings. I glance down and see Pete's name on the screen. I'm not expecting his call with the final decision on the building until tomorrow, so I'm quite surprised to see his name appear. "Hello?"

"Hey, Latham, it's Pete. I have news," he says.

"Hold on," I say into the phone. "Excuse me a minute," I then say to the guys, excusing myself from the small group. "Okay, what's up?" I ask finally when I'm alone away from the party in the backyard.

"I've heard from Mrs. Morton's family. She made a decision. You win. The building's yours, man," he boasts. Pete goes on, but I don't hear him. I turn around, my eyes immediately seeking her out. Harper's beside her cousin and sister, laughing at something one of them says. She looks completely carefree and full of life. So beautiful and happy.

Until we get back to her place and I tell her the dream of expanding her business isn't going to happen.

"Did you hear me, man?"

Clearing my throat, I answer, "Yeah. I heard you."

There's silence before he asks, "Aren't you happy? This is what you wanted."

"Yes, of course. I'm happy."

Am I really?

"She wants to do this ASAP. Her lawyers will draw it up Monday, and as long as the financing you were preapproved for goes through, you could own that building by end of the week. Do you hear me? End of the week!"

I hear him. Loud and clear.

My heart pounds in my chest, but I'm not sure if it's from happiness or dread. Both, probably. With this one phone call, I have a feeling the entire course of my future has been altered. Something tells me everything I wanted, hoped for, planned is about to erupt in my hands, like a grenade with the pin already pulled.

"...when you have confirmation from the bank. I'll get back with you when I have everything lined up," he says, earning a noncommittal noise in response.

He signs off, leaving me standing there with my phone in my hand. Dropping it back into my pocket, I take a few moments to collect my thoughts. The bed and breakfast is positioned in a clearing of trees. You can hear the distant sound of the ocean, and any other day, I might actually enjoy my surroundings. But not now.

Not since the phone call.

Scrubbing my hand over my face, I turn back toward the beauty with auburn hair. The sun hits the crown of her head, illuminating the smile she wears on her face. The face I love. The one who won't be very happy with me when I tell her about the building.

But she needs to hear it from me.

As soon as we can get to her place, I have to tell her. She'll be disappointed, definitely. Maybe a little upset. But she'll understand it was business. If the shoe were on the other foot, I'd feel the same way. Then, maybe after I tell her about the building, I'll tell her how I really feel about her. That I'm crazy about her.

Totally and completely in love with her.

I'll even be able to help her with her spacing problem. I could help her build more shelves or redesign the space to optimize room. This could work out, maybe even better than expected. She'll see that, right?

Something tells me I have a better chance of walking on water than getting Harper to understand this is a good thing.

I better wear my nut cup for this conversation.

Just as I start to make my way back to Harper, Jensen stops me. He's visiting with Marissa and Rhenn. "Latham, did I hear Douglas Hardware is trying to stock a few new lines, including outdoor yard tools?"

My throat tightens as I think about the new lines we'll be able to carry now that we have more space. "Well, we're always on the lookout for ways to better serve our customers," I reply, politically.

Jensen laughed. "You sound like your dad," he replies with a smile. "I hope you guys can get it done. I have a few new pieces of equipment in my budget for next spring. I'd rather buy them local, if I can."

"We'll see what we can do for you," I comment to Harper's younger brother.

"Good deal."

"How's work going?" Rhenn asks Jensen.

"Busier than shit," Jensen comments with the shake of his head. "I was considering adding another employee for summer help, but after the call I had Friday, I'm thinking I might need some permanent help quickly."

"What does that mean?"

"Someone bought the Elliott house," he says, his posture suddenly ramrod straight, his body radiating tension. If memory serves me correctly, I think I know why.

"They did?" Marissa asks, watching her brother's reaction closely.

Jensen shrugs. "It's a job."

"Do you know who?"

He shakes his head.

"It's sat empty for several years. I don't think they kept up with the landscaping, right? That's going to be a big job," Marissa says, not telling her brother what he doesn't already know.

"It is, but I'm ready. If I get it, I'll have to take on another employee. I've been doing too much lately because I haven't wanted to take someone on this late in the season. I might have to now," he says. "I meet with the lawyer of the new owner next month. If I get the job, I'll start right away. It's going to take a lot of work to get it ready for whoever bought a million dollar home."

Rhenn whistles. "That's a pretty big chunk of change. Are you talking about that big house across town by the waterfall?"

"Yeah," Marissa says, keeping one eye on her brother.

If memory serves me correctly, Jensen dated the Elliotts' only daughter, Kathryn. She came from money – a lot of it – and he, well, didn't. When I left for the military, they were dating and planning a future, even though they were both in high school. I remember hearing the Elliotts left town, but I don't recall the circumstances. Considering Jensen married someone else from school and had a son, I'd say the forever Jensen and Kathryn had planned didn't work out so well.

"Well, I'm updating some electrical wiring and installing all new kitchen lighting first of August. I'm happy to not have to drive too far for a bit," Rhenn says, pulling Marissa into his arms.

"Aren't you coming from Harriston?" Jensen asks.

Rhenn and Marissa share a look. "Actually, Rhenn is moving in with me."

Jensen watches his baby sister for a few long, tense seconds before pulling her into a hug. "I'm happy for you two." Jensen kisses his sister's forehead and reaches for Rhenn's hand.

"What am I missing?" Harper asks her siblings, clearly noticing the exchange from across the yard. She slides in beside me, standing nice and close. I can smell her sexy perfume and a hint of jasmine from her shampoo.

"I'm shacking up with your sister," Rhenn says, throwing his arm over Marissa's shoulder. They both wear matching smiles.

Harper rolls her eyes. "Duh, Cowboy. You've been shacking up unofficially for weeks. 'Bout time you made it official," she says, giving a pointed look to her sister's boyfriend.

"Yeah, yeah," he teases, goodheartedly, throwing her a smile.

"Hey, guys!" Freedom says as she comes around the corner, carrying a bundle of balloons and a wrapped package.

"Hey!" everyone replies as Harper's best friend comes over to our group.

"What's that?" Harper asks, trying hard not to smile.

"Something special for the birthday boy!" Free hollers, loud enough to draw attention from most of the party.

"Oh, he's going to kill you," Jensen says with a chuckle.

"He loves me," Free says with an evil grin and a wink.

"Who's birthday?" Aunt Emma shouts from across the yard.

"Sammy's!" Free yells, making a beeline toward the oldest Grayson. Samuel, of course, turns and tries to bolt for the kitchen.

"No way, Samuel," Orval says, grabbing him by the arm with strength that completely catches everyone off guard – especially Samuel. Orval then proceeds to pull Samuel to the middle of the yard, where his embarrassment can probably be seen from space.

"Open it!" Emma claps as Free hands Samuel the balloons and gift.

He glares at Harper's spitfire friend, but she seems to pay no attention to his irritation. Instead she takes the balloons from him and sets them on the nearest table. Then, she returns to watch Samuel open his gift in front of the entire family.

"He's about to freak out," Harper whispers.

"Yeah?"

"He hates anything that draws attention to him, and Free knows it. She loves to push his buttons, including calling him Sammy as much as possible. But that gift? He's going to have a coronary right there in the middle of the family barbeque."

My hand wraps around her hip as we watch her brother open his gift. The entire yard is quiet – even Sawyer and Max have stopped playing catch to watch. Samuel slowly pulls the paper off the small box, which looks like a tie box. He pulls open the lid, gazes down at the contents, and slams the lid back on the top.

"Samuel!" Mary Ann chastises her oldest. "Don't be rude."

"Oh, stop being a sissy," Free says, grabbing the box from his hands and peeling it open. "Look!" she bellows, holding up a pair of men's trouser socks.

"She got him socks?" I whisper, not really understanding why he'd hate a pair of trouser socks. I mean, the guy wears suits all day, every day – probably even to bed or the pool.

"Not just any socks," Harper giggles, but doesn't have to continue because Free takes care of the question on everyone's mind.

"They're alien sex socks!" Free announces.

"They have aliens and twenty different sex positions on them." Harper finally loses her composure and bursts into laughter. I'll admit it's quite comical. Especially when you glance at the look of mortification on the eldest Grayson sibling's face.

"Let me see those," Emma says, grabbing the socks and proceeding to describe the positions to Free and Samuel.

"So, I was thinking, after the party, we can head back to your place," I tell her, keeping my eyes on the people milling around the cookout.

"Alien sex does it for ya, huh?"

"Totally," I reply with a smile. My eyes lock on hers, and my heart hammers in my chest. "I have something I want to discuss with you," I tell her, not wanting to give too much away.

Her eyebrows arch. "Everything okay?"

"Yeah," I reply automatically, that single word thickening in my throat and making it hard to breathe.

"Okay," she says with a slight grin, reaching down and taking my hand in hers. She opens her mouth to say something, but the ringing of her cell phone halts whatever words she was about to say. She glances down at the name on the screen. "It's Mandy," she adds absently, and brings her phone to her head.

My entire body runs cold.

Mandy is her realtor. What are the chances she's calling her to tell her the same thing Pete just informed me?

Yeah, pretty fucking good.

I watch her face as she takes the call. Within seconds, her smile is wiped away, replaced with shock, and yes, a few tears. "Oh, yeah. And that's it?" Pause. "Okay, thanks," she says quietly, dropping her head. "Wait! Do you know who won the bid?" she asks, turning and glancing my way. She listens, but doesn't take her eyes off mine. "Thanks for everything, Mandy. Bye."

Her blue eyes hold my gaze as she slides her phone back into her pocket. I open my mouth, but nothing comes out. The hurt I just saw in her beautiful eyes is quickly swept aside and replaced with an edge, a hardness.

She knows.

Chapter 25

Harper

"WERE YOU GOING TO TELL me?" I ask without moving a step toward him.

"Can we talk about this in private?" he asks quietly, his chocolate brown eyes pleading with me to go somewhere to discuss this.

"In private? Why? You don't want everyone to know what you've done, Satan?" I spit out as if the words have a vile taste.

"What I've done? I haven't done anything but win a bid on the building I was trying to purchase," he tells me calmly, even though I can tell he's anything but.

"Really? You *stole* it from me!"

He takes a step closer to me, but I immediately take a step back and out of his reach. "I didn't steal it, Sweetheart."

"How long have you known that I was the other bidder?" I ask, crossing my arms over my chest.

He swallows hard, his Adam's apple bobbles beneath his few-day-old stubble. I can tell right away I'm not going to like what's about to come out of his mouth. "Since I installed your new laptop and heard you and Free talking about it." The admission is painful to hear.

"And you didn't think to say something to me?" Before he can open his mouth, I continue. "You knew I was the other bidder, but you never said anything. You used me."

He stares at me, his face hardening and his jaw ticking. "Harper—"

And then I feel my face pale as realization sets in. "Oh my God, is that why you slept with me?" I take another step back, not wanting to get too close.

He takes two steps forward until he's standing directly in front of me. My eyes burn with threatening tears, but I will them away. No way am I going to let him see my cry. He stands there and watches me. Latham looks like he's about to say something, but I stop him. "No. Do not speak to me!"

The ugly truth finally sets in.

He's worse than Joey, worse than the jerk in high school who only wanted to sleep with me at prom. I told him about Keith. I shared my horrid past that I spent years trying to forget. I shared because I trusted him.

Because I was falling in love with him.

My heart beats wildly in my chest as I look at the man I thought I knew, but didn't know at all. I had suspected he was the one bidding against me, but didn't know for certain. But now? How will I ever trust him again? The entire timeline isn't in his favor. It's damaging, in fact. He shows up, wines and dines me, and then sleeps with me? I guess you really do keep your friends close and your enemies closer.

He watches me, his eyes like steel and his body tense. And my body? It cries for his. I yearn for him to tell me it's not true, that it wasn't all a lie.

"Harper, please —" And my heart breaks wide open.

I glance to my right and realize the entire party is standing there, watching. I hold up my hand to stop him. "Well, congratulations. You don't have to pretend to like me, sleep with me anymore, just to get a leg up on the deal." I swallow hard, sucking down all of the painful emotions that have bolted to the surface. "You win." The words are barely audible as I take a step away and turn.

Before I make it more than two steps, I glance over my shoulder. "Goodbye, Latham."

"...and I really think you should just come back to my place tonight," my best friend drones on and on from the driver's seat. I'm ignoring her, of course, but not because I don't care about what she's saying. I'm ignoring her because my drunk mind can't seem to stop spinning enough to wrap around her words.

"I just wanna go home," I tell her quietly, my hot cheek pressed firmly against the cool glass of the passenger door.

I have no idea what happened with Latham after I went inside the bed and breakfast. Part of me really hopes all of the men in my family took turns using his kidneys as a punching bag – especially Rhenn. He's a black belt in ass-kicking, and I really hope he got in a few good shots, defending my honor. But the other part of me hopes no one kidney punched him because I'd never wish any amount of pain on him.

Stupid heart.

Why must it care about the Devil?

Free keeps talking the entire ride back to my place, and I continue to ignore her. The shots of tequila have done a number on my head, but it has failed to do the one thing I set out to achieve: numbing my heart. It still beats wildly in my chest, crying out in both love and pain. And that's exactly what love is. Pain.

We pull into my driveway, her car fitting easily without mine taking up space. I almost fall out of the door when I open it, but fortunately, the still-fastened seat belt keeps me from eating gravel. It suddenly releases, and I sway forward, the ground getting closer and closer. My best friend grabs my arm, saving me from a gravel makeover, and eventually comes over and helps me out of the car.

She takes my keys and opens the door, Snuggles happily greeting me the moment I enter. Just the sight of her has me on the verge of tears. "I'll take her out back," Free says, leading my puppy toward the backyard.

The walls move as I stand still, praying for the darkness to swallow me whole. No, drinking definitely wasn't my brightest idea, but it was there and I was looking for anything to quickly numb the pain. I'm not worried about Snuggles. I know Free will take care of her before she goes. All I want is to lie in bed and let the drunkenness finish me off.

As soon as I step into my bedroom, I smell him. His cologne, his aftershave, his soap. Whatever it is, it's everywhere. The sight of my bed sends the tears I've been fighting tumbling down, and they don't stop. They consume me, just like the pain.

Knowing I can't sleep in my bed, I reach for the pillow and head to the spare room across the hall. The sheets are clean and won't remind me of the man who shared my bed the night before. I don't undress, I can't. I have no strength or will to even remove my shoes. Instead, I crawl on top of the bedspread, curl my body around my pillow, and close my eyes.

He's here.

I feel him.

I smell him.

When I open my heavy eyelids and glance around the room, I find it as empty as my heart. He's not here. But his scent is. In my haste to get out of my bedroom, I grabbed the pillow Latham always used. The material is wet as I place my head back down and hold it tightly against me. It's not him, but for a moment – a beautiful second in time – it makes me feel like he's here with me.

As I fall into the darkness, I pray for the pain in my chest to subside just a little. I pray for my heart to forget all about one Latham Douglas. And most of all, I pray he's missing me as much as I'm missing him.

Latham

"YOU'RE IN A FINE MOOD again. You've been acting like a bear with a thorn in his paw all week. What gives?" Dad asks as he sits down in the empty chair across from the desk. The desk that used to belong to him.

"Nothing," I grumble.

I've been a bear, I know. I've been in the worst mood since everything with Harper came crashing down around me last Sunday afternoon. It about killed me to leave her there, to walk away without actually defending myself, but I tried. She wouldn't hear me out, not when her mind was already made up about me sleeping with her just to get the building. It wasn't true, but she wouldn't let me get a word in edgewise, and I didn't try hard enough.

Biggest mistake of my life.

The only reason I slept with her was because I was in love with her, not because of the building. I need to tell her that, but it hasn't exactly worked out the way I had planned. I had hoped we'd be able to discuss this after cooler heads prevailed, but she won't answer her phone or her door, even though I'm pretty sure she was home at the time. I've gone to the gym, but she's not attending her stupid 90's spin classes either. The only place I haven't gone is next door – to her shop. The last thing I want to do is disrupt her there in the middle of a workday.

Apparently we haven't gotten to the cooler heads part yet.

"Could have fooled me, Lath. So what gives?"

I rest my tired head in my hands and close my eyes. I haven't slept for shit in the last few days, mostly because every time I try, I see her face. I see her tears. And it hurts too fucking much. "I fucked up, Dad."

"With the building? We sign the papers in an hour."

"No, not with the building. I mean, yes, with the building." I let out a long, frustrated growl. "I don't know."

"Start at the beginning."

So I do. I tell him about overhearing Harper and Free discussing their plans for the space, and how I didn't tell her I was the other bidder. I end the tale with our explosive exchange (okay, she was the one exploding) on Sunday and how I tried to rebuff her claim on exactly why I was sleeping with her, but she wouldn't hear it. Dad doesn't say a word, not even after I finish spilling my guts.

"What should I do?" I ask him, kicking back and putting my feet on top of the desk.

"Do you love her?" he asks, not even commenting about my dirty boots in the middle of the desk calendar.

"Yes." No question.

"Then you work it out," he says, shrugging his shoulders.

"But how? She won't speak to me."

"Do you blame her?" he asks, the corner of his mouth tipping upward.

"No," I state, running my hands over my several-day-old stubble. I haven't shaved in more than a week, and I'm definitely beginning to look like the wooly mammoth.

"Do you think it's a coincidence that she knew about that building being available and no one else did?"

His question catches me off guard. I glance up into his dark brown eyes and notice a certain sparkle that wasn't there before. "What do you mean?"

"Well, Harper knew about the building, and you knew about the building. No one else knew it was for sale," Dad says, crossing his arms over his chest and waiting for me to catch up.

"You told her," I say aloud, finally understanding what he's getting at.

"I did."

"Why?" He knew we needed that space for our expansion. Why else would he tell someone else about it? We could have been the only bidder, securing us that space in no time. Instead, he told Harper. Why?

"Because you have always loved her."

Okay. Wasn't expecting that.

I clear my throat and try to think of something to say, but come up empty. He's not wrong, not even close. I just hate he's known all this time; hell, he knew before I even realized it. I mean, it's a little embarrassing that your dad knows you fell in love in high school with the girl you lost your virginity to, ran off and joined the military, and returned fourteen years later in the same shape as when you left.

"You don't have to say anything. Your face says it all," Dad says with a little more of a smile.

"I don't understand why telling her about the building is a positive, Dad. You knew we needed it for expansion."

He shrugs his shoulders. "We would have figured something out without that building, Lath. You're a smart man and one hell of a businessman. I saw it when you were working here part time after school and on weekends. You love this place and what it represents. If push came to shove, I knew you'd do whatever it took to keep the doors open – with or without the building next door."

His words sit heavily in my gut as I take in his compliment, as well as trying to figure out his motives.

"There is a way for you *both* to have your dreams, Lath. You just have to figure out how."

I close my eyes again, her face instantly filling the darkness. "I don't know how."

"Yes you do," he says as he stands up. "Let's go sign those papers. We have a big undertaking in front of us and we need to get the ball rolling. Plus, you have to figure out how to win back the woman you love."

Sure, Dad.

Easy.

The next two weeks fly by in a flurry of tearing down walls and rebuilding new. Replacing the old front window into something more modern and more energy efficient is top priority, while trying to decide how to tell the woman I love I'm an asshole is the other.

No, wait.

Check that.

She already knows that.

I need to tell her I was wrong, plain and simple.

I stay late, trying to help get our expansion ready. The contractor we are using has made great progress these past two weeks, and now the plumber is coming in to update the plumbing in the small bathroom in back. We're going to make this one a public bathroom for customers, something we don't have on the larger, original side of the business.

The worst part is knowing she's on the opposite side of the wall, and I can't do a damn thing about it. I've caught sight of her a few times, entering or leaving her shop, but she doesn't look around – doesn't even give one over the shoulder glance at the building positioned between her business and mine.

The pranks have stopped. Those petty tricks between two sworn enemies, turned lovers, I've come to love and expect as part of my day...gone. It's been almost three weeks without them, without her. Each day is hell, but it's also one day closer to getting her back.

Will she have me?

That's the big question, one I try not to dwell too much on.

Instead, I focus on what I *can* control.

The expansion.

I move to the front of the building. With my hands shoved in my pockets, I glance around the new space. This might very well be my favorite part of the upgraded building. The floors are hardwood, a deep, rich walnut that complements the freshly painted earthy taupe walls. The interior space is nearly complete, and then the contractor will work on refinishing the roof, and I'll put the finishing touches on the room.

Flipping off the lights, I head back through the brick archway into our existing space. Dale is finished closing down the register, so I flip the last of the light switches, and gather the moneybag for tonight's deposit. "I'll drop it off. I'm gonna head out back and work for a while."

Dale gives me a pointed look, but doesn't say anything. He knows what project I'm referring to, knows how late I've been working into the night to get it all completed. But it beats the hell out of tossing and turning all night long in my piece of shit bed, wishing my arms were wrapped around Harper.

"I'll take it, Lath. I'm parked on the side. It'll be easier for me to head out the front and drop it in the night deposit box," our faithful employee says.

"If you insist. I don't mind, though," I say, engaging the lock.

"You just want to walk by the undies store and catch a glimpse of the pretty owner," he teases, knowing full well he's one-hundred-percent correct.

I shrug my shoulder. "Maybe."

Dale snorts. "Ain't no maybe about it, boy." Dale takes the bag from me and heads toward the front door. I follow so I can lock up behind him. Before he exits the building, he turns back and says, "You're doin' the right thing, Lath. She'll see it."

Swallowing over the lump in my throat, I nod. "I hope so," I finally reply.

He grabs my shoulder and gives it a light squeeze. "Have faith, boy. Just have faith."

And then he's gone, heading down the sidewalk, past Harper's store and to the bank on the corner. I lock up behind him, make sure everything is shut down, and make my way out the back. I bypass the stairs leading up to my apartment, since there's nothing up there for me anyway except a week's worth of dirty clothes and some moldy leftovers.

Outside, I spy her car still in the lot beside the alley. It takes everything I have not to go pound on her door and force her to talk to me. But if my dad has taught me anything, it's that actions speak louder than words. I just pray she sees my actions as a positive, rather than a negative.

Ignoring the pull to go to her, I head into the building where our lumber is stored. It's a tight fit in here, but Dad was able to keep a small area open for cutting wood and small projects. For the last few nights, I've been out here making new shelving units for the addition. I didn't want your typical metal storage systems for the entire space, though we are using it for the back area that'll house chainsaws, leaf blowers, and hedge trimmers.

Leaving the big door open to let the warm August air blow through, I head to the corner of the shop and grab the sander. The two large pieces are done, but I'm working on a small unit that'll fit directly under the front window. It has cubical bins for merchandise and a padded bench for sitting. I've never had a seating area in the store before, but I can definitely see the benefits. How many times has a man brought his wife along into the hardware store, and while he browsed for his purchases, she looked bored out of her mind, like she'd rather be anywhere else but there? When I told my mom about the idea, she volunteered to make the cushions.

My mom's the best.

I finish sanding the entire unit and get ready to apply the second coat of stain. Once it's dry, I'll add a few coats of polyurethane, to make sure it's well protected and sealed, and then figure out how to haul it inside. I've got a few buddies I could probably call, but most of them I haven't talked to yet since I returned. My mind instantly goes to Jensen and Samuel, who would probably rather drop the wooden units on my dead body than actually help me carry them inside the new space.

Headlights fill the alleyway, but I don't look up. It's probably Harper leaving for the night, and I don't really want to see her ignoring me (not that I blame her). A car door opens and closes, which tells me it's probably my dad. Mom has been sending him over with extra food lately, ever since I fucked everything up with Harper.

Dad steps into the doorway, but doesn't say a word. I'm not really in the mood for a lecture, so I keep on stirring the stain as if it's the most fascinating thing in the world.

"You just going to pretend I'm not here?"

I know that voice, and it definitely doesn't belong to my father.

Glancing up, my eyes connect with those of Harper's oldest brother. He's wearing a charcoal gray suit, and his black shoes look like they cost my last paycheck. "Samuel," I state, standing up straight and setting down the stain.

Neither of us speaks as we continue to stare at each other. I have no clue why he's here, but he clearly has something to say. Hell, he probably wouldn't mind taking a swing at me, not that I'd blame him. Not that I'd fight him off, either. I deserve any punches thrown my way.

"Was it an act?"

My throat tightens. "No."

"No?" he asks, stepping inside the warehouse and walking my way.

"Not one moment of being with your sister was an act."

He crosses his arms and continues to watch me. "I have a hard time believing that, especially after she outright asked you about it, and you didn't deny it."

I come around the table and lean back against it. He's only a few feet in front of me now, his dark blue eyes boring into me. "I admit, I didn't handle things right where Harper is concerned, but I *did* try to talk to her. She just wouldn't hear it. I had planned to tell her about the building that afternoon, but she got the call from her realtor before I could."

"You were going to tell her you were the bidder or that you had won?"

The air thickens around me. "Both."

"Why did you start seeing her?" he asks, taking another step forward.

"Why?" I ask with a humorous laugh. Sobering, I tell him exactly why. "Because she's the most beautiful woman I've ever known, inside and out. She's fiery and bossy. She knows how to get under my skin faster than anyone ever has before. She doesn't put up with my crap, and doesn't expect me to put up with hers either. She's cagey when it comes to men, mostly because the ones in her past have jerked her around, but when she finally gives you her heart, it's the most glorious thing I've ever experienced."

"Yet you fucked it up."

I hold his stare. "Yeah, I did. I didn't get a chance to tell her about it at the party because she was already so pissed off and hurt, nothing I said would have mattered. I was a fucking idiot. I thought if I let her cool down a little, we'd be able to talk, like reasonable adults."

Samuel snorts. "When have you ever known Harper to be reasonable?"

The corners of my mouth curl upward for the first time in ages. "True." I stand up straight and face her brother. "I fucked up, I know. I love your sister, and have for pretty much my entire adult life. If I could go back in time and redo it all, I would, but I can't. So now I'm trying to right my fucking wrong, trying to undo the pain and hurt I caused her. I'm going to explain and make her realize how much I love her."

He watches me for several long seconds, and I'll admit, I start to sweat a little. Not that I need Samuel's approval on anything, but it would definitely make it easier in the future. A future I hope to have with Harper.

"You love her?"

"With everything I am." My words are the dead truth.

He glances down and then around the workspace. "What's this?" he asks, pointing to the storage bench I'm making.

"A few things for the new addition."

And then I tell him all about my plans for the space. He even takes off his suit jacket, rolls up his sleeves, and grabs a paintbrush. For the next few hours, Samuel and I work in unison, finishing up the final piece of new furniture for the store, leaving the final coat of sealant to dry overnight. When he goes to leave, he sticks out his hand and offers me a small smile. "For what it's worth, I hope you two are able to figure this stuff out. You're good for her," he adds, just before heading over to his car and disappearing into the darkness.

I glance to my left, saddened to see her car gone. She probably left hours ago.

My body is starting to ache as I make my way up the stairs to my tiny little apartment above the hardware store, wishing she were here. Wishing I could wrap my tired arms around her. Wishing I could kiss her one more time.

Wishing everything was different.

Chapter 27

Harper

THE MUSIC IS A LITTLE louder than normal, but I'm desperate to drown out the hammering and drilling next door. Every day, it's a painful reminder of the lengths someone would go to just to get what they want.

Well, he won.

The building is his.

I don't even really care anymore that he won the bid, and I didn't. I mean, did it suck, finding out? Hell yeah, it did. I had plans for that space, dreams even. This expansion would have meant the potential influx in business for Kiss Me Goodnight, by bringing in more local product and expanding my inventory. I can probably figure out how to still make some of that happen in my current space, though it'll be a little more challenging.

What hurts the most is being made the fool. Being duped. Trusting someone and having him let you down. Should I have questioned him after I started to suspect he was the other bidder?

Yes. I know that. But he should have told me. Maybe not in the beginning, but the moment we started sharing a bed (or a wall or floor, in some cases), he should have come clean about everything.

Instead, he kept it to himself.

And slept with me.

My gut starts to churn with anxiety as I think back to our fight. He tried to defend himself, though I really didn't give him much of a chance to speak. That's one of my faults, not to listen when I get so worked up. I blame my dad for that fun trait. But in the end, I just couldn't get past the truth: he slept with me for the building.

That was the most painful realization of them all. That someone I care about, someone I fell in l-word with, would do something so dirty. So cheap.

Yes, l-word. I refuse to say it.

Instead, I'm going to put it all behind me. I'm going to make a few changes to my shop and inquire about a small loan to remodel and expand my product line. Rhenn has already given me a few suggestions, and even offered to have Ryan Elson, my cousin Jaime's husband, come by on their next visit, to give me a few ideas. I have space here; I just need to figure out how to maximize it.

I've been working late into the evening, most nights, to make the most of my space. Well, that and because I can't sleep. When I'm at home, I think about Latham, and he's the last person I want to think about. Even Snuggles has been sad. She mopes around, setting her head on my leg and giving me the worst case of puppy-eyes I've ever seen.

She misses him.

Just like me.

The weather is as crappy outside as my mood. Even the upbeat tunes of the Backstreet Boys can't seem to bring me out of my Saturday morning funk. Free should be here anytime, and her objective was this: largest mocha with as many espressos as she can legally add and something sweet that could induce a sugar coma. I don't care about healthy anything this week (or the last two, if I'm being honest). When I finally feel up to it, I'll go back to the gym. For now, I'm going to continue eating crap and drinking too much caffeine, the way my mama told me not to.

The bell over the door chimes, pulling my attention from the super soft pajama sets I just got in. There's no doubt these babies are going to fly off the shelves when I get them priced and on display. I glance up, expecting to see my best friend blowing through the front door like a hurricane, but it's not Free.

It's Felicity.

"Well, good morning," she coos in her fake, over-the-top voice that makes me want to stick pencils through my eardrums.

I swallow the reply I long to give, and turn on my own sugary-sweet greeting. "Good morning." Even though I'd rather tell her to turn right around and walk into traffic, I decide to be the bigger person here. I mean, if she's willing to fork over a little money to outfit her next conquest, who am I to turn that profit down? "To what do I owe the pleasure this morning?"

I literally hurts to be nice.

"I have a date tonight, and I need something...amazing," she replies, glancing around at the nearest displays. There's no missing the look of disregard on her face as she glance at the soft pink nightgown on the mannequin. She quickly bypasses the timeless, breathtaking piece (the one I have at home – that Latham seemed to love so much) and hurries over to the leather and lace section. Clearly this is more her speed, not that I'd expect anything less.

There's also no missing the Douglas Hardware Store T-shirt she's wearing, that she clearly found in the kids' section of the store. Her fake boobs look like they're going to rip the sides of the shirt at any moment.

"We have plenty of items to fit your date night needs," I tell her, abandoning my new pj's and meeting her on the far side of the store.

Felicity quickly picks up a black bra with gold edging. The cups are sheer, as is the matching thong panties. "This looks a tad cheap, doesn't it?" she asks, her mouth in a nasty little sneer.

"Are you referring to the undergarments or the woman potentially wearing them?" I ask before I can stop myself.

She looks up and pops her gum, rolling her eyes so wide, there's a good chance she just saw her brain. Felicity tosses down the bra and panties on the table, completely disregarding the outfit. She makes her way over to a red corset – the only one left in the store – and pulls it off the shelf. She fingers and plays with the material, running her hand over the cups, and essentially fondles the shit out of the bustier. "This is nice."

"There are matching panties too. I only have the one size left though. I could probably order something for you, if that doesn't fit."

She checks the sizing. "It's a small. Are you saying I can't fit into a small?"

"Not at all," I tell her honestly. "Every woman is shaped different, and sometimes you wear a certain size shirt but a different size bra."

Felicity rolls her eyes. "I'm sure I'll be just fine," she growls as she takes the red ensemble and heads to the dressing room. Just the thought of her trying on the pieces makes me want to fumigate the store. I'll definitely have to hand-wash them in the back if she doesn't purchase them. And something tells me, that outfit isn't going to fit her the way she's expecting it to. She's too...top heavy.

I stand outside the dressing room, like I always do, ready to offer assistance, if needed. Felicity, however, is a professional at getting in a bustier, and before I know it, she rips open the curtain and struts into my shop, wearing nothing but the red corset and its matching red lace thong.

I should be completely shocked she just struts out into the store, where anyone can see her, wearing next to nothing, but I'm not. First, it's Felicity, and I'd expect nothing less. But mostly it's because the outfit looks...bad. Like really, really bad. Like a busted can of biscuits BAD!

"Umm," I start, not really able to find the right words.

If I were being completely honest, Felicity actually has a lot in her favor. She's pretty when she doesn't completely overdo her makeup, her hair has long, natural curls that everyone fawn over, and her body isn't bad. It's not perfect, but hell, whose is?

What draws my attention though is how *bad* this outfit makes her look. It doesn't complement her natural curves and beauty – at all! As expected, the top is too small. Her boobs look painfully uncomfortable and lack the natural plump appearance a corset can give you. And her waist? Oh, God. It's way too tight and gives her a horrible muffin top over the panties. I'm almost embarrassed for her.

"Well, I'm not really sure it's right–" I start to say, but am cut off.

"I'll take it!"

My mouth opens, ready to argue with her. I know the customer is always right, but this outfit just isn't for her. Maybe if it were in a medium, it wouldn't look like a marshmallow seeping out of the sides of a s'mores graham cracker. I'm saved from trying to talk her out of it when she turns to face the mirror on the wall (not the one in the actual dressing room, mind you) and says, "Latham is going to swallow his tongue tonight when he sees it."

And that's when everything around me seems to crumble. My vision blurs (probably from the tears I didn't know were so dangerously close to the surface) and my ears fill with static. Getting air into my lungs seems like the hardest job in the world right now.

"Oh, you didn't think he was over there, pining away for you, did you?" she sneers, a vindictive grin on her face.

I don't say anything. I can't.

"Lathy and I have been spending a lot of time together lately," she continues, shrugging her shoulders and running her hand seductively down the bodice of the corset. "We've been dancing around each other for too long now. When he asked me out, I knew it was time to take our relationship to the next level." She stares at her reflection in the mirror, but I can feel her eyes on me. When they connect in the reflection, she adds, "He's been over you since the moment you walked away."

My throat closes and my vision blurs again. I open my mouth to speak, but nothing comes out. I look at the woman in front of me, wearing horrible lingerie and a malicious smile, and I realize I'm not angry. I'm sad.

For her.

I take a step closer, ignoring the ringing of the bell over the door. "You know, Felicity, someday, you're going to meet someone who loves you for who you are, not who you're trying to be. Quit with the manipulating and the man-stealing. That's not love. In fact, you'll never know what love is because you don't love yourself first. Maybe when you finally realize all of your evil and nasty isn't who you really want to be, you'll finally experience the life and love you're meant to have. Until then, you're just a shallow, horrible person who gets off on making everyone around her miserable." I glance down at the hideous red outfit. "I feel sorry for you."

Then, I turn around, coming face to face with my best friend, and say, "I'm going to take a break. Can you finish helping this customer?"

Free doesn't say anything, just gives me a reassuring smile as I head toward the door. I don't grab my purse or my keys, I just need air. I need space.

I need a hug, dammit.

Chapter 28

Latham

I'M PISSED.

Samuel, Jensen, Rhenn, Dad, and I have been setting up the new space all morning, getting everything ready for the big reveal and grand opening next week. It's hot, tedious work, but it's going smoothly, considering I have a lot of extra hands to help move in all the new shelving units, build the metal display structures, and start to stock the shelves – or most of them. We've put our noses to the grind and have gotten shit done.

Until Felicity disappears.

"Where the fuck did she go?" I bellow in the empty (fortunately) store.

"Latham, settle down. I'm sure she's around here," my dad says, always trying to appease me. He heads to the back of the store once more, while I head out the back to see if she's in the lumber yard.

She's not there, of course, so I head back inside. "Anything?" I ask, coming in the back door.

"No," Dad says, scratching his head.

"Knowing Felicity, she went for a coffee run or something," Jensen says, and he's probably right.

"Did she tell you she was leaving?" I ask my dad, who just shakes his head.

"You guys go back to the addition and finish up. I'll stay up here and man the counter," he says.

"You're retired, old man," I smart off, a smile on my face.

"Pfff, that might be the case, but I was running this place when you were still shitting yourself at home. I think I can manage to ring out a few customers over the next hour or two," Dad retorts with a wide smile that matches my own.

"Thanks," I tell him, following Harper's family into the new part of the store. It doesn't go unnoticed when I called in for reinforcements this morning, her family came running. I called Samuel, who was all too thrilled to help put the finishing touches on the building. He had stayed last night to help, and it was only fitting he was here for the final steps. And when he told me he'd make a few calls for manual labor, I wasn't surprised to see Jensen and Rhenn in tow.

"Let's get this done," Rhenn says, slapping me on the upper back and heading back into the other room.

I follow the guys, loving the nearly finished product of a long week's hard work. The building itself was in great shape. It was an open space, which didn't require much demo. The biggest part of tearing out the old drywall and exposing the beautiful brick underneath, just the way Harper and Free suggested. The rest of the interior work was a quick refinish of the floors and some updating in the storage area.

Now, we're setting it all up – or at least, most of it.

Some of the areas, primarily the front of the room, will have to wait. New product is expected to arrive very soon, but I'm still taking extreme care of making sure the area is just right. Rhenn helped me carry in the two large units, and they're positioned front and center, facing the new window. I can practically see the new stuff on the shelves, in prime location for patrons.

Jensen and Samuel have been focusing on the back half of the room. The younger brother was like a kid in a candy store when he started unboxing and setting up all the new outdoor tools. He knew my general concept, and from what I saw each time I popped back there, he's following my ideas to a T. He's also made a few tiny changes, grouping items together that are more logical, and arranging items on the shelves for convenience of the shopper.

Rhenn and I bring in the final touches to the front half of the room: the bench storage. Dad helps hold the doors, which is a tight fit, but we make it. Just as we're setting it down by the window, I hear the bell sound over the door. I pay no attention to who's coming in, especially because Dad's over there to help, and keep my focus on reassembling my bench.

"I'm back!"

My back straightens and I glance to the doorway between the two buildings. Felicity comes flitting in, shaking her hips like it's her fucking job. She's wearing a bright smile, flashing her pearly whites at anyone who glances her way. It's what's in her hand that has my full attention now. She's carrying a white bag with a familiar logo on the side. My heart starts to beat like a fucking snare drum in my chest.

"Where the fuck have you been?" I ask, my tone harsh and aggressive.

"Shopping!" she coos, waving her Kiss Me Goodnight bag in front of my face.

"Why? You're on the clock," I state, crossing my arms over my chest.

Felicity rolls her eyes. She actually fucking rolls her eyes at me, and it takes everything I have not to wrap my hands around her neck and squeeze. "I was taking a little break," she says with big doe eyes.

"You had already taken your morning break, right? You aren't scheduled to take lunch until one. Why the fuck did you leave without telling someone?" I know I'm being a dick, but you know what? I don't care. She has proven to be a subpar employee, at best, and frankly, I'm fucking done.

"I'm sorry," she whines, twirling her hair with her available hand. "But hey, good news! I found something for later," she smiles widely and bounces, her hand now resting on my chest. She steps forward, way too fucking close for my liking, and digs her fingers into my pec. "Maybe you can come over later tonight. You know, and see what I bought?" Then she bats her I-want-to-suck-your-dick eyes and smiles seductively.

I shiver, but not in a good way. Just the thought of seeing her in whatever's in that bag has me seeing red. No way in hell. The only woman I ever want to see wear something from that store is the owner.

"You're fired." The words fly out of my mouth before I can stop them, not that I'd want to.

"What?" she gasps, tears welling in her heavily made-up eyes.

"You heard me. You're fired. Get your shit and go," I state bluntly before turning around and heading back to my current project.

Felicity starts to argue and cry, but I ignore her. I hear my dad talking, hopefully taking care of escorting our former employee from the building. Rhenn doesn't say a word, just tries his damnedest to hide his smile. He fails.

We get the rest of the bench in place and anchor it to the floor. When I'm sliding in the last screw, Dad comes over and stands next to me. "That was blunt."

"She needed blunt," I tell him, glancing up at him for the first time. "She gone?"

He nods. "Yeah, I helped her to her car with her bag and purse. She was a bawling mess, probably more for my benefit than because she's that torn up over losing her job."

"She'll be fine. A woman like that will find something else before the end of the day."

Dad laughs and slaps my back. "You're probably right. Now, come on, guys. Kitty brought some lunch for all of us."

"And I can't wait to see if the cushions fit the bench," Mom says as she walks up behind Dad, wrapping her arms around his waist. My gut clenches as he gazes down at her as if she hung the moon and all the damn stars. They have the perfect relationship, one I've always secretly admired. It's what I've always strived for, wanted for myself, just wasn't sure I'd ever have.

After eating a quick lunch with the guys and Mom, making sure the cushions fit and are positioned perfectly, and cleaning up the addition, my parents head home to enjoy the rest of their Saturday afternoon. The guys aren't too far behind them and start to make their way to the door. "Thanks for helping," I say to each of them, reaching out and shaking their hands before they go.

"Just make this right," Samuel says with a pointed look.

"I will," I reassure him, praying I didn't just tell a lie.

"Good luck," Jensen adds, slapping me on the back before stepping outside.

"Thanks."

"You're gonna need it," he teases with a wolfish grin.

"According to Marissa, she's working on inventory tonight," Rhenn says quietly, yet making sure he's loud enough I hear.

"Thanks, man," I tell him with a nod.

As I lock the door, I watch the guys get in their vehicles and head home. Rhenn's heading home to Marissa, Jensen to his mom's to get Max, and Samuel off to shower and head back to work. Before flipping off the lights, I take one last peek at the new space that will officially open to customers on Monday.

Hopefully.

There's one minor tweak yet to be made, or at least I pray like hell it'll be made. If it doesn't, then that means I failed. That Harper's not in my arms. That she's not in my life for good.

And that's unthinkable.

I head up to my tiny apartment to shower and get ready for the biggest mission of my life: Operation Win Back The Love of My Life.

It's going to be a bitch, but I won't settle for anything less than her in my arms again.

Chapter 29

Harper

AFTER LEAVING THE STORE, I find myself wandering through the trail on the edge of town that leads to the falls. Rockland Falls, the very waterfall our town was named after. I've always loved it here, with its breathtaking view, lush green plants, and fragrant scent of the outdoors. It's one of the things I missed the most while I was in New York.

After firing off a text to Free, letting her know I was going to be a little bit and I was fine, I take some time to sit, watching the water beat against the rocks before smoothing out to the stream, and reflect on everything that's happened. Seeing Felicity in my shop, hearing her talk about her date tonight with Latham just pushed me over the edge. It was a blatant reminder things don't always work out the way you plan.

Me? I started to plan a future. One with the sexy closet computer geek next door, who runs his family's hardware store with the singular goal of turning around a struggling business. I never heard that from Latham, but from Mr. Douglas. Not too long before he announced his retirement, he mentioned business was down. Everyone would rather drive a half hour away to a larger city to shop at a big box chain store just to save a few dollars. I understand it, really I do, but it still sucks balls.

Then, Latham stepped in, bringing with him ideas and dreams of expansion. More space means more product. More product means more consumers, a bigger draw of customers. That part I understand. I get why he needed the building. As hard as it is to admit, I think their business needed it more than my own, and in a way (not that I'll ever admit it aloud), I'm glad they won, and I pray it all works out for them in the end.

The part I don't get is the lies. He didn't need to sleep with me to get information. Hell, he never asked for it. What could he have possibly gained by sleeping with me, if all he wanted was information?

As I gaze up at the cascading waterfall, the light bulb goes on.

He didn't need to.

He didn't sleep with me for information or to get the building.

He slept with me for *me*.

Then why the hell didn't he say that? When I asked him, he never spoke a word. He never told me I was way off base, never told me to shut up and listen to him, never told me to stop with my crazy nonsense.

He kept quiet.

Probably because I wouldn't let him speak, and he tried.

I sigh deeply, wondering how in the hell I'm going to get out of this heart aching mess I'm in. Maybe I should stop by, give him a chance to come clean. Even if he tells me he really *did* screw me for the wrong reasons, at least I'd know and I could move on, instead of being trapped in this perpetual state of limbo.

Checking my phone one last time, I hop off the rock I'm perched on and set out for the walk back to work. Thank God I wore somewhat comfortable sandals today. No, they're definitely not hiking appropriate, but at least I won't have huge blisters on my feet like most of my other shoes.

By the time I make it back, Free's already gone and the store locked up tight. She took care of everything for me, including closing out the receipts and backing up the laptop, dropping off the deposit in the slot next door, and tidying up the mess I made when I was pricing the new pajamas. I head over to where they all sit on the counter and find my size. They're made from a thin, breathable cotton you'll probably be able to see through, but that's okay. In the heat of summer, sometimes wearing just the thinnest layer of material is the best way to sleep.

Knowing I have several hours of inventory to complete, I head to the back and decide to get comfortable. I throw my long hair up in a high ponytail and strip off my work clothes. Underneath, I'm wearing a basic white cotton bra and matching white cotton boy cut panties. I didn't even have the energy to put on anything pretty this morning. It was all about the comfort.

Ripping off my bra, I slide the tank top over my head. I opt to keep the panties on as I pull the shorts up my legs and tie the drawstring around my waist. I glance over at the mirror and can't help but smile. Sure, the reason I bought these pajamas is because of the soft material and super amazing comfort value, but that's not the only reason. Written across the black tank top in a rainbow of colors are the words Kiss Me Goodnight. It was fate when I saw them in the online catalog, and at a discount to boot, considering we're already approaching the end of the summer shopping season.

After getting into the appropriate 'ready for inventory' outfit, I head to the mini fridge for a bottle of water. When I open the fridge, I spy a new container with a note attached.

In case you get hungry later. Love, Kitty

My eyes well up with tears as I think about the woman I've come to care a great deal for. I wonder if she knows how stupid her son is, or if she has yet to find out we're not...together anymore. Not that we were anything official before, but we're definitely not anything now.

Popping the lid off, I slip it in the microwave and set it for one minute. Instantly, the scent of deliciousness starts to fill the room, making my stomach growl angrily, and reminding me I missed lunch. It's after four, so I guess technically, this is an early dinner.

I shove the first bite of chicken and broccoli casserole into my mouth, moaning with absolute pleasure as it explodes against my tongue. There's cheese too in her dish, and before I know it, I've shoveled the entire thing into my face as if it were an eating competition. As I take a quick drink of water, I make a mental note to send Kitty a thank you for the food. Then, I turn on my favorite boy band playlist and get to work.

Inventory is busy work, plain and simple. It probably doesn't need to be completed quarterly, as I've always done it, but you'd be surprised how many pairs of nice panties get up and walk away.

By eight in the evening, Free sends me a text.

Free:	You still alive? You haven't hung yourself with a lace bra, have you?
Me:	Why would I waste something so pretty on something so horrible?
Free:	I was joking. I don't think you'd actually do something like that. I just wanted to make sure you're actually counting thongs and not sitting on the floor, surrounded by pretty things, and eating a tub of chocolate mint ice cream.
Me:	Never! I don't even like chocolate mint.
Free:	*gasp* How are we even still friends?!?!? *insert shocked face emoji*
Me:	Because of the awesome discount you get at KMG!
Free:	Oh, yeah. That. I do love the discount. *insert heart-eye emoji*
Me:	Anyway, is there a real reason for you bugging me at eight at night on a Saturday? I do have a life, you know.
Free:	You do know you're texting ME, right? I know, for a FACT, that you're probably wearing pj's and blasting your horrible 90's boy band playlist.

Me:	That's creepy.
Free:	*sigh* At least put on a bra.
Me:	What?!?!? Why?!?! No one is here and it's practically a law when you get home, you're supposed to strip off your bra and fling it somewhere in the room!
Free:	You speak the truth.
Free:	Except...
Free:	Wait for it...
Free:	You ready?
Free:	Here goes...
Free:	You're not actually at home. *gasp*
Free:	I'm sorry to have to be the person to tell you! I know you've given your heart and soul to that business, but it's okay to go home every once in a while. In fact, it's highly recommended.
Me:	Shut up. I go home. I have a dog to take care of.
Free:	But you don't deny that you're wearing pj's and your bra is flung somewhere in the back room, right?
Me:	*insert middle finger GIF*
Free:	That's what I thought. Anyway, inventory can wait. I think you should go home, open a bottle of wine, turn on some Kardashians, and relax in the comfort of your own space for the evening.

Me: Kardashians?

Free: They make everyone feel better about their own lives. We all know this. Why do you think everyone watches their programs?

Me: *grumbles* Fine. I'll put my clothes back on and head home.

Me: But you're finishing this inventory next week.

Free: Deal.

Me: I love you.

Free: I know you do. I love you too. That's why I'm rescuing you from...you.

Me: *insert Grey's Anatomy hugging GIF*

Free: You're my person. Now, go home and shower. Drink wine. Watch bad reality TV. And don't even give Mr. Bad In Bed another thought.

I can't help but smile.

Me: Done.

Me: Except...

Me: He wasn't bad in bed.

Me: He was actually really, REALLY good...

Free: I knew it! He totally has that "I can rock your world in five seconds flat" look to him.

Me: He does.

Me: Anyway...

Free:	Stop thinking about him.
Me:	I can't.
Free:	I know.
Me:	I miss him, and I hate that.
Free:	Because you love him.
Me:	...
Free:	It's okay to love him, Harp.
Me:	NO IT'S NOT! He hurt me!
Free:	He did. He's a guy and he's stupid and his dick isn't big!
Me:	But it is! Really big!
Free:	I figured. Share a pic next time? *insert devil smiling emoji*
Me:	No! And there will be no next time.
Free:	If you say so.
Me:	You are all over the place.
Free:	Yet, you still love me.
Me:	I do.
Free:	Go home.
Me:	Fine

I toss the phone onto the floor beside me, rubbing my eyes. I glance down at the pj's I'm wearing (she totally called it) and at the bins of panties around me. She's right. This can totally wait until Monday.

Standing up, I stretch my tight back, hating how my muscles protest the movement after spending the last couple of hours on the floor. I slowly make my way to my laptop, shutting down the playlist, bathing the room in silence.

Only, it's not silent.

There's music.

And it's getting louder by the second.

The twangy country vocals of Tammy Wynette billow through the wall. My body instantly straightens, my blood swooshing in my ears. I stand there for several seconds, making sure I'm not hallucinating. Nope, definitely not. Coming through my wall is the exact same song the Devil next door downloaded on my laptop to play on repeat.

"Stand by Your Man."

The irony isn't lost.

"Oh, hell no!" I yell, angrier than a mama bear whose cub was just kicked.

I grab my keys, only seeing red, and take off out the front door. I barely remember to lock the door before I storm down the sidewalk, not even noticing my feet are bare.

When I get to the front door of the hardware store, I yank it hard. It doesn't give, though. It's locked. I pound on the door until my fist hurts and I'm worried I'm about to break the glass. But no one comes to the door. How could they hear over that stupid song blasting at full volume?

I turn around and head back to my store. There's a back door and one that leads to the apartment upstairs. If I throw on my sandals, I can head out back and beat down the door until the jerk answers.

Just as I approach the building that's positioned directly between his store and mine, I notice the door cracked open. The windows are covered with paper, but I can see a sliver of light shining through the crack and landing on the sidewalk before me. I don't even give myself a chance to talk myself out of it. I reach for the door and fling it open.

When I step inside, I stop in my tracks.

The building is done.

And it's...beautiful.

Two large display cases sit directly in front of where I stand, both empty. There's a matching rack on the left wall, with satin covered hangers. Those are empty too. What draws my attention next is the stunning bench positioned directly beneath the window. It's stained to match the displays, and has beautiful etchings on the side that remind me of a flower.

Huh.

I definitely didn't think Latham was the flower kinda guy, but whatever floats his boat.

The music is loud, but I'm able to ignore it. I step farther inside and see the back half of the room filled to the brim with product. There's tons of new items all on new displays, and I have to admit, it looks amazing. Latham did a great job at turning this space into a showroom for his new lines. While I might hate his guts and wish I could twist them with a fork like noodles, I'm proud of him for turning this old building into something useable again.

I don't hear him, but I can feel his eyes on me. It also dawns on me the music suddenly isn't nearly as loud as it was before. In fact, Tammy is at a much lower, respectable volume. I glance to the right, and there he is.

Latham.

He's leaning against the wall, his hands stuffed in his pockets as he watches me. I'm so overwhelmed with seeing him I can't even seem to find words. He looks...good. His scruffy jaw is a little longer than normal, but it totally works for him. His gray T-shirt is still molded to his impossibly hard chest, and his jeans fit in all the right places. He looks as gorgeous as he did the first day he strutted into my store, ready to give me a hard time.

I've missed that.

I've missed our stupid pranks.

I've missed the sass and the frustration.

I've missed him.

So much.

His eyes have me trapped in a trance where only he and I exist. I couldn't look away if I tried. He doesn't move from the wall, but there's no missing the way his jaw tightens and his back straightens. "What are you wearing?" he finally asks, his voice familiar, yet so different at the same time. It's thicker, as if he's pained.

That's when I glance down.

And gasp.

I'm wearing the tiny little pajamas that say Kiss Me Goodnight across the chest. And speaking of chest, my nipples are hard, the ring clearly visible to Latham, God, and anyone else who wanted to see.

"You went outside like that?" he growls, his jaw ticking as he says the words. He pushes off the wall, taking a step in my direction. Then another. He moves until he's standing directly in front of me, his eyes burning with passion and need.

Crossing my arms over my chest, I take a step back, but it doesn't help. I can still smell his soap and feel his eyes raking over my body.

"That doesn't help," he pleads. I glance down and realize I'm pushing my girls up and out of the tank top.

I quickly straighten, drop my arms, and adjust the top. "Sorry."

"No need to apologize," he whispers, the words kissing my skin like a breath of air. "I'm the one who needs to apologize."

I quickly avert my eyes, not really knowing what I should say or do. Who would have thought? Me, Harper Grayson, unable to find words for probably the first time in my life.

"Will you hear me out?" he asks softly.

Part of me wants to say no. Run away. Hide from the apology.

But the other part – the bigger part that sings to my soul and has my panties already wet – really wants to know what he has to say. In fact, I need the answers. I don't say anything, but nod my head.

He places his hand on my lower back and guides me to the bench. The feel of his hand on my skin, burning me through the thin material, has my body going haywire with need. It's been almost three weeks since he's touched me, and dammit, if I haven't craved his touch.

Latham waits until I'm seated before sitting next to me. He keeps a respectable distance between us, even though I'd rather have the touch. I don't move, though. I'll have a clearer head if he's not touching me, and I don't need the distraction his touch evokes.

"You look beautiful," he finally whispers, raising his hand and setting it on the side of my face. His warm palm soothes my soul and brings tears to my eyes.

I shake away the emotions. "You were saying?"

He sighs and drops his hand, but only to take mine. Latham sets our joined hands on this thigh and takes a deep breath. "I fucked up. Bad."

I sit back and wait. Wait for the moment he confirms what I suspected: he was using me.

"I lied to you, but not with my words. I lied by omission."

That has my attention.

"The day I installed your new computer system was the day I overheard you and Free talking about the building next door. I had just come back from my realtor's office a few days before and was told I was the only one who knew about the building being for sale. So when I overheard you and Free making plans, I was confused. And a little upset. I thought the deal was as good as done, but all of a sudden, it wasn't.

"I should have told you I was bidding against you, but we were barely tolerating each other then, and I couldn't see past that. You drove me absolutely crazy, but only because I wanted you so fucking bad that it hurt."

I look into his eyes, gauging his sincerity, and find nothing but honesty.

"Even when I wanted to fucking kill you, I wanted you more than I needed my next breath," he continues, the hint of a smile on his lips.

My hands start to shake a little at his admission, but he doesn't say anything about it. He just holds them tighter, gently rubbing circles over the tops of them.

"When we were lying in bed that last night and you confessed what happened in New York, I knew I needed to come clean about the building. Even if I lost it, I was more afraid to lose you."

"Then why didn't you?" I asked, interrupting.

He sighs deeply and closes his eyes for a second. "Because I was stupid. I was planning to tell you when we got home from the cookout. I got a call from Pete while we were there and found out

I had won the bid. I knew I needed to tell you, before your realtor could give you the bad news. Unfortunately, she was quicker than I was."

I hold his gaze and ask the question that has been burning in my mind for nearly three weeks. "Were you sleeping with me for information?" I'm pretty sure I'm not breathing as I wait for his answer.

"No. Absolutely not. I was sleeping with you because I had fallen in love with you."

My eyes widen at his confession.

"No, cancel that, it's not entirely true. I was sleeping with you because I have been in love with you since high school." He blurs in front of me and I realize it's because of tears. "That was the only reason I was sleeping with you, Sweetheart. Not to get information. Not to get a leg up on the building. Not because I needed to scratch some itch. Because I was in love with you and it was the only way I could tell you."

His finger swipes at a tear that trails down my cheek. "Why didn't you tell me that?" I ask with a sniffle.

He laughs, but it lacks humor. "Well, I tried, but you kept cutting me off. But the short of it is, I was an idiot. I knew you were pissed, and rightfully so. Somewhere in my stupid, pea brain, I thought it would be better to have that conversation in private, after you'd calmed down so when you kept cutting me off, I just shut up."

I gape at him. "So you just let me think and believe you were sleeping with me for intel?"

"I've already admitted to being an idiot, Harper. It was the wrong thing to do, I know. I should have tried harder to come clean and confess right there, but I didn't. I could feel everyone's eyes on me, and I panicked. I tried to get in touch with you after so we could talk, but you wouldn't answer. That's when I realized I had truly fucked it all up."

Glancing down, I confess, "I was too hurt to talk to you."

"I know."

"That's why I didn't answer the door either."

"I know that too."

"But then you stopped trying," I remind him, realizing just two days after our fight, he went radio silent.

"I didn't stop trying, Sweetheart. I just realized I needed to bring out the big guns," he says, waving his hand around him.

I follow the movement, trying to piece together what he's saying. "What does that mean?"

He quickly stands up, taking my hands in his, and leads me to the middle of the room. "Welcome to the new addition of Douglas Hardware...and Kiss Me Goodnight."

Chapter 30

Latham

I CAN'T BREATHE AS I wait for my words to sink in.

Harper glances around, first to the back half of the building that's filled with product for the hardware store. Then her eyes swing to the front half of the building, the part that's still empty of merchandise. "I don't understand," she whispers, tears filling those gorgeous blue eyes once more.

"This is ours. Together."

Her eyes meet mine and her mouth falls open, but no words come out.

So I keep going. "See, we both had a dream. Yours was to expand your business so you could bring in more product, right? Local vendors and new things that would cater to more than just those individuals seeking lingerie," I say, watching as she nods her head in confirmation. I already knew that, though. Yeah, I figured it out on my own just by being around her, but I'm not ashamed to admit I recently talked to her best friend for a little more intel.

"Well, I bid on this building for much of the same reason. Numbers were down, and the business was suffering. Dad was worried our small family-owned business wouldn't survive without some sort of change. He mentioned the building being for sale, and I sort of went with it. I felt like it was my only option to save the business I had grown up in."

"I'm glad you won," she says, catching me off guard.

"You are?"

"Yeah," she replies with a small smile. "I would hate to see it close down. It's a staple for our community, and whether the residents realize it or not, this place needs your store."

I swallow over the lump that forms in my throat. "Well, thank you. But I also realize if you had won, I could have still made it work. I could have reorganized the store and figured out how to carry more product in our existing space. I could have gotten rid of the stuff that wasn't moving. I just had it in my head I needed this in order to achieve it. I was wrong."

She glances around, really taking in the building again. "This is stunning," she says, a smile on her totally kissable lips.

I turn us both so I'm gazing directly into her eyes. "I want to share it with you. Because I love you and want to spend my life with you."

Again, those tears fill her eyes. I hate them, honestly, especially because I'm the dick who put them there. Unless they're the good tears, the ones my sister has talked about. The ones that actually mean she's happy and not sad.

"Lingerie and hardware really don't mix," she says, her lip barely curling upward.

"Are you kidding? Something sexy from your store and maybe some new rope or bungee straps actually sounds like a good time," I reply with a wink.

Her laughter fills the space, and my soul, making it shine like the sun for the first time since she walked away. "Maybe, but I'm thinking you'll be the one tied to the bed," she whispers, wrapping her arms around my chest and leaning her head against my shoulder.

"If it means you're back in my arms, I'd let you tie me up anywhere," I reply, leaning down and kissing the top of her head.

Her shampoo assaults me, reminding me of just how long it's been since I've been this close to her.

She glances up, her eyes shining with happiness. "I love you too." Her words make me smile, make my heart do a double backflip in my chest. "But I have a confession to make too."

I gaze down at her intoxicating blue eyes and wait.

"I knew you were bidding against me too. I figured it out when I went to see Mrs. Morton and you were leaving. In fact, both times, you beat me to the punch. You even wined and dined her better than I did."

I can't help but snort. "I'm sorry I went behind your back like that."

"Don't be. I did the exact same thing. I could have asked you, but I didn't. I'm at fault here too."

"Maybe," I tell her, squeezing her a little tighter in my arms. "I guess this all could have been avoided if we had just communicated a little better, huh?"

"Oh, I believe we communicated just fine."

"Glitter doesn't count as communication," I tease, drawing a small laugh from her lips.

Then, finally, after the longest twenty-one days, my lips are on hers, soft and sure. She tastes like heaven. *My heaven.* My hands slide to her head, threading into her ponytail, as I devour her mouth with my own. She gives just as good as she gets, using her tongue to pretty much send me straight over the edge of sanity.

Pulling back, we're both panting and trying to catch our breath. "Did you really go outside like this?" I ask, glancing down to where her nipples poke through the material.

She blushes as she glances down. "I wasn't thinking. As soon as I heard that stupid song, I just flew out the door."

"Well, I'm glad it was nearly dark. I'd hate to have to kill someone for seeing what's mine," I state, moving my hand to cradle the back of her neck.

"Yours, huh?"

"Fuck yes, Sweetheart. For as long as you'll have me."

I kiss the smile off her face, taking my time to memorize the way she feels in my arms and the way her nipples slide against my chest. It takes every ounce of strength I have not to throw her down on the floor and have my wicked way with her. But before I do just that, I remember the door was open and unlocked. All it would take is for one person to waltz inside and see her naked, and I'd be arrested for murder.

"Come on," I say, throwing her over my shoulder like a sack of potatoes.

"Wait, what? Where are we going?" she gasps, slapping my ass with her hand.

"Upstairs," I state, making a quick stop at the door to close and lock it.

"But... what about all this?" she asks, swinging her hand around to the still empty space.

"We'll get to this tomorrow. Besides, we have a doorway to knock out in the morning so your customers can see your addition," I reply, taking a swat at her ass in return.

"Tomorrow?"

"Yeah, Sweetheart, tomorrow. We've got to get that wall opened up for Monday's grand opening," I tell her, flipping off the lights as I head toward the stairs.

"But... Snuggles!" she hollers.

"Is already out for her sleepover with Jensen and Max. You don't have to worry about her," I say, taking the steps two at a time.

"I think my lights are still on," she adds when I reach the top of the landing.

"Free already stopped by and turned them off. Your purse is safely tucked away in your office." I set her down, her face red from being upside down.

I open the door and she starts to take a step inside. "But wait. What about your date tonight?"

Date?

"Yeah, your date. Tonight," she says, confirming I actually said that out loud.

"The only person I have a date with tonight is you." I take her in my arms, kicking the door closed behind me.

"But Felicity said you guys had plans later," she glances down, avoiding my eyes.

"I wouldn't touch that with someone else's dick, baby. You don't have to worry about her being here anymore. I fired her for her stunt earlier. She left the store without telling anyone and went fucking shopping in the middle of her workday. The only plans I had for tonight involve you, some groveling, and hopefully, some make-up sex."

Her smile is bright as she wraps her arms around my neck and pulls me toward her lips. "I think that can be arranged," she whispers, gently swiping her lips across mine.

My hands find their way up the pajama top, her glorious tits filling my hands. I give the nipple with the ring a squeeze, loving the way she gasps in pleasure and wiggles against my erection.

"Latham?" she whispers, leaning her head to the side and exposing her neck. My tongue immediately finds its way to the delicate spot where her pulse pounds.

"Yeah?"

"There's something I really want to do tonight," she gasps, reaching down and cupping my dick in her hands.

"Anything."

She glances my way and bats her eyelashes. She gives me a coy smile as she lifts her tank top up and over her head. Then, she leans in, rubbing herself against my shirt and whispers, "Go get some rope."

Epilogue

Harper

THE SUN IS BEATING DOWN on me as I flip over to color my back. Snuggles is snoring loudly in her doghouse, while I enjoy a few hours of sun and tunes on this gorgeous Sunday August afternoon. The back door closes and I can hear the heavy footfalls of Latham's boots on the steps.

"You're gonna burn, Sweetheart," he says, dropping down into the shaded chair beside me.

"I just flipped over," I reassure him, moving my sunglasses up a little to take him in.

Holy hell, this man is total sex.

He's shirtless, his hard muscles and new tattoo on full display. He got it a week ago and it's healed enough it no longer itches. He sits just out of the sun, making sure it doesn't fade his new, fresh ink. He's also wearing board shorts and his trusty ol' work boots, unlaced. I don't know why, but it's sexy as fuck, and so totally Latham.

"Stop ogling me. I feel so violated," he says, throwing me a cocky smile.

"I believe you were begging for me to *violate* you last night. Or was that this morning?" I tease, knowing full well it was both.

"Umm, I believe it was *you* who was begging for it. All three times," he says, winking at me.

I just smile in return, knowing he's completely right.

Latham has all but moved in over the last three weeks. It's too soon, I'll be the first to admit, but frankly, I just can't find the gumption to care. I love him, and I've discovered I much prefer having him in my bed at night than anywhere else. Since his apartment is so small, and since Snuggles is as much a part of the relationship as he or I, it's just natural we'd come here after work every night.

Together.

"You may be right," I tell him, closing me eyes and soaking up the sun. As a redhead, I don't stay out in the sun too long, but I was craving the vitamin D.

"What the hell are we listening to?" he asks, taking a drink from his water bottle.

"Hanson."

"Okay, I guess the question I should have asked is why the fuck are we listening to one-hit wonder teeny boppers?"

"Umm, how in the hell do you know they were one-hit wonders? This wasn't even their big song."

Latham scratches his stubbled jaw. "What do you want for dinner tonight?"

I immediately sit up, swinging my legs around and face him. "Why are you changing the subject?"

"I'm not. I'm ignoring it. That's different."

I get up and walk over to him, straddling his wide hips and the chair. His eyes dilate beneath his sunglasses. I can see the whites of his eyes burning into me. I lean forward and lightly kiss his jaw. "How?"

"How?" he croaks, adjusting his hips until my pussy is against his hard erection.

I run my hands down his bare chest, tracing his eight-pack abs, and around his back until my boobs are pressed against him. There's no doubt he can feel my nipple jewelry through my bikini, especially because my nips are definitely hard. "How do you know who Hanson is, babe?" I whisper, sliding my tongue down his neck, tasting a hint of sweat mixed with his soap.

"I don't know," he grumbles, rolling his hips and driving his cock into the apex of my legs. Dammit, why does he have to be wearing shorts?

"No?" I nip at his Adam's apple, dipping my tongue into the dimple below his neck.

"No."

I roll my hips, riding him seductively. My bikini bottom is completely soaked, but I don't care. It feels too good to care. "You sure?"

"About?"

"About Hanson," I encourage, wiggling just enough as I thrust my boobs in his face.

"Fuck," he groans, gripping my hips in his big hands and grinding into me.

"If you tell me, I'll fuck you right here in the middle of the backyard." I won't but he doesn't know that.

Latham grits his teeth and hangs on, letting me continue to squirm against him like a stripper. I reach up and slowly pull down my left bikini cup, exposing my ring. "Fuckshitdammit," he moans, both in pleasure and in pain.

"Fine. You win," he grounds out. I pull off his sunglasses so I can see his eyes. They're completely on fire with desire, yet hold a hint of pain. My heart gallops in my chest, but nothing prepares me for what he's about to say. "I used to like Hanson."

I gasp, pulling back in total shock. "Latham Douglas, are you...are you a closet boy bander?"

"No!" he argues, making me bust out laughing.

"Oh my God, you are! You used to listen to "MMMBop" in high school, didn't you? Holy shit, I can't believe this! Latham Douglas listened to Hanson. I can't wait to tweet this," I state, trying to swing my leg over his lap to grab my phone, releasing my bikini top as I go.

"Don't you fucking think about it," he says, making a grab for my phone. He's too slow though. I get it before he can and hold it out of his reach.

"Give me the phone."

"Mmm...no," I sing, much like the lyrics of the beloved 90's song. "It's going in a group text to the whole family."

Then he moves, pouncing on me so fast I drop the phone. He tosses me over his shoulder, Snuggles happily barking at our feet, thinking it's time to play. Something tells me it's definitely time to play, but not with the dog.

He slaps me on the ass, most likely leaving a stinging red handprint. "Ouch!"

"You deserve it," he says, strutting to the back door.

"Why?"

"For making fun of my horrible taste in music in high school. For teasing me with your delicious nipple. For making me so fucking hard I could cut glass with my cock right now."

I giggle, reaching down and grabbing two handfuls of his ass. "No one could see us. The fence is high enough," I argue as the door slams.

"Snuggles, go lie down," Latham demands politely, while continuing to carry me to our bedroom. When we get inside, he shuts the door and tosses me on the bed like a sack of potatoes. "What if one of the high school kids down the street was peeking through the fence?" he asks, his eyes blazing with lust, as he toes off his boots.

"They wouldn't do that," I argue.

"Fuck yes, they would. They're horny teenagers and you're fucking hot. They probably sneak peeks of you in your bikini every chance they get and go home to jerk off," he replies, reaching down and pushing at his shorts. They fall quickly, exposing his very hard, very thick cock, which he takes in his hand and slowly strokes.

I gasp, but I'm not sure if it's because of what he said or what he's doing. "That's wrong."

"I was a horny high school boy myself. I'm not at all off base," he says, stalking the rest of the way to the bed and slowly climbing on, pulling off my bikini bottoms as he goes. My legs automatically fall open and my breathing comes a little faster.

"You know, it's kinda funny," I say, wrapping my arms around his back and my legs around his waist as he comes down on top of me.

"What?" he whispers, placing open-mouthed kisses along my jaw and reaching his hand to my bikini top and exposing my breasts.

"That these were the first set of boobs you got to touch...and they'll be your last."

Latham chuckles. "You're right."

"I know I am," I tell him, lifting my hips until we're lined up perfectly.

Slowly, Latham starts to push inside. "That wasn't my only first, you know," he grunts as he fills me completely.

"First and last of that too," I confirm, knowing there's no way in hell I'll be able to ever give him up.

He takes my lips with his and whispers, "You know, I might not have been your first, but it's the last one that matters the most."

I tilt my pelvis upward, taking him even deeper. "The only one that matters," I confirm. His lips are a little more urgent now, and his hips start to speed up. "You know what else matters?"

He glances at me, uncertain where I'm going in the middle of his forward thrust. Then, he wraps his arms around me and holds me tightly against him. "What?"

I nuzzle his neck, kissing him in all the right places, and driving him closer and closer to release. "That you're Hanson's biggest fan. That totally matters, babe."

Laughter spills from his lips as he lightly bares his teeth and sinks them into my shoulder. "I love you. And your sass."

"I love you more," I whisper, right before he thrusts forward, burying himself to the root.

"Doubtful, Sweetheart. Totally doubtful."

I spend the next fifteen minutes showing him just how sassy I can be.

the end

About the Author

USA Today Bestselling Author Lacey Black is a Midwestern girl with a passion for reading, writing, and shopping. She carries her e-reader with her everywhere she goes so she never misses an opportunity to read a few pages. Always looking for a happily ever after, Lacey is passionate about contemporary romance novels and enjoys it further when you mix in a little suspense. She resides in a small town in Illinois with her husband and two children.

Website: www.laceyblackbooks.com
Email: laceyblackwrites@gmail.com

Sign up for my newsletter
so you don't miss a single sale, reveal, or release!
www.laceyblackbooks.com/newsletter

www.ingramcontent.com/pod-product-compliance
Lightning Source LLC
Chambersburg PA
CBHW051527290626
47170CB00016BA/2524